MERCHANT OF JUSTICE

The 13th Juror

A Jack Merchant Medical Mystery
Book 2

BRUCE HENNIGAN

Print ISBN: 978-1-968321-00-0

Ebook ISBN: 978-1-968321-01-7

An imprint of 613media,LLC — Area613

Cover and layout design by ebooklaunch.com

All scripture quotes are from the NIV version.

Websites:

hopeagainbooks.com

brucehennigan.com

 Formatted with Vellum

For Nicky who has helped me understand the processes and nuances of the courtroom.
For Cliff — We miss you!

Foreword

No person in this story is based on real people. It's important to understand this. The trials and tribulations Dr. Merchant endures are endemic to life in general. My readers should not assume that any one person depicted in this novel is based on a real person from my life experience with my medical colleagues.

First off, I would never try and benefit from my patients illnesses. The cases that are discussed in these stories are based on possible but very likely illnesses and the manner in which these illnesses are handled by radiologists.

Second, I would never try and benefit from my partners' personalities and quirks. The only exception was Dr. Montana and the person he was based on gave me permission to do so before I wrote the first book in this series. Unfortunately, on October 30, 2023 Dr. Cliff Coffman perished in a deadly accident. He is greatly missed because his presence was larger than life itself!

And so, any resemblance to any other person or circumstances is purely coincidently and not deliberate. However, the daily routine of practicing radiology is very accurate and intentional. Most patients have no idea who their radiologists are. But if you have any imaging studies in a hospital or outpatient setting, there is a radiologist behind the curtain making sure you get a speedy and accurate diagnosis from these studies. We serve in the shadows — true shadow merchants!

Bruce Hennigan, M.D.
June, 2025

He has told you, O man, what is good;
    and what does the Lord require of you
    but to do justice, and to love kindness,
    and to walk humbly with your God?

Micah 6:8 (ESV)

Chapter 1

"Dr. Merchant, when's the last time you actually saw a dead body?"

Dr. Sam Francisco peered at me through her cat-eye glasses. In the light of the rising sun, one half of her glass frames glittered with gold and the other half with bright purple. She had dyed one half of her mane of curly hair bright green and the other purple to celebrate the upcoming Mardi Gras. Sam loved holidays. Sam dressed *as* holidays. I figured it was to offset the gloom and doom of being a medical examiner. Today, she wore a bright green overcoat over eggplant purple scrubs. As the medical examiner for Talako parish in north Louisiana, Sam had upended the "good old boy" network of law enforcement when she took the position a little over a year ago.

I, on the other hand, was a radiologist with no training in forensic medicine other than an uncanny ability to study imaging studies and discern the underlying disease process. Since becoming a "consultant" to the medical examiner's office a couple of months ago, I had solved four cold cases after examining the evidence. Was I that good? Or was the prior medical examiner that incompetent? More likely the latter. I pushed my gold rimmed glasses up on my sweaty nose and ran a hand through my unruly hair. After a night of radiology call, I had slept only two hours. Too early for hygiene, I had been roused out of bed by a call from Sam to meet her on the riverfront in Talako, Louisiana.

"Sam, I'm a doctor. I've seen dead people." I avoided looking directly at the body a mere fifteen feet away. Did it look like our cadaver from medical school? Our study group had named our cadaver Ernest so we would always be working in "dead earnest". I had kept his face covered most of the time.

Sam chuckled. "But never in the wild, eh?"

Conversation drifted to us from the two patrol officers nearby and my friend, homicide Detective Jerry Langley. They questioned a young man in coveralls standing next to his delivery truck filled with portable potties.

"Jack, you said you would help Trenda Gayle while I am in New Orleans for Mardi Gras. For that, you will need some field experience." Sam said. Trenda was the assistant M.E. with a Ph.D. in physiology. "I don't expect you to pronounce the victim or determine cause of death. Although, as a physician, you are imminently qualified. But the paperwork will need an M.D.'s signature. Don't worry. Trenda has been with the department for five years. Thank God she didn't pick up my predecessor's sloppiness." She leaned toward me. "Truth is, she was far more competent than that man ever was."

I tore my gaze away from Langley and studied the jogging path before us. A parkway ran along this side of Choctaw River and this early in the morning, traffic was light. Trees stretched away to the riverbank. Across the river in Bayou City, I spied the towering hotels and their attached riverboat casinos. For a moment, I was inside the casino. The cloying odor of cigarette smoke and whiskey filled my nostrils. I felt the burn as I guzzled my drink. Saw the spinning lights of the slot machine. I closed my eyes and chased the memories away. I had been sober for almost two months now. No alcohol. No gambling. I nodded and stepped toward the body. Sam grabbed my arm.

"Gloves, rookie." She said.

I pulled blue, vinyl gloves from my pocket and put them on. The body was draped over a park bench. I avoided the face just as I had with Ernest. The body was clothed in a rumpled raincoat. Curiously, its lower legs and feet were bare. Yeah, I said 'its'. I had to remind myself this was a person. At least it had recently been a living, breathing person. Unlike the bodies I had seen in the hospital when, on rare occasion, I had been asked to declare them dead, this one seemed unearthly, stiff, almost posed.

"Who's the newbie?"

My heart skipped a beat at the sound of THAT voice. I whirled. Langley and a woman had joined Sam. She wore a long, beige coat over jeans and a Saints jersey. Her blonde hair was pulled back in a ponytail. Sanchez!

"What are you doing here?" I blurted.

"Oh, no, Merchant. That is my question. Why aren't you huddled over your laptop gazing at CAT scans or PET scans or Dog scans? Shadow merchant, right? Ply the shadows. Study the shades of gray?"

"Field training." Sam said with authority.

The woman glanced at Sam. "You're kidding? After blowing up an MRI at the Institute? You trust him in the field?"

Detective Gloria Sanchez referred to our recent encounter with a murderer in the Biotechnology Institute. While attempting to kill me, the magnetic field of an MRI had sucked him in. The ensuing release of gas and electricity had been, to say the least, dazzling. They still hadn't replaced the MRI which had been a boon to my practice. MRIs originally scheduled there were now done at my hospitals. Truth was, if

Sanchez hadn't fired her gun at the MRI and hit the oxygen tank, the Institute would still have a functioning MRI.

Sam crossed her arms and glared at Sanchez. "And why aren't you back on desk duty in Colorado Springs?"

Detective Sanchez had come to Louisiana on an unsanctioned investigation suspecting I had killed my wife while we were on our anniversary in Colorado Springs. A little over a year had passed and I had not yet recovered from losing my wife!

Sanchez drew a deep breath and nodded. "Touché. Let's just say I like Louisiana. Love the Cajun food. Dig the Saints. I asked for a transfer."

"You mean, we were desperate for help and we took you in." Langley said.

I smiled at that one. "Got in deep with the Secretary of Health and Human Services?" Just before Christmas when Sanchez and I stopped an attempt to, let's say, influence the Secretary, we were NOT rewarded with accolades. Sanchez had inappropriately recruited a government aide and had carried out her own secret agenda. Results were good. Response was not good.

"Okay, so they asked me to find somewhere else to go." She held a cup of coffee and sipped it. "Jer, here, needs me. I have years of experience in homicide." She looked down at her coffee. "Oh how much I love New Orleans blend. Now, can we get on with it?"

Langley sighed. "That fellow over there was unloading portable potties for the parade this afternoon."

"Wait!" Sanchez interrupted. "I thought the Mardi Gras parade was in New Orleans."

"We have five parades in Talako. Louisiana towns celebrate Mardi Gras statewide." Sam said proudly. "But none compare with New Orleans."

Sanchez looked down the parkway at the line of portable potties along the road. "All of this for a handful of beads?"

Sam tensed. "Don't be disrespecting the parade, Sanchez. I'll see that you are cleaning out cells in Bunkie!"

Sanchez raised an eyebrow. "Spunk. I like it."

"As I was saying," Langley went on. "He pulled over on the shoulder to unload and saw the body on the park bench. Went over and tried to wake the guy but realized he wasn't going to wake up. Called 911 and here we are."

I turned back to the body. "Okay, I'll take a look." I swallowed back bile and approached the bench. The bare legs intrigued me. I lifted the bottom of the coat and gasped. I stepped back.

"He's naked. Under the coat."

Sanchez chuckled. "A flasher? Sweet."

Sam stepped in front of Sanchez. "Listen here, Sanchez. You can disrespect me. You can make fun of Louisiana. But have respect for the dead. I speak for them since no one else can."

Sanchez sipped more coffee and nodded. "Noted."

"Look for a wound, Jack." Sam said.

I lifted the coat, and the rising sun illuminated the man's torso. "Oh my! He's been cut open! A gash from right to left through his umbilicus."

"Umbi who?" Sanchez asked.

"Belly button." Sam moved up next to me. She donned her gloves and unbuttoned the man's coat. She threw it open and I almost put my gloved hands over my mouth. An incision stretched from the man's right flank across his abdomen to his left side.

"Help me lift him, Jack." Sam said.

I put my hand under the man's hip. The skin was freezing cold. We lifted and rolled his stiff body toward his left. The incision spread all the way to his spine. The wound gaped open and bowel protruded out.

"Good thing it's cold today." Sam said. "Otherwise, the gas in his bowel would have pushed his guts out. You can lay him back. I'll have to take a closer look when we get to the lab. There's something significant, Jack." Sam said behind me.

I straightened. "Where's all the blood?"

"Exactly. This isn't where he was killed."

"He was killed somewhere else and left here." Langley said.

I stepped back and for the first time looked at the man's face. "Jerry, do you have an I.D. on the man?"

"Not yet. Nothing in his coat pockets."

I glanced at him. "So, you already looked."

"I did." Sanchez said quietly. "I saw the slash."

I wanted to ask her why she hadn't said as much. But it was our job to be objective and examine the body. I paused. I had said 'our'. I leaned over the man's face. His eyes, empty of life, were directed toward the heavens, hopefully his eternal destination. He looked so familiar.

"I know who this is." The realization hit me like a lightning bolt. "Dr. Lawrence McVay. Retired surgeon. He taught me in medical school. It's been a few years since I saw him at our staff meetings."

"Hey, dude, can I move my truck, now? I got a deadline." The truck driver said behind Langley.

"Yeah, fine." Langley said over his shoulder. "Are you sure, Jack?"

"Yeah, Jerry. It's Dr. McVay." I looked around at the trees along the riverfront. Was the killer there? Were they watching as we floundered around trying to imagine why anyone would to this to Dr. McVay? A chill ran over me.

Behind us, the truck beeped as it backed up. The rear wheels lunged up onto the curb and one of the portable potties toppled sideways. I saw it fall toward Sam and tried to push her aside, but it fell right on top of her. She put up a hand to try and push it away as she went down and then rolled off to the side.

"Sam!" I screamed.

Sam slowly sat up, holding her right arm. "I'm alive. But I think my wrist is broken." She held up her right hand now sitting at the wrong angle at the end of her arm.

"Won't be throwing beads after all." Sanchez said.

I glared at her. She shrugged. "Too soon?"

Chapter 2

My name is Jack Merchant. I am a radiologist. No, that isn't someone who fixes radios. And yes, I am an actual doctor. After getting my M.D., I spent five extra years after medical school in radiology residency and another year of fellowship in body imaging and nuclear medicine. I sit around all day and interpret shadows, shades of gray, images produced from the human body with various kinds of radiation or magnetic energy or ultrasound waves. Along with my eight partners, we work in the shadows.

Our group covers three major hospital radiology departments in the Fairmont Medical Center system in north central Louisiana. The main campus is called Fairmont Central, referred to simply as Central, in downtown Talako, not far from the Choctaw River. Talako is the Choctaw word for eagle.

Fairmont East was the newest hospital on the northeast side of the city in the ritzy part of town. It was built to compete with the oldest and most prestigious of Talako's hospitals, St. Alexander, also called St. Alek. Since it was in stiff competition with the Fairmont hospitals, we called it Smart Alek. In return, physicians at Smart Alek referred to

Fairmont East as the Death Star. It would amaze you the level of vicious competition between the two competing health care systems in a moderate metropolis like Talako. In north central Louisiana, Talako didn't rank with the likes of Dallas or New Orleans or even Shreveport to the west. But, as one native put it, Talako was a great place to visit from. Two universities and the oil industry provided the economic foundation for the city. Of course, oil wasn't the black gold it used to be, so other industries had moved in along the river.

Bayou City sat on the west side of the Choctaw River. Rumor was Fairmont administration planned to build a new hospital in Bayou City to beat Smart Alek to the punch and take business away from the smaller city run Bayou City Medical Center. Bayou City thrived because of its riverboat casinos. That's the other industry I referred to. And, finally, there was General University Hospital-Talako and its associated Institute of Biotechnology south of the interstate in Bayou City. Medical students rotated through GUT, as it was called. The aging hospital sat on the other side of the new Institute from the local private medical school.

A few weeks before the end of the year, Detective Sanchez had accused me of murdering my wife, Janice. I agreed with her about the murder. But it wasn't me. The following days were filled with intrigue, mystery, and the surfacing of a national conspiracy. I barely escaped with my life. Wait! I did die. Had one of those near death experiences and I'm still trying to wrap my mind around it. Come to think of it, Sanchez died, too. So we thought.

In the aftermath, I had tried to put aside my sorrow for losing my wife. It wasn't easy. Janice and I had something special. Now, her maiden name graced a floor of the Biotechnology Institute, the Manning Nanotechnology Wing. Few people knew that Janice's groundbreaking nanotechnology had been appropriated by the United States government and the events surrounding the mysterious explosion at the Institute during the president's visit were attributed to a leaky MRI gas container. I knew the truth, and so did Sam. The threat of an arrest for treason does wonders to keep one's mouth closed!

(Author's shameless commercial spot: For the full story of Jack Merchant's first appearance, check out "Shadow Merchant" at hopeagainbooks.com. Jack also appears in his own future timeline in "The Chronicles of Jonathan Steel". Now, back to our story.)

After leaving the riverfront, I had returned to my apartment, showered and put on some warm clothes. Sam had been taken to Fairmont East, the 'nice' hospital in our system. I picked up the envelope and its letter and tucked it into my jacket pocket. I had to talk to Sam today!

RIGHT BEFORE NOON, I stopped in at Sam's hospital room. Dr. Ballard, an orthopedist, stood beside her bed. He was tall with gray hair and towered over Sam, lying in her bed.

"Dr. Francisco, reduction and casting would be enough." He bellowed.

"Nope. I want surgery. Today! Now!" Sam said. A shapeless blue surgical hat covered her multicolored hair. Bandages wound around her right arm and wrist. She looked past Ballard at me. "Jack! Tell this moron I will heal quicker with surgery. A plate and a few screws. If I wait for it to be stable in a cast, I can't do my autopsies."

Ballard glanced at me with a reddened face. "Hey, Jack. Can you talk some sense into her?"

"Never could. Never will." I shrugged.

Ballard shook his head. "I'll post you for three this afternoon. It is a Saturday, you realize. The surgical crew will be one that was on call last night. They won't be at their best."

"Quit trying to scare me, Bobby." Sam said. "It's a simple

surgery. Even you can handle it. Now, get out of here and get things rolling."

Ballard sighed and stormed from the room. I pulled a chair up beside Sam's bedside. "Do you think it was wise to call your surgeon a moron? He's the one holding the scalpel."

Sam shook her head. "Don't care. If he plates and screws my fracture, I'll be able to toss beads in ten days on Mardi Gras."

"In New Orleans." I said.

"Yes!"

"Why is that so important to you?"

Sam glanced at me. I realized she wasn't wearing her glasses. Without them, she was less intimidating. "I've told you before, Jack, no discussing my private life. I haven't missed a Mardi Gras in New Orleans for ten years now. A fractured wrist will not derail my plans." She grimaced as she inadvertently gestured with her broken wrist.

"Who's going to do autopsies in the meantime?" I asked. "It won't be me."

"Dr. Wang from the medical school. He does most of them, anyway. The man is very meticulous."

"Speaking of meticulous, you should know."

Sam glared at me. "Okay. I deserved that. Wang has an incredible mind and a meticulous manner. He misses nothing. He's posting Dr. McVay right now."

I grimaced. "Any idea of what happened to him?"

"I haven't heard from your friend, if that's what you mean," Sam said testily.

"Which one?"

She glared at me. "Langley. He was supposed to give us a preliminary police report by now."

"It is Saturday, you know."

"As everyone keeps reminding me." She growled and groaned. "Where is the nurse with my pain meds?"

I touched the envelope in my jacket pocket and stoked my

bravery. Maybe now was not the best time, but I had no choice. "Sam, uh, Dr. Francisco, I need to talk to you about something."

Sam nodded toward the bedside table. "My glasses."

I handed them to her, and she put them on with her left hand. They sat crookedly, and she blinked. "Can you help me?"

"Sure." I straightened her glasses. How to approach this? Maybe ease into it. "Can I tell you a story?"

"Sure. Put me to sleep since I'm not getting the pain meds right away. I need a nap."

Chapter 3

Choctaw Parish Courthouse
    Nine years ago

"DR. MERCHANT, are you aware that you are the last physician to see Mrs. Dixon alive?"

Ms. Kosinski sauntered toward the witness stand. Her sleek, black dress hugged her body, and the effect was totally intentional. Distraction was her middle name. I swallowed hard to clear my throat and pushed my glasses up my nose. I tried not to wipe the sweat beading on my brow. Never let them see you sweat, my attorney had told me.

"I was not aware of that. What is your point?"

Kosinski paused and glanced at the jury. "You claim that Mrs. Dixon was stable and communicating with you when she left your angiogram suite for surgery."

"That is right." I said hoarsely. I tried my best to keep my eyes focused on hers. "Vital signs were stable. She had no complications during the arteriogram."

"Which took how many minutes?"

"Roughly twenty minutes from the time she rolled into the angiography suite until we put her back on her stretcher to head to surgery."

Kosinski nodded and walked back to her table. She shuffled through a stack of papers. She paused and sighed. "Well, I can't, for the life of me, find any record of Mrs. Dixon's condition while she was in your care."

She approached the witness stand holding a sheaf of papers. "I would ask you to look through this entire one hundred and twenty-four pages of medical records but since I have already entered it into the record, I would hope your attorney would not mind me stating there is no record of Mrs. Dixon's time in your care. Where are there records of her vital signs? Or did you even bother to check them? Did you destroy the form, Dr. Merchant? Are you lying to this court?"

She slammed the sheaf of papers onto the railing before me. Everyone in the jury box flinched. I glanced at Peter Brantley, my attorney, sitting in the front row of the courtroom. He was studying his fingernails. Even though I was not the subject of this malpractice suit, he should have objected. Or something.

On trial was the late Dr. Saul Reynolds. Dr. Reynolds had passed away six months ago. But his death had not halted the malpractice suit and the subsequent trial to which I had been called as a witness.

Dr. Reynolds had been on call the night Mrs. Dixon had been brought into the ER with a gunshot wound to the upper abdomen. The assailant, who had never been caught, shot Mrs. Dixon in the abdomen and the bullet had tracked up and out the back of her mid chest. I had been on call that night for radiology and had to come out and perform an arteriogram to evaluate Dixon's aorta and inferior vena cava. The aorta supplied high pressure blood flow from the heart to the body and the inferior vena cava returned all venous blood flow to the heart. Reynolds needed to know which vessel had been impacted by the bullet and was responsible for filling Dixon's left lung cavity with blood. If the aorta, the surgical approach would involve "cracking her chest" and he would need the aid of a thoracic surgeon. If the inferior vena cava, he could approach from within the abdomen, a much less invasive surgery.

My face warmed with anger, and I glanced toward the jury. Some of them glared at me. I was not the bad guy! The shooter was! And I had only performed a quick aortogram and inferior venacavagram, taking less than ten minutes!

The realization hit me like a ton of bricks! I focused on Kosinski. She wore a Mona Lisa smile. Or, if a black widow had lips, a spidery grin. She had weaved a web of innuendos and lies. Dr. Reynolds was dead. His estate was under review. But I was fresh meat. If she could prove I was incompetent and I was ultimately responsible for Mrs. Dixon's demise, then the suit could be expanded to include me! I had only been in private practice for a year and already was in danger of my first lawsuit.

"Can you give me a minute to think?" I said quietly.

Kosinski tilted her head like a spider examining her prey. "You don't have to answer right now. Take your time. We have all the time in the world."

I glanced over at Dr. Reynold's attorney, a young African American woman, sitting alone at the defense table. What I was about to do was throw a deceased colleague under the bus. Better Reynolds than me. I closed my eyes and recalled an encounter from six months before.

▭

"DR. MERCHANT?"

I looked up from my PACS monitor to find Alec Stanford standing beside me. "What is it Alec?"

"It's kind of complicated." He was a short, thin man with a blonde goatee and bald head.

"Have a seat." I motioned to the chair beside me.

"You remember that arteriogram case from about a few months ago where the patient had been shot, and we came out at midnight to do an aortogram?"

"How could I forget? What's up?"

"Well, it has to do with medical records." He produced a folded paper and placed it on the desk before me. "We always fill out paper forms during the procedure and then send them with the chart back to the floor. They send the forms to Medical Records where they're scanned in and become part of the digital records."

I unfolded the paper. "Okay, so what seems to be the problem?"

"Well, the medical records department refused our form." He tapped the paper. "They sent it back to us."

"Why?"

"They said we used an outdated form. But we didn't. Turns out they made new regulations starting the first of that month that we had to use the new forms. But the new forms were not available to be printed out from the medical records system. Only the old forms were available. Some kind of problem with I.T."

The form showed the ongoing monitoring of the patient's vital signs during her brief time in radiology. I could toss it in the shredder, but something told me to hang onto it. "Have our secretary scan it into our PACS system along with the other returned paperwork. That way, WE have a copy of it in case medical records ever wants to add it to the final records." Radiology departments used PACS systems dedicated to the storage and display of diagnostic studies and their associated documentation. Because of its complexity, PACS systems differed and were separate from the more comprehensive Medical Records systems.

"Okay, doc."

I MIRRORED Kosinski's smile and for a moment I thought her cheek flinched. "Ms. Kosinski," I tapped the medical records. "You seemed to have incomplete records."

Kosinski crossed her arms. Her dark eyes glittered with anger. "How is that?"

"These are the records from HIM." I turned to the jury. "That is Health Information Management." I smiled at Kosinski. She crossed her arms impatiently.

"Perhaps you can explain?"

"There are two records in the system." I turned to the judge, a young, dark-haired woman with bright green eyes. "Your honor, may I explain this to the jury?"

Judge Keller smiled. Was she enjoying this as much as I was beginning to enjoy it? "Please, Dr. Merchant."

I ignored Kosinski and put on my best teaching voice. "The HIM module is the centralized collection of all medical records in the hospital. As such, it obtains any important information from pathology, radiology, surgery, etc. Now, in radiology, we have what is called a PACS system. It's a digital collection of the information regarding our imaging studies and those associated studies. For instance, I work in front of three monitors, two of which are high resolution for X-Ray studies. My PACS module loads a list of all patients who have had studies on to the information monitor. When I choose a name, a second list shows the studies they have recently had performed. For instance, an MRI of the brain. When I choose the study, all the pertinent images show up on my viewing monitors. I review the study and dictate a final report and diagnosis for the ordering physician."

I leaned forward as if about to share a great secret. "But, without the health information regarding the patient, I wouldn't know why they had a study or what the doctor who ordered the study is looking for. Patients come into our system from all over and our hospital cannot expect that kind of information to be shared from another HIM locations. Sometimes, doctors fill out a paper order with pertinent information. How am I going to see that information? The patient brings the written order, and it is scanned into the PACS system and shows up in the information list. I can choose the doctor's order from the document list and read what they are looking for. I can learn the patient's symptoms, which can be big clues why they are having that particular study. There, I hope that explains it." I looked at Kosinski expectantly. "Do you understand, Ms. Kosinski?"

She looked like she had swallowed a toad. "Are you telling me there is a lost sheet with information taken during the arteriogram? And somehow this information is not available? Isn't that inconvenient?"

"Not for the doctors who are taking care of our patients. We knew exactly where to find that information." I pushed the medical records gently toward Kosinski. "You can have these back. As I said, they are incomplete. If you had subpoenaed the PACS information, you would have the complete record." I pulled my cell phone from my pocket. "Your honor, may I access my cell phone?"

"Please." She almost smiled again.

"I can reach my PACS system through my phone app." I tapped on the screen. "Ah, here we are. I put in the patient's name and do a search." I glanced at Kosinski. "You can come closer so I can show you the flow sheet with the vital signs."

Kosinski's look almost took the top of my head off. She leaned into the witness stand. As opposed to the heat she had radiated earlier, her demeanor was as cold as ice. I pointed to the screen. "Here it is. The angiogram flow sheet and if the bailiff would be so kind, I can print it out on the court room printer for all to see." I sat back. "In the interest of doing what is best for your client, I will gladly share this information without the need for a subpoena. And you will see I was not lying to the jury when I said Mrs. Dixon was stable when she left my care."

I tapped the screen, and the printer whirred. The look on Kosinski's face was priceless.

Chapter 4

"What happened in court?" Dr. Sam Francisco had not taken a nap after all. She sat up in the bed.

"Kosinksi had no further questions. The jury found in favor of the family of Mrs. Dixon." I sat back. "That was nine years ago. The only time I caught an attorney with their pants down." I cleared my throat. "Figuratively speaking."

"Time ran out for Mrs. Dixon before she could get to surgery."

"That is what I thought." I sighed. "So, right before the end of last year, our chief technologist asked me if it was okay to erase Mrs. Dixon's imaging files. We're only required to keep them for ten years. I asked to take one last look at her file and guess what I found?"

Sam lifted an eyebrow. "What?"

"A note attached to a portable chest X-Ray performed five minutes after I completed the arteriogram. The X-Ray technologist placed a note in the PACS system saying the time was incorrect on the image because they had to wait and run it later. Turns out the elevator to surgery broke. They had to take her down the hall and up another elevator. Delayed her getting to surgery by about ten minutes."

"A broken elevator cost Mrs. Dixon her life?"

I nodded. "Maybe. We'll never know. The truth is, her injuries were so bad, it was a wonder she lived long enough to have an arteriogram. I had the records locked, so they will never be erased."

Dr. Francisco relaxed back into the hospital bed, resting her broken wrist on her chest. "So, Jack, why are you telling me this fascinating story?"

I waved the envelope in the air. "I've been summoned for jury duty."

"And what has that to do with your story?"

"I have been on the witness stand five times in the last ten years. Every time I considered myself a hostile witness because the attorney was trying to get me to implicate a colleague. Every time the experience was as bad as the first one. Only I haven't been able to pull a rabbit out of my hat since that first time. I don't want to be on a jury. I need you to talk to the judge and tell them I have a conflict of interest."

Sam frowned. "What kind of conflict of interest?"

My eyes widened. "I am a consultant for the medical examiner's office? I work for the medical examiner's office! Doesn't that make me an insider to the legal system?"

Sam smiled. "Well, technically, you work for me. Didn't you read your contract?"

My mouth fell open. "What? You recall what state I was in when you handed me that contract?"

"You were asking to have your wife's body exhumed, and you were under the weather."

"Symptoms of what could have been leukemia!"

"And you still saw something of interest on a victim's X-rays that revealed the person had been murdered." Sam said. "I saw potential in you, even at your worst. Jack, you signed a contract as a consultant to the medical examiner, *ME*. You are *MY* private consultant. I have my own private practice. I review cases for other parishes. I spared you having to go through the civil process of approval. I expedited your position because I needed you. You don't work for the parish. Or the state. There is no conflict of interest."

I slumped in my chair. "Great! What am I going to do?"

"So, you've never been on a jury?"

"No."

"Good." She yawned.

"Good? What are you talking about?"

"You need to do this, Jack. You need to see the process from the other side of the fence. Working for me, and, yes, *with* me, you see the inside of the process. I want you to experience it from the layperson's point of view. It will be good for you." She pushed the nurse button on the side of her bed. "Where is my pain medicine?" She glared at me. "Go home! Get some rest."

"Rest? Not likely. We have our monthly practice business meeting tonight." I slid the envelope back into my pocket. "Well, they have to choose me for jury duty first. I'll figure out a way to get out of it."

Chapter 5

Our practice's business meeting occurred each month. But once a quarter we treated ourselves to "fine" meal at Frank's Italian Gardens, one of the best Italian restaurants in town. It served good food, but my partners went for the wine selection. Unfortunately, with my history, that option was not open to me.

Let me introduce you to my partners. Rolly McBride was a stout man with red hair, with Scottish heritage and a temperament to match. Rolly headed up our IR, interventional radiology division along with "Moondog" Taylor. Dog, as we called him, came from California and left behind a life of sand, beach, and surfing to become an interventional radiologist in our group. Rumor claimed he had fallen in love with a southern girl in Shreveport who left him after he joined the group. Few women could resist his tanned complexion and wavy blonde hair.

Maximillion or "Max" Wu came from a mixed Asian heritage. Raised in the United Kingdom, he came to the United States to study MRI research. We had lured him away from the medical school and had "made a capitalist" out of him. He covered our neuroradiology needs, interpreting complex MRIs of the brain and spine. Sonny Robicheaux came from south Louisiana. Rene Dupuis, from France, had immigrated to the United States during medical school to take care of his ailing parents and had never left. Along with the last few, Ronald Charles, like me, covered general radiology with some subspecialty interests. Mine was nuclear medicine and mammography. Our boss, Roger Montana, shared the nuclear medicine duties with me. Fairmont recently opened a diagnostic breast imaging center and Marilyn Pence had joined our group as our main breast imaging expert.

Our meeting room teemed with all my partners except for Charles. I was the last to show up. The wine was already flowing freely as my partners milled around the room. Montana spoke to a short, African American woman, Sheila Cummings. Sheila ran our practice and oversaw collections and other details. We didn't really have an office, per se. We practiced out of the hospitals' imaging centers and hospital campuses.

"About time you showed up." Rolly bellowed, clapping me on the back. "Don't worry about your share of the wine. I'll take care of it."

"I hope you're not on IR call tonight." I said hoarsely.

"He's not, dude." Dog frowned. He drank sparkling water. "I am."

I looked around. "Where's our newest partner?"

"Marilyn is in Washington, DC for a breast meeting." Dog said. "Hey, she might meet your old friend, the Secretary of HHS." He grinned and slapped me on the shoulder.

"She's not my friend." I growled.

"Jack." Montana gestured to me with a hand holding a wine glass. Montana was tall and wiry with salt and pepper hair. I joined him. "Sheila has something to say to you."

Sheila looked at me with intense brown eyes. "I wanted to make sure you are keeping your reimbursement from the medical examiner's office separate from your compensation from the group."

"Of course I am keeping it separate. It's not much money."

"You have set up an LLC, haven't you?" She asked.

I blinked. "Well, no, I haven't."

"Oh, my! I'll get the group's lawyer on that right away. We don't want any liability from that job bleeding over onto the group."

I blanched and my heart raced. "I never thought of that."

"You can get sued for missing something with the M.E.'s office, Jack." She glanced at Montana. "I told you we shouldn't have let him do this."

"I thought he would need extra compensation for all the days he has to pay back." Montana said.

I froze. "How many days do I owe?"

"27 days from last year." Montana said. "The entire group pitched in to cover for you, but now you need to make this right."

"I was grieving." I said quietly. At the casino, I should have added.

Montana stood a good six inches taller and his intense gray eyes bored into mine. "Jack, over the last year, your performance sucked. Everyone had to sacrifice time off to cover for you. There was even talk of letting you go."

I swallowed down nausea. "I did not know, Roger."

Montana put a hand on my shoulder. "I told you once you are a good radiologist. I had to have faith you would work through your grief, Jack. But I wouldn't be a good business man if I didn't realize how much you had failed over the last year. You've cleaned up your act. I know it's hard losing someone you love."

I wiped sweat from my lips and looked around the room at my partners gleefully and unknowingly laughing and chatting. Had they really wanted to fire me? And I never knew? I had been so steeped in my grief, I never realized what I had done to my partners.

"Fine, Roger." I had to be humble. "Thank you for sticking up for me."

Montana smiled, a rare sight. "Good. I knew you could do it, Jack."

"How much longer will it be before I pay back all the extra time the group had to work?"

Sheila handed me a piece of paper. "Here's the document we need you to sign. You have two choices: pay back the days by working for your partners or have your monthly salary docked to pay everyone for the days they worked. The compensation is based on an average day's net compensation."

My mouth fell open when I saw the amount I owed. "This is more than half of my current salary!"

"You'll notice it is only until the end of July." Sheila said. "Paying back from your time off will be spread out over the next year."

"Your choice, Jack." Montana said. "Realize the group could have forced it either way. We're giving you the benefit of the doubt."

Twenty-seven days of work would be five work weeks and two extra days. No more time off after paying them back! "I don't seem to have much of a choice. Take it from my salary."

Montana called for us to sit down and I settled into a seat next to Rene Dupuis. Rene was a rollicking, free for all spirit and I struggled to imagine him wanting to fire me. Had I been that bad? Truth was, I couldn't remember many of the awful weeks of the last year. Steeped in grief and depression, I really was blessed to still have a job. The chair next to me was empty.

"Where's Ronald?" I leaned toward Rene.

"His wife may be in labor, *mon ami*." Rene said in his heavy French accent.

The next hour droned on laboriously as Sheila covered endless financial minutiae and problems with billing and problems with insurance companies and problems with Medicare. Dinner came and went. Wine flowed.

The second part of the meeting consisted of our usual gripe fest. Complaints about other physicians. Complaints about the performance of some of our technologists. The complaints about St. Alex taking business away from us. Complaints about aging equipment. Unlike surgeons or cardiologists, we couldn't make threats like taking our patients to St. Alek to force the hospital to buy us new equipment. As hospital-based physicians, we were often viewed more as a necessary evil than an essential asset.

As the 'old business' portion ended, I stood up. Silence filled the room. "I just realized how much this group has stepped in to carry the extra load because of the last year of my poor performance. I want to thank you for taking up the slack when I couldn't perform. I promise this will never happen again." I sat back down, and the awkward glances finally ceased.

A server entered the room pushing a cart. After dessert was served — as Montana and his impossibly sleek physique always had dessert — he dropped the bombshell.

"As of this afternoon." He looked around the table. "The administration of the Fairmont System has acquired Bayou City Medical Center and will convert and update it to Fairmont Bayou City."

We all started talking at once and Montana had to bang his glass with a spoon. "I know what you're thinking."

"Yeah, *how* do we cover another hospital? *When* will we have to cover it?" Robicheaux asked.

"The conversion and update will take months, maybe a year." Montana said. "But Dr. Lamb wants us working over there now and has asked us to absorb one of their radiologists." Dr. Lamb was the genius administrator behind Fairmont's success. Once a well-known surgeon, his skill with a scalpel had been supplanted with his skill as an uncanny business man.

"I hope it's Gabriel Masters." Wu said. "Man's a genius."

"Yeah, but is he a work horse?" Robicheaux asked. "We got enough geniuses already."

The murmuring and talking carried on for a while until my eyes were crossing. I raised my hand. Montana tapped his glass.

"Jack, this isn't first grade."

"What about the PET scanner? Is it still coming to us?"

Montana grimaced. "Well, that is a problem."

Silence fell. Just before the disaster at the Institute, Lamb had promised Fairmont would get the newest PET scanner in town. PET scanners were very expensive and indispensable for cancer imaging. "It's just that acquiring an entire hospital system will cost more than a PET scanner."

"Did he make a deal?" I said. I knew how Lamb worked.

Montana leaned back in his chair. "Yes, he did. The PET scanner will go into the new 'Fairmont Bayou City'. Don't worry. You'll still be interpreting those images." Montana paused. "And I was considering posting you physically over there during the transition. We'll start covering there next week. Along with Masters."

Voices rose again and my face grew warm. "Wait a minute! I know I should be the one to take up the slack." I tried not to look at my partners. "But I've heard those doctors over there are, well, mavericks! The reason they are at Bayou City Medical is because they can't get along with anyone at any other hospital."

"It's more than a rumor." Montana said. "And you and Ronald Charles have the best temperaments. I need the two of you over there."

I looked around at the faces of my partners and what I

saw was relief. They didn't want that rotation any more than I did. But I was now the low man on the totem pole!

"That could be a problem, next week." I swallowed hard. "I have jury duty, and I tried to get Dr. Francisco to get me out of it and she can't." Or, won't, I wanted to say.

Montana put up a hand as the rest of the group talked all at once. "I remembered you might have jury duty, Jack. It shouldn't last over a week. Who can switch with Jack for next week?"

We worked out a compromise and Robicheaux agreed to work for me in exchange for one of my weeks off in the future when I would cover for him.

Montana drew a deep breath and ran a hand through his short, graying hair. "I'll go to BCMC next week. I was slated to go to a meeting in Colorado, but I'll cancel it."

By now, my lack of sleep had caught up to me. I wanted nothing more than to collapse in my bed. As we left the restaurant, Montana met me at the door.

"Jack, wait up."

After everyone was gone, he motioned toward the parking lot. We walked through the chilly February air. One street over, I could hear the jazz music and see colored lights flashing up in the night.

"A Mardi Gras parade." I said. There were at least a half dozen scheduled throughout the last two weeks of February.

"Sorry to dump that on you, Jack. Truth is, working with Masters might be the thing you need."

"Because he doesn't know me." I said. "Or my recent history."

"Yes." Montana paused as we reached his truck. His penetrating gray eyes focused on me. "It will give you a break from the rest of the group for a while. Give you some breathing room. As to the maverick doctors, they're the ones who asked Lamb to take over the medical center. They'll be SOB's for a while but Lamb will keep them in line because they owe him."

"Just hope it won't drive me to drink." I said.

"Oh, the jury duty will do that." Montana slid into his truck and unceremoniously shut the door. His window slid down, and he cut his gaze at me. "But, don't let it!"

I stepped back as his truck rumbled into the night. As I eased in behind my steering wheel, I watched the lights play along the trees lining two streets over. The music drifted in the cold air. And for a moment, I saw Dr. McVay's lifeless eyes, and I shuddered. I would be glad when my eyes closed on this day!

———————————

Chapter 6

———————————

It took a hot shower and two cups of coffee before I could get dressed the next morning. My mind had been a maelstrom of emotions through the night. Betrayal. Disappointment in myself and disappointment in my partners. What could I expect at Bayou City Medical? Sorry, Fairmont Bayou City Medical Center. I had a hungering desire to abandon it all and head to the casino. My phone rang around 9 AM and I dreaded looking at the caller ID. It was Jerry Langley. Was there another dead body?

"Jack, better today?"

"Some, Jerry. Another body?"

"No, Jack. Just offered to meet you in the coffee shop at church before the 10 AM service, remember?"

I groaned. Sunday! Jerry had been doing his best to get me back into church lately. I had considered going to a gambling relief group, but I made a deal with Jerry to go to church instead and he would be my sponsor, so to speak. So far, it had worked to keep me out of trouble. I hadn't missed a Sunday since the first of the year. I massaged my forehead and nodded. "Sure. I'll meet you there."

I changed out of my sweatpants and tee shirt into some

jeans and a button-down long sleeve shirt. Standing in front of my bathroom mirror I assessed the damage. During the past year, I had lost almost forty pounds. Most of it, I could do without. I had gained about ten pounds back since the first of the year. I ran my hand through my dark brown hair. Was that a streak of gray? At thirty-five, it shouldn't surprise me. After what I had put my body through in the last year, I was fortunate if that was the only damage. My eyes were bloodshot from restless sleep, and I had a little too much beard to be fashionable. I shaved and put drops in my eyes. I looked almost presentable. I would definitely get back to working out after the coming week.

I still felt way out of place at Burnwood Community Church. But Jerry's friendship and the warm embrace of his family kept me coming back. Maybe, in the far-off future, I might actually feel accepted. And forgiven.

Burnwood sat at the intersection of I-20 and a major north-south highway. While not exactly a mega-church, it still felt big to me. I had grown up in a small, rural community and attended a church with less than a hundred members. My mother and father had raised me to go to church and my father had been a deacon. Mother had been a "WMU" member supporting missionaries. I still recalled a young missionary couple stationed in South Africa spending a week with us when I was ten. Their tales of life in Africa had always enchanted me. One day, I would go to visit Africa. I wondered if they were still there. I doubted it. Memories of my mother and father were always welcomed. I missed them. They had died in a fiery car wreck just a month before I was to graduate from medical school and they never got to see me walk across the stage. They had never met Janice.

A greeter shook my hand at the front doors to the church and I made my way through the milling people toward the coffee shop. People filled the "Inkwell" as it was called, a combination coffee shop and bookstore. They stood in line for their lattes and cappuccinos. I spied Jerry sitting at a table in the corner talking to a woman whose back was to me. He stood up and had the strangest expression on his face.

"Jack! So glad you're here." His artificially expansive smile took me by surprise until the woman turned around.

"Sanchez?" I blurted.

"Yeah, the roof didn't cave in." Her hair fell around her shoulders, and she wore a dress. She stood up and motioned to her chair. "Sit. Jer got you a latte. I'm going to the ladies' room. If Jer can direct me in the direction."

"It's to the right." Jerry pointed down the hallway.

Sanchez winked at me and sauntered away. Yes, sauntered! Swagger and everything. Way out of place in the milling crowd of mixed age groups, blue-haired old ladies included.

I collapsed in her chair and finally closed my mouth. "Jerry! I mean, really?"

Jerry sat down slowly and exhaled slowly. "Yeah. I invited her. Didn't think she would come."

"You should have mentioned to her we aren't at a night club." I grabbed the latte and drank deeply. It didn't have enough bourbon. It didn't have *any* bourbon. We were in a Baptist church, remember?

Jerry wiped the sweat from his lip. "I was just being kind and doing what any good Christian should do and reach out to see if she would like to come to church, you know? And she said she would love to."

"Jerry, it's okay. Woman at the well, and all. Jesus welcomes her here. Just like He did me. After all, I'm the prodigal."

"It ain't Jesus I'm worried about." Jerry nodded toward two elderly women huddled outside the bathroom door. Their voices carried through the people moving down the hallway.

"Did you see that woman's dress?" One lady said.

"Yeah, tighter than a seal's skin."

They both looked back at the bathroom. The first lady shrugged. "Well, I used to look like that."

"I never did." The second lady said.

"Well, let's greet her in the name of Jesus." The first lady said. "We need more young adults around here, you know."

I raised an eyebrow and glanced at Jerry. "That was unexpected."

"Yep." Jerry said and sighed in relief as Sanchez emerged from the bathroom. She talked to the two ladies and then came to our table.

"Those two grandmas were so nice to me." She sat in another chair at our table. "They invited me to the sewing club next Tuesday."

Sanchez drank some of her coffee. I glanced at Jerry, and he shrugged. "Well, are you going?" I asked.

Sanchez shrugged. "I might. If I survive today. So, what happens in the main hall?"

"It's called the sanctuary." Jerry said. "A worship service."

"Worship service? I grew up Catholic and if it is anything like mass, punch me to wake me up."

"You won't have any problem staying awake." I sipped more coffee hoping AND praying I could stay awake!

The sanctuary was anything but a cathedral. Instead, the multi-use space felt more like a warehouse with padded chairs in rows before an elevated stage area. Behind the stage, a choir loft spread out across the back of the sanctuary just in front of a baptistery.

Six people spread across the stage formed the praise team with our worship leader, Musaka, leading the songs. We entered from the back and sat in the back row. In case we had to bail, Jerry said. His wife, Faye, sat between Jerry and Sanchez. The second service of the morning had a contemporary slant. The music began, loud and percussive. Musaka, a tall, thin man of Asian descent, led the congregation in a praise song. Hands went up among the crowd.

Sanchez leaned toward me. "Are they asking permission to go to the can?" She said with a wry grin.

"No, just raising their hands in worship."

"What's wrong with your hands?"

"I was raised different. Doesn't feel comfortable."

She nodded. "What's wrong with the lead singer?"

I glanced at her. "What do you mean?"

"Looks like he has gas."

Musaka's face was pinched as if in agony. "He's just feeling the spirit."

"Where did he get spirits from? The coffee shop? All I saw was coffee."

I rolled my eyes. "Just go with it, Sanchez."

She shrugged and started moving with the music. The back row had leg room for people to move down the aisle. We were already standing and Sanchez stepped forward and began to dance. Yes, to dance!

Jerry's face paled and his eyes widened. He looked at me and mouthed, "Stop her!"

I shook my head. Faye saved the day. She stepped up beside Sanchez and took her by the hands and joined in. They danced back and forth, swaying to the music until Faye pushed Sanchez's hands up. Sanchez grinned and the music stopped. The congregation applauded, eyes still fixed on the stage. Thank you, Lord, we are in the back row, I thought.

"Now that's the spirit!" Sanchez winked at me. "Puts my masses in the shade. I think I'm going to like going here, Jer."

The praise team led us through two slow, more prayerful songs before our pastor took center stage behind the pulpit. Sanchez remained subdued and halfway through the sermon, I heard her snoring. I punched her and she almost bolted up from her chair. She glanced at me with glassy eyes.

"Sorry. When do we take communion?"

"We don't do that every Sunday."

"Too bad." She sat back. "I'm hungry. And thirsty."

I glared at her, and she grinned.

After the service, Donald Holcomb, our pastor, made his way through the crowd milling in the foyer and took me by the hand. He was a tall, thin man with short, gray hair and bright blue eyes.

"Jack, it is so good to see you here today. How are you doing?"

"Much better, pastor. Thanks for asking."

His eyes turned to Sanchez. "And who is your girlfriend?"

Sanchez laughed out loud. "Please, padre. We are NOT a couple."

His smile faded a bit. "My bad. Donald Holcomb."

"Gloria Sanchez. I'm Jerry Langley's partner. Homicide detective."

Donald nodded. "Well, you killed it with that dance routine."

Sanchez tilted her head. "I didn't see any LOLAs pass out."

"Lolas?" I asked.

"Little old ladies with an attitude." Sanchez grinned. "I hope it wasn't too shocking."

"Shocking? Sometimes I would take anything, within reason, to shake up the status quo. After all, David danced naked before the Lord."

Sanchez blinked and I put a hand on her arm. "Don't give her any ideas!"

Chapter 7

Jerry invited me and Sanchez to lunch with his family. We invaded the local pancake house. Jerry and Faye had four kids ranging in age from 4 to 13. The next hour was one of barely controlled chaos. Jerry and Faye spent the time herding cats. Feral cats!

Sanchez leaned toward me once. "You ever want kids, Merchant?"

I paled at the suggestion and held my breath. Janice and I had tried several times to get pregnant. If fact, seeing a fertility specialist had led to the circumstances that inadvertently led to her death. "We tried." I said quietly.

I felt her hand on my arm. "Sorry. I shouldn't have asked. What about you and Keri?"

I glared at her. "We aren't supposed to talk about her."

"Jack, we're with Jerry and his family. They aren't going to tell anyone about your old girlfriend."

"Who has re-entered the witness protection program." I hissed.

"Have you heard from her?"

I breathed slowly, avoiding panic. "No, Sanchez. And I don't think I ever will."

Sanchez nodded. "Too bad. I liked her. She was good for you." She went back to eating her pancakes and bacon.

"Uncle Jack," Reagan, the six-year-old daughter, pointed to my plate. "Can I have your waffle?"

"Honey, there's plenty of waffles at the buffet." Faye said to her daughter.

"But Uncle Jack put sprinkles on his. And they are out of sprinkles." Reagan pouted.

I pushed my plate toward her. "I haven't touched my waffle, Regan. You can have it, and I'll go get something else. Without sprinkles."

Reagan pulled the plate to her. "Thanks, Uncle Jack. You're the best!"

I got up from the table and wandered over to the busy brunch buffet. Jerry joined me. "You okay?"

"Sanchez brought up Janice. Asked if we had kids." I said.

"Oh! Sorry. Maybe asking her to join us was a mistake."

I shook my head. "No, I've got to get used to these kinds of questions and comments, Jerry. I avoided them for a year, choosing to bury myself at the casinos and numb my brain. I'm overdo for a reset." I put my plate back on the counter. "Listen, I'm going. Give my regards to everyone."

"Don't rush off, Jack." Jerry said.

"It's fine, Jerry. Thanks for inviting me. Tell Reagan I said goodbye. I need to go check on Dr. Francisco and see how her surgery went." I left the restaurant before he could stop me.

———

SAM WAS STILL in the hospital and fast asleep when I arrived at her room. Her blue surgical cap was missing and her normally well-coiffed hair was flat with the "positive bed sign". She stirred when I sat by her bed.

"Jack?"

"Just checking on you. How did the surgery go?" Sam cursed, and I flinched. "That bad?"

She pointed to her right arm above the bandage. "See those red streaks?"

"Yeah."

"A porta-potty fell on me, Jack. Contaminated with poop! Scratched my arm and now I've got a rip-roaring infection. They can't operate until it's under control." She pointed to an I.V. hanging by her bed. "Antibiotics. Ballard won't operate until tomorrow. I've got to spend one more night in his hellhole!"

"What's the alternative, Sam?"

"Reduction and casting. Can you imagine having that infection inside a cast? No thank you."

"Then be patient and wait until tomorrow. What did you tell me? It might be a good thing to experience the things you don't like but have to deal with every day." I smiled.

Her looks could have killed at ten paces! "I was talking about jury duty. Not surgery."

"But you deal with dead people all the time. They come from these places, you know?" I motioned to the room. "Might do you good to be around sick people who get well. Spend too much time with the dead and you might get a little wonky."

"Just because my hair is purple and green doesn't mean I'm wonky! You got nothing better to do than irritate me?" She said. "Go tell the nurses I want some pudding or gelatin or something. And make sure it's not sugar free."

Before I could leave the room, a short, lean man in a three-piece suit walked in. His hair was gray, and his eyes revealed his Asian heritage. He bowed toward me. Dr. Wang worked in the pathology department of the medical center. His job as professor provided him ample opportunity to serve as part of the medical examiner's office. His attention to meticulous details made him the perfect person to perform autopsies on murder victims.

"Jack Merchant, how are you?" He said in his monotone.

"I'm fine, Dr. Wang."

"I see you are here to make sure our medical examiner will be back at work soon. I understand you are now her worthy assistant at crime scenes?" He smiled stiffly. "I just finished the autopsy on Dr. McVay."

"So, the body was Dr. McVay?" I said, a chill running down my spine.

"Come over here and tell me more." Sam said.

Wang stood, almost at attention, at her bedside. "His kidneys were removed with almost surgical precision. His blood work revealed the medication often referred to as 'roofie' although I do not understand why the roof of a house is used in its designation."

"He was drugged and then someone took his kidneys?" My skin crawled. "Why would anyone do that?"

"Motivation is not part of our investigational responsibilities, Dr. Merchant." Wang said crisply. "Motivation, method, and opportunity are the province of the police department. Our job is to uncover sufficient details regarding the manner of death to allow them to build their case. I have long ago stopped questioning the why. I can comment only on the how. But I did not come here to report those findings, Dr. Francisco. I came to check on your ongoing progress. I understand your surgery was delayed?"

"Yes, because of a toppling toilet." She held up her right hand. "Cellulitis has to clear up first. Surgery is on for the morning."

"So, I would assume Dr. Merchant will handle any declarations deaths until you are well?" He glanced at me with emotionless features.

"If he is free. If not, Trenda can handle the actual examination, and all Jack has to do is sign the papers. Once I get out of here after surgery, I can show up and supervise."

"I would point out, Dr. Francisco, the potential danger inherent in this approach. If the defense questioned the presence of a medical doctor affiliated with the medical examiner's office and discovered he was not present, it could jeopardize the entire prosecution's case." Wang stated mechanically. "Such circumstances would nullify my autopsy results. All would be for naught."

I sighed. "What is one more night? If Trenda needs me, I'll be there."

Wang nodded toward in me in a diminutive bow. "Excellent. Now, Dr. Francisco, will you be well enough by Friday?"

"Yes! I wouldn't miss it. I won't be able to toss many beads, but I can wear my crown. Are you sure you won't join me as the king?"

I raised an eyebrow and Wang cleared his throat. "Perhaps an explanation is in order. Dr. Francisco has agreed to serve as queen for our Krewe of Aesculus parade on Friday afternoon. And, no, I will not assume the mantle of royalty. A queen will suffice."

"I didn't think you approved of our local Mardi Gras parades?" I said to Sam.

"I never meant to imply that. The REAL parades are in New Orleans. This will be a good test run for me. Besides, I was, what, fifth choice?"

Wang nodded. "There were others in the running to represent the TBCMS, but they all had prior obligations."

"Ah, the Talako Bayou City Medical Society." I nodded.

"Yes, and you have yet to come to our monthly meetings. They are quite robust and intriguing." Wang said.

"I'm sure they are." I rolled my eyes at Sam. She grinned.

"Well, Dr. Francisco, I will take leave of you and hope all goes well tomorrow." He bowed toward Sam and then paused as he passed me. "Dr. Merchant, I hope you do not hear from the M.E. office tonight. Good evening."

"Queen?" I smiled at Sam.

"Yes, and I will toss beads with all my gusto using my left hand. Don't stand on the sides, because I'll probably hit you in the face. Now, my pudding?"

"Yes, your highness!" I bowed, and she cursed. I put a hand to my mouth. "Dr. Francisco, such language."

I laughed, and on the way out, asked a nurse to bring her a snack. I made it back to my apartment and fell onto my bed. Perhaps a small nap? I was asleep in seconds.

The ringing of my cell phone woke me up. I floundered around the bed until I found my cell phone. How long had I been asleep? My phone said 8:30 P.M.! I had been asleep for almost five hours! I glanced at the I.D. and groaned. Trenda!

I DROVE through darkness and misting rain toward downtown Talako. Maxine Chandra and Chuck Wilkins met me at the crime scene. Several ancient "high riser" buildings populated downtown Talako, with a few scattered newer buildings. The once booming oil industry in Louisiana had once caused a flourishing business atmosphere but now, most of the buildings were only partly occupied. The Tiger's Tail had become famous because of a visit from Johnny Cash in the 1970's that put the nightclub in the national spotlight. Sadly, the Tiger's Tail had lost its fur! A tiger in orange and white neon lights flickered over the doorway to the nightclub. A fading sign with "Geaux Tigers!" in orange and purple sat at an angle beside the door, a vain attempt to entice LSU fans to the club.

"Dr. Gayle is already inside." Chandra motioned to the doors. She was short, with black hair and dark eyes. "Dr. Merchant, right?"

"Yes. Where's Jerry?"

"He's off today. We get the graveyard shift." Wilkins growled. His bald head reflected the light from the tiger. Bags surrounded his eyes, and his pale skin matched his comments about the graveyard. Rumor was he had only a couple of months until retirement. "Let's get on with this so I can go home to my fireplace." He shivered beneath a loosely hanging raincoat.

"Can you tell me what to expect?" My breath steamed in the cold air.

"Let's just say whoever left the body yesterday wasn't finished." Wilkins coughed wetly. "I need a smoke." He walked away from us.

"He okay?" I asked.

Chandra sighed. "Smoker's lungs. Work for the force for thirty years. Give your life to the force. Then you retire and you can't walk twenty feet without coughing your lungs out." She studied me with her dark eyes. "It's bad, Jack. Just warning you."

"Anyone else here at the time of the death?"

"Club is closed on Sundays. Janitor found the body."

Patrol officers milled around us, and I leaned under the yellow crime tape and went inside. Muted light inside left the interior in shadows. An officer nodded to me, avoiding meeting my eyes, and pointed to the back. "Just past the dance floor in the ladies' room off the hallway."

I crossed a wooden tiled dance floor covered in scratches and splintered wood. Cold air tinged with the mixed aroma of alcohol and cigarette smoke reminded me of a run down casino. I should know!

The door to the restroom hallway had been propped open and the open door to the women's restroom allowed sickly yellow light into the hallway. I heard water running and noticed an inch of water on the hallway floor.

Inside the restroom, water ran from a sink hanging at an

odd angle. The glass from the broken mirror lay in shards beneath the water on the floor. Trenda stood outside an open stall, her shoulders heaving as she sobbed. She had pulled her dark hair up into a ponytail, but strands of it hung in the air. Her discarded blue gloves floated in the water at her feet. What I thought were water stains on her scrubs turned out to be blood.

"Trenda?"

She froze and looked at me with tear-stained cheeks. "Oh, Jack, it's horrible!" And then she reached out to me with her bare hands and hugged me, pressing her face into my chest. I held her, unsure exactly what to say. Our "relationship" had always been purely professional, and truth was, I didn't know much about her.

She pushed away suddenly and wiped her face. "I got blood on your clothes." She said. "I'm sorry. I don't usually act this way, but it's bad." Her gaze focused on me. "Very bad."

I looked down at the blood on my jacket, zipped up, thank goodness. "It's fine, Trenda. If it's that bad for you, I hate to even look."

"Crime investigators are on their way. All I need you to do is put your eyes on her and sign the form. I'll fill it out." She walked past me and out of the room.

I stood alone in the restroom, water running around my feet. The ancient fluorescent lights cast bluish light that reflected in the broken mirror shards and cast moving flashes of light around the room. It was like being in a demented reverse mirror ball at an old disco. And that fit this establishment perfectly.

Once I realized I would occasionally have to venture out "into the wild" as Sam had put it, I had put together a "go" bag. I wore an old jacket I could easily discard and tonight would be the right time to do so. I pulled on blue vinyl gloves and turned on the flashlight mode on my cell phone.

Swallowing back bile, with heart racing, I moved to where I could see inside the stall. When I was a teenager, for a short period of time as I considered becoming a surgeon, I had read up on the history of Jack the Ripper. My young, imaginative mind tried to picture the horrific scenes described in the literature of prostitutes murdered and slaughtered like cattle. My imagination proved to be my worst enemy and my dreams had become nightmares. I would awake, hot and sweating night after night until I realized putting such ideas into *MY* head was not the best thing for me. I abandoned reading about Jack the Ripper and decided I would never become a surgeon.

The victim had been staged for maximum shock. The murderer had far exceeded expectations. The woman had been slaughtered, indeed, and her insides draped and hung about the interior of the stall. A white plastic bag covered her head. For a moment, an image from an anatomy textbook I had used in medical school surfaced with an illustration of a body opened and organs pulled out to the side for demonstration of their size, shape, and location. The killer had duplicated the image perfectly.

I ran from the restroom, my stomach contents spewing in the hallway. I made it out into the cold February air. Chandra and Wilkins stood quietly by their squad car. Police officers waited patiently for us to release the scene. I took off my glasses and hunched over, wiping vomit from my lips. My cell phone flashlight lit up my features. Trenda put a hand on my back.

"See what I mean?" She said.

I looked around me, expecting laughter or derision for my "rookie" reaction. There was no such reaction from the surrounding officers. I realized I had just expressed everyone's feelings perfectly. If it hadn't been for the fact I owed over half of my salary to my partners, I would have walked away from my obligation to Sam that night.

"Oh, my Lord!" I said, expressing a heartfelt need to understand why God would allow such evil to exist.

Wilkins coughed and spit phlegm on the sidewalk. "God had nothing to do with this, Doc. You're looking at the work of the devil."

Chapter 8

I spent the night sitting in my recliner nodding off and on while the nightmares from my teenage years resurfaced, only now painted in actual blood and gore. I awoke an hour before I was to appear at the courthouse, and I spent fifteen minutes under a hot shower trying to wash away the blood from my memory. It didn't work. I dressed in jeans and a comfortable flannel shirt. On the way out to my car, I dropped the trash bag with my blood-stained jacket in the dumpster.

The parish courthouse in Talako once knew its splendor in 1922. Built in deco style, the courthouse made history with its daring design. Over five stories tall, its arches and sharp-edged windows became well known in architectural circles. Now the building slumped under decades of aging, with an empty courtyard once featuring a well-known general from the Confederate army. The statue had been removed at the turn of the 21st century. Lack of funds for the planned fountain left the courtyard barren except for the towering oak trees along the walkway.

I turned my collar up against the cold February wind and hurried up the stairs to four huge brass doors. Once inside, I made my way up marble stairs to the foyer. A guard met me at the security booth. After showing my summons for jury duty, I emptied my pockets, removed my overcoat and made my way through the metal detector.

Old, stained marble stairs led down into the basement to the hallway of the jury gathering room. The nondescript door bore a printed paper sign, "Jury duty here". Inside, the room smelled of mildew and body odor. Dozens of people filled old, straight-back chairs with cracked vinyl seats. Silence ruled the room, and I signed an attendance sheet on an empty desk. I made my way to a chair and settled for what would be a long, long day. The door opened and in walked one of the last people I expected.

Virgil "Gill" Brown worked at Fairmont medical system as an engineer, keeping our machines running and tuned up. Duct tape and paper clips held some of those machines together and Gill was the miracle worker of the Starship Fairmont. He was a six and a half foot tall African American with short, black wiry hair shot through with gray. He was hard to miss and tipped the scales at over three hundred pounds. And all those pounds were muscle! Rumor was, he had been on track for the NFL when he was a linebacker at LSU until he blew out his knee. During the past couple of months, Gill had become a close friend. His eyes widened when he saw me, and he hurried over to sit in the chair beside me. It groaned under his weight.

"What's up, Doc?" He grinned.

I rolled my eyes. "Not funny! You know what's up. Jury duty!"

"Well, it just got tolerable for both of us because we are here for each other."

"If we get picked."

"Oh, we'll get picked, all right. This is my third jury duty in the past seven years. See, Doc, once you serve, you don't have to come back for two years. But on that first day after two years lapses? Bingo! You lose!"

I sighed. "I have to admit, I'm glad you're here, Gill. Tell me what to say to get out of jury duty."

"Well, if I knew that, I wouldn't have been on two juries already!" Gill crossed his arms. "Just be honest with them, Doc. They do this every day. You can't pull the wool over their eyes. They've heard every excuse imaginable, and they know how to see through the bull."

A tall, blonde-haired woman with an ankle length denim dress and long sleeve blouse called for everyone's attention and took a roll. Her cheery tone did nothing to dampen the feeling of doom and depression hovering over everyone in the room. Most kept their eyes glued to their phones.

She led us out of the room and up the stairs to the first floor and down a long hallway. The stained marble floors and dark wooden framed doorways led to a dozen court rooms. We lined up along a wall like children waiting for recess. A thick chested African American man in a dark blue uniform made his way down the line. He wore his hair in an afro straight out of the seventies.

"I am Joe, your bailiff. I will lead you into the courtroom in a moment in single file." He paused in front of me and studied the group. "Once inside, fill up all the pews on the far side of the room from front to back. A roll will be taken once the judge takes charge. As of this moment, you must turn off all cell phones." He walked to the end of the line and pointed to a door.

"This will be your jury room. If you are chosen, you will be brought to this room. It will stay locked at all times, and you must show a photo ID to get into the room. You may leave valuables in the room while in the courtroom, including your cell phones. We will not take them now, but if they are not turned off while in the courtroom and you get a text or call, you will be considered in contempt of court. A fine, or possibly imprisonment, can be the result."

Joe moved back along the line as we hastily turned off our

phones. He went to a double door with the sign above, "Courtroom 3" and disappeared inside. I kept my eyes directed across the aisle to the blank wall, conscious of Gill standing next to me. The last thing I wanted was to get to know anyone else.

Joe opened the door and motioned us inside. I followed along and my stomach clenched with memories. This was the same courtroom I had been grilled in so many years ago. It had not changed. The ceiling far above bore stained acoustic tiling and harsh fluorescent lights. Tall windows covered the far wall of mahogany wood. Wan light seeped through the closed slats. The air smelled of old paper and dust. I ended up at the back of the courtroom as we filled in the pews. Gill settled beside me and leaned over.

"Say a little prayer, Doc."

I had prayed most of the night in a futile attempt to erase the images of the victim from the Tiger's Tail. Nausea took me at that moment, and I swallowed hard. Maybe I should let the nausea take its course. Surely a prospective jury member who hurls during selection is enough to allow them to go home! Probably not. I leaned back and fought back bile.

Silence filled the air with a sense of foreboding. Two tables sat before the judge's elevated bench. On my far end of the left table, a man sat with his back to me. He wore a dress coat, and his long, black hair was all I could see of him. A man and woman sat next to him. Another man and woman sat at the right table, the prosecution no doubt. Facing them in the center of the tables at a small desk sat a woman at a computer. Apart from the tables, a woman in a three-piece suit sat in front of the witness stand at a small desk, the court recorder. I recognized her instantly. Her face had grown more wrinkled in the years since she had presided over my last deposition. Dirty brown hair wreathed her tired face.

Joe stood like a sentinel before us as the last of the potential jurors filled the back pews. He walked around the tables to a door on the far left-hand wall and opened it. He turned back to the room.

"All rise for the Honorable Judge Tamika Ford."

We stood as Judge Ford made her way through the door and up a set of stairs to the judge's desk. She was an African American woman with straight dark hair surrounding her face. Her skin seemed ageless as she sat.

"You may be seated." Joe said.

Judge Ford placed a set of reading glasses on her nose and studied documents before her. She glanced at a laptop to her left and then looked out over the courtroom.

"Thank you, ladies and gentlemen, for coming today. I know you had no choice, and we are very much aware of the importance of your time. Many of you will try your best to get out of jury duty. However, I am asking that you consider the importance of serving on this most important jury. Imagine, if you will, that you were brought before this court for justice. I believe each of you would hope for a jury willing to perform its civil duty to the best of your abilities. The court clerk will now call the roll."

Our names were called again, this time by the woman sitting before her computer. She was heavyset with blonde hair and a bright orange blouse. When she was finished, Ford took off her glasses.

"Now, if there is anyone who believes they cannot perform these duties because of health issues, now would be the time to raise your hand and you will be allowed to approach the bench."

About five people raised hands. Joe came to each, one at a time, and escorted them to the attorney's table. Inaudible conversations ensued. I longed for my phone. I wished I had something to help me pass the time. For a fleeting moment, a strong desire to sit before the slot machine gripped me and I tasted a Manhattan in a glistening, wet glass with floating round ice cubes. I shook my head to get rid of the images. I had put those things behind me.

Of the five, two were sent back to their seats, and the others left the courtroom. I glanced at my watch. We had been in the courthouse for almost two hours and had only gotten this far. My stomach growled. I had ignored eating breakfast and wondered how long I could last. The pressure in my bladder was growing. This was not good!

Judge Ford donned her glasses and studied the laptop. "Now, fourteen of you will be called by name. If you are called by name, please make your way to the jury box and have a seat. Understand that this is only a preliminary list for now. Of the fourteen, some will be chosen and some will be released. Understand that if you are released today, this does not mean you are free from jury duty. We have seven trials this week, and if you are not chosen for this trial, you will be chosen for another."

I cringed. If my name was not called, I would have to come back? What was worse, getting chosen now or having to return later in the week? I looked down at my shoes and closed my eyes. What should I pray for? Pick me now or wait, only to return later in the week?

The clerk of court in the orange blouse called my name on the third person. I sighed and made my way down the aisle to the jury box. I sat on Judge Ford's left side in the third chair in the front row, behind a low wooden divider. The same witness box from the trial nine years ago was directly before me. The woman sitting next to me overflowed her chair. She had dark skin and maroon hair and wore a pair of red-rimmed glasses too large for her face. She would have gotten along with Sam just fine. She glanced at me and whispered a curse word. Her head bobbled back and forth as she shook her head in dismay. Bobble Head, I would call her for I had no idea of her name.

A tall, skinny woman with pale skin and a dirty blonde

hair in a bowl cut sat beside me. Her hawkish nose protruded beneath jade green eyes that blazed with anger. She forced her purse into her lap and crossed her arms. What a snarky attitude! She was Snarky Woman!

By the time all fourteen names were called, Gill remained in the audience. I glanced at him and shrugged, and then I noticed the woman sitting next to the accused. She had not aged a day since she had accosted me on the witness stand. Ms. Madeline Kosinski led the defense!

Judge Ford turned to us. "The fourteen of you are potential jury members. It is now almost noon, and we will take a forty five minute lunch break. Joe can direct you to the snack bar downstairs. Please return to the jury room by 1245 PM." She turned to the rest of the potential jury members. "As for the rest of you, it is likely not all these fourteen people will make it onto the jury. Once instructions are given after lunch to this group of people, we will call forth another 14 potential members so each of you must return to this courtroom by 1245 PM." She tapped her gavel and stood up.

"All rise!" Joe said. We rose. Judge Ford left the courtroom. For the first time, I glanced at the accused sitting at the far end of the table. His dark eyes glared at me. He had a Hollywood actor's features with a straight nose, high cheek bones surrounded by his shoulder length hair. He wore a white shirt with a red bowtie and a dark blue blazer. As his eyes fixed on mine, something happened. I couldn't exactly describe it. A wave of cold? A sensation of unspeakable unease? Oppression? I shivered. Did I know him? Did he know me? Unlikely. But his gaze never left my direction as I followed the rest of the jury members out of the courtroom. Then, it hit me. Two different colored eyes stared at me. Kosinski noticed and touched him on the shoulder. His gaze drifted away and then Kosinski looked straight at me. Her eyes widened. She remembered me! Knowing her might be my ticket out of this thing!

Chapter 9

Gill followed me out the door of the courthouse to the empty courtyard. Dull gray clouds hung over downtown spitting cold rain. I stood under an ancient oak tree to get out of the rain. The snack bar had one person cooking and taking orders at the same time. I had grabbed a protein bar and a water from a vending machine.

"Doc, you okay?" Gill asked.

I shook my head, munching on the bar. "Sorry, Gill. I am helping out with the medical examiner's office this weekend and I had to observe two dead bodies in the last two days." I glanced at him. "They were murdered, Gill. Horribly. Dissected like lab rats."

I shivered and he leaned up against the tree and I drank some water. "Sorry about that, Doc. But you took on that job, didn't you?"

"Thinking all I would be doing was reviewing medical records and imaging studies of cold cases."

"Yeah, there's always more to a job than you expect. I never thought I'd have to help Dr. Lamb's wife with her salt-water aquarium." Gill sniffed. The administrator of the Fairmont Health Care System was well known to ask his employees to do work for him.

I glanced at him. "What?"

"She has this huge saltwater aquarium. She had a service in town set it up. They went out of business. Go figure. How many saltwater aquariums are there in Talako?" He raised an eyebrow. "One! Now, zero! Dr. Lamb came down to Bioengineering and asked Lester who knew how to fix the pumps."

Lester Whittle was the head of the "Bioengineering" division and worked for radiology. But his expertise was wide, and the department had taken on more work than just radiology.

"Let me guess. Lester volunteered you?" I smiled.

"Yep. I won the lottery!" Gill shrugged. "But, in the end, a pump is a pump. I fixed it with some parts from Home Depot. She gave me a nice tip and an apple pie." He looked at me and grimaced. "The apples were raw. Not my Mama's apple pie. And she put raisins in it? Who puts raisins in an apple pie?"

"No good deed goes unpunished."

"I'm sorry you've gotten in over your head, Doc. Looks like you got raisins in YOUR apple pie!"

"It's more than that. My partners are ticked off because I missed so much work last year. They had to step up to the plate for me. Now, I owe them big time. Which means I'm not leaving the M.E.'s office anytime soon." I swallowed hard. "I'll just have to stomach the gore."

"Gore?"

I shook my head and refused to meet his gaze. "It was bad, Gill. Saturday, the murderer left the victim in plain sight on the riverfront parkway. And last night, posed the body for maximum shock. Gruesome. I lost my food. That's all I can say." I tossed the rest of the protein bar in a nearby trash can and finished the water.

"I understand. Confidentiality and all that." Gill squinted into the misting rain. "Doc, the world is full of evil. We are about to see it up close and personal, detail by detail, more than you would ever want to see or hear. I've been in two of these murder trials and it can get, like you said, gruesome. It's one thing to see a dead body." Gill looked at me. "It's another to get inside the head of a murderer."

My phone rang and the caller I.D. showed Ronald Charles. "Gill, I got to take this."

"I'm heading back in. Too cold for me." He headed for the stairs.

"What's up, Ron?"

"Jack! I know you're not working today but I need you to take call tonight!'

"Ron, I'm on jury duty!"

"Oh, that's right. But Melody is in labor and at 7 centimeters. She's a week early and I really need to be with her. Everyone else has plans. Are you free tonight?"

"I don't know, Ron." None of my other partners could take his call? Was this more punishment for the last year? I glanced to my right and spied Joe smoking a cigarette.

"Just a minute, Ron. Let me ask someone." I hurried over to Joe huddled beneath an overhang. "Joe, I have a partner requesting I take call tonight. I'm a doctor and I need to know if I'll be tied up tonight."

Joe blew out a huge plume of smoke in the cold, moist air. "My friend, I can guarantee the jury will not be filled until 8 PM at the earliest. And if it isn't, we'll start the whole process over in the morning. Judge Ford will have you return at 9 AM at the earliest and noon at the latest tomorrow. The first round of selections, of which you are a potential, should be done by 5 this evening." He sucked on his cigarette and blew smoke from his nostrils. "Then, my good man, I get to do this all over again until we have fourteen on the jury."

I nodded and turned away just as Joe's phone chimed. Time to go back in. "I can cover just tonight, Ron. I don't know when I'll be done, so stand by your phone. I should be free by 5 PM. But the rest of the week is definitely out of the question."

"Thanks, Jack. I owe you big time." And he was gone. I glanced down at the other numbers and recognized a long-distance number from south Louisiana. Sam had also called and left a message, but I had to hurry back into the building before I could listen to it.

Joe waited by the metal detector and smiled at me as he leaned toward me. "I will tell you one thing, Dr. Merchant. I've been doing this for thirty years and I can guarantee this murder trial will last all week. So, plan accordingly." He winked and headed through the metal detector.

"LADIES AND GENTLEMEN, I am Frederick Mansfield with the district attorney's office. This is Maria Zuniga, my associate." Mansfield wore a three-piece gray suit and a dark blue tie. His dark hair was flawless, and he wore gold-rimmed glasses and had a clean-shaven face. Zuniga wore a teal-colored dress, a simple gold chain and cross. Her black hair touched her shoulders as she nodded towards us.

"The state will take some time to ask you questions about your possible service on this jury. I would ask that you simply answer as truthfully as possible so we can determine if you are a good fit for this jury. You will note there are twelve seats in the jury box and two over to the side. Two of you will end being alternates and you will be here for everything that takes place until the jury recesses for final deliberations. If the original twelve members are present for the final deliberations, alternates can leave before those deliberations." He nodded toward Zuniga.

She assumed a position behind a podium stand and beside her, a large flat screen monitor came to life and showed a list of our names. "My task for the next few moments, ladies and gentlemen, is to ask you more about yourselves. Let me go through the roll." She read off each name and waited for each of us to raise our hand.

"My first question to you is: Is there anyone here who has served on a jury before?"

A man sitting in the alternate chair raised his hand. Zuniga glanced at her paperwork. "Mr. Fullgut?"

The man grimaced, and said quietly. "Falgout. Pronounced Fowl-Goo."

"I'm sorry. Tell me about your prior jury experience."

"I have been on two juries in other parishes." He said.

Zuniga asked more questions about the nature of those trials, and my gaze drifted to the defense table. The accused? Perp? Whatever he was called, he stared straight at me. Not at Fowl Goo. At me. When our gazes met, he never flinched. I blinked a few times and nervously looked away from his two-toned eyes. My heart raced and my spit dried up. Something about the man troubled me. Well, it should, I reasoned. He was being tried for murder. A woman sitting behind me with poofy eighties' hair raised her hand and answered similar questions. We finally moved on with the next question.

"Has anyone been a witness in a trial?" Zuniga asked. I looked up at her. This could be my ticket. I raised my hand,

"Yes, Mr. Merchant." She looked up from her paper.

I tried to speak, and my voice squeaked. I cleared my throat. "I am a physician, and I have been a witness in a few malpractice trials. Not as the doctor being sued. But as an expert witness. But not by choice. I didn't want to be *there*." I pointed to the witness stand and sweat popped out on my fore-head at the memory of Kosinski. "An attorney called me a liar in front of the jury. In fact, it was right there in that witness stand. So, I have very bad memories of this place. I do not want to be here." I tried to slow my breathing. Bobblehead leaned toward me.

"Honey, you need a paper bag?" She whispered.

Zuniga, totally unfazed by my little act, looked right into my eyes. "Mr., I mean, Dr. Merchant, do you think being IN the jury will keep you from making a reasonable conclusion about the innocence or guilt of the man seated at the defense table? Be honest, please."

I swallowed hard. Tell the truth, Mansfield had said. "No." I said and looked up at the judge. She pulled her glasses off as she looked away from her laptop and, frankly, studied me for a moment. "Dr. Merchant, I can assure you as a member of the jury, you will never have to worry about being mistreated in my courtroom. I will not put up with an attorney calling a witness a liar just to inflame the jury." She glanced over at the two people seated at the defense table. "Will I, Ms.Kosinski?".

"I will, of course, conduct myself as always in the most professional manner toward any witness, but especially Dr. Merchant." Kosinski refused to make eye contact. Did she remember me? A chill ran down my spine as her client leaned around her standing figure to glare at me again. Great! Now everyone knew who I was! I should have kept my mouth shut!

Zuniga droned on, asking if anyone had been arrested, to which a tall bald man in camo shirt and dark green pants raised his hands. The discussion that ensued went on far too long. "Dodger," as I pegged him, wanted to be off the jury. I remembered him as one of the five who asked to be relieved before we were chosen.

"I been in jail three times." He stood up.

"Mr. Donaldson, please sit down." Zuniga said with admirable patience. "What were your crimes?"

Donaldson sat down and his hands danced nervously in front of him. "I, uh, shoplifted. Got two months for that. I, uh, hit an officer of the law. Got a week for that. And I, uh, jaywalked."

Zuniga nodded and smiled. "I will note that for the record."

More questions surfaced regarding prior litigation,

possible political protest attendance, and so forth. Finally, Zuniga walked away from the podium and Mansfield took her place behind the podium.

"What I will do now, ladies and gentlemen, is to go over some basic information you will need in order to perform your duties as a jury. Let me first introduce you to the facts of this crime."

A screen appeared on the monitor. He pointed to the screen. "Our victim is Mrs. Paloma Preston of Talako, Louisiana. On February 14th of last year, Mrs. Preston was found in her home after a 911 call alerted authorities to a fire. Her body was discovered in her living room after the fire was extinguished. Upon investigation, she was discovered to have been shot with an arrow prior to the fire. The fire appears to have been set to cover up the murder."

Nausea gripped me and I looked away from the words on the screen at the perpetrator. The man sat calmly at the defense table; his eyes fixed on something in the distance. For a second, his gaze flicked in my direction, and he smiled. I looked away as the image of my wife's body surfaced in my memory. The smell of burned flesh and charred bedding filled my nostrils. I leaned forward and fought to keep from vomiting.

"Dr. Merchant? Are you okay?"

I heard the words drift into my memory and I glanced up at Judge Ford. She leaned forward over her desk. I realized everyone was looking at me. I straightened and swallowed back bile.

"I'm sorry, your honor. It's just that my wife died in a motel room fire and the memory is disturbing."

Judge Ford nodded and tapped her gavel. "Why don't we take a fifteen-minute recess? Bailiff, will you bring Dr. Merchant to my chambers?"

We stood and Ford left for her chambers. As I stumbled from the jury box, Joe met me and motioned for me to follow.

We moved around the tables, and I passed right behind the defendant. I avoided his gaze and followed Joe through the doorway into a short hallway. He motioned to an open door.

"I'll wait for you outside."

I stepped into Judge Ford's chambers. She sat behind a huge mahogany desk. Shelves were covered with ancient books and photographs of her family.

"Dr. Merchant, you may not remember me." She looked up from an open folder on her desk.

I fidgeted and swallowed hard again. "No, I don't."

"I was on the defense team when you testified nine years ago in the Dixon affair. Very smart move, bringing up a medical record the plaintiff's attorney missed. Didn't take me long to move on and run for judge. You were a big part of that decision. I realized I didn't want to continue to be involved in low hanging fruit such as litigations."

I nodded. "Okay," was all I could manage.

"I'm not supposed to talk to you outside of the jury selection process. In fact, this conversation may get you off the jury. But the truth is, we need you on this jury if you will persevere."

"I'm sorry for the reaction." I said. "My wife died in a fire."

"And I understand you are now a consultant with the medical examiner's office. We could use that perspective in this case. It will be a challenging case for both the prosecution and defense. Let's face it. Most juries lack the level of education and professional knowledge people like you bring to the process. I will give you the opportunity, when the time comes, to remove yourself from this jury." She stood up. "But, as a favor to me, please consider staying on the jury. That is all I ask."

I didn't know what to say. She was handing me a "get off the jury free" card. I nodded slowly. "I will consider it."

She moved to the door. "Then let's get on with it."

Chapter 10

I joined the jury as they re-entered the jury box. I glanced over at the remaining potential jury members sitting listlessly in their pews. Gill gave me a thumbs up and I nodded toward him. Two people sat in the front row, Detectives Langley and Sanchez! Jerry saw me and quickly looked away. Sanchez ignored me as she chewed on a toothpick. Why were they here? Were they involved in this case?

Madeline Kosinski took to the podium. "My name is Madeline Kosinski and along with my associate Robert Xavier we represent Mr. Eagleson. Like Mr. Mansfield, I have questions I would like to ask of each of you."

I groaned inwardly. More questions from the one attorney I never wanted to see again. Kosinski went through a number of other banal questions about our personal beliefs, some of which touched on religion. Then she paused.

"I have one last question I will ask each of you. If the evidence is not convincing and you are not certain of Mr. Eagleson's guilt beyond a reasonable doubt, would you have a problem finding him not guilty?" She looked at the first person in the front row of the jury box and called her by name. She answered 'no'.

Kosinski went down the line repeating the question every time. Oddly, she skipped over me. I glanced at Ford in confusion but she did not make eye contact. A woman sitting behind me shocked us all. After repeating the question, she said, "No!"

Kosinski wasn't prepared for that answer. "Pardon me? What did you say?"

"I said, no." The woman stiffened. I glanced over my shoulder. She had straight black hair and dangling green ear hoops. "Look at him. He's guilty as sin. If he got caught, he did it. No matter what you say, I'm finding him guilty!"

Everyone whispered around us. Bobble Head leaned toward me. "Dang it! I should have said that."

Kosinski nodded and drew a deep breath and went on to the next person. Finally, Kosinski paused.

"And the final prospective jury member, Dr. Merchant. " She looked directly at me. "If the evidence is not convincing and you are not certain of Mr. Eagleson's guilt beyond a reasonable doubt, would you have a problem finding him not guilty?"

I stared directly at her. "I'm not lying when I say if the evidence is there and presented to me in a believable fashion, I would have no problem finding him not guilty!"

A muscle twitched in her cheek. She nodded and looked down at her list. "I have no further questions."

MANSFIELD once again took the podium and for the next two hours lectured us on the details of Louisiana law regarding murder.

"I would like to acquaint you with the types of murder in the legal system of the state of Louisiana."

I wanted to groan. I wanted to get out of that chair and run screaming from the room. I was hungry and tired. At almost two P.M., the remaining candidates for the jury still sat in the pews, eyes vacant and empty. Anger radiated from some. Others merely sat in quiet resignation.

Mansfield continued. "Potential members of the jury." He addressed us and then turned to the remaining people in the room. "Pay very close attention to what I am about to say. The distinction between the types of murder is very important and directly impacts your verdict." The screen filled with words.

"First-degree murder represents the most serious homicide charge in Louisiana's criminal code. What distinguishes this charge from other homicide classifications is the element of specific intent to kill or inflict great bodily harm, combined with at least one aggravating circumstance. Under Louisiana law, first-degree murder includes killings that occur when the offender has specific intent to kill more than one person. Or, during the commission of certain felonies. Or, when the victim is under 12 years of age. Or, when the victim is a police officer, firefighter, or correctional officer engaged in their official duties. And, finally, when the killing involves torture or particularly cruel methods."

Mansfield read from the monitor. "The penalties for first-degree murder in Louisiana are exceptionally severe. Upon conviction, a defendant may face life imprisonment without the possibility of parole or, in certain cases, capital punishment."

"Second-degree murder also involves killings committed with specific intent, but without the aggravating circumstances required for first-degree murder. Louisiana law classifies certain unintentional killings as second-degree murder under specific circumstances: Killings with specific intent but without premeditation or aggravating factors. Deaths resulting from the intent to cause serious bodily injury. Killings that occur during the commission of felonies not listed under first-degree murder. Deaths resulting from the distribution of controlled dangerous substances.”

“Manslaughter represents a lesser homicide charge that typically involves killings committed without specific intent to cause death. Louisiana law recognizes several forms of manslaughter. The first is voluntary manslaughter and this classification typically applies when a killing occurs in ‘sudden passion’ or ‘heat of blood’ caused by provocation that would deprive an average person of self-control. Common examples include discovering a spouse in an act of infidelity or responding to significant physical provocation.”

“The second form of involuntary manslaughter involves unintentional killings that result from criminal negligence or during the commission of a non-felony crime. This might include deaths resulting from drunk driving accidents or reckless handling of firearms.”

“Negligent homicide represents the least severe form of criminal homicide in Louisiana. This charge applies when a death results from criminal negligence without any intent to harm. Examples include: deaths resulting from grossly negligent handling of firearms, fatal accidents caused by extreme recklessness, or deaths occurring due to serious safety violations.”

My mind instantly went to that phrase: heat of blood. I tried to listen, but my mind kept drifting to memories of Janice’s body on the burned motel bed. First degree murder! She had been murdered by a man who had paid the ultimate price for that crime. He had died in an explosion at the Biotechnology Institute thanks to me and to Detective Gloria Sanchez. The state did not have to waste its money trying the man. But his death left loose ends. He was working with the mysterious “Shadow Man” as part of an international conspiracy. My former girlfriend, Theresa Douglas, also known as Keri, had been placed back into the witness protection program after the incident. What would have come out of a trial if the murderer had survived? What would we have learned about the technology Janice had created now appropriated by the federal government?

"Dr. Merchant?"

I flinched and glanced at Mansfield. "Can you answer the question, please?"

"I'm sorry. Can you repeat it?"

"Can you give me an example of second-degree murder?"

Second degree murder, I thought? What had he said about the definition? "Does it have something to do with premeditation?"

"In the state of Louisiana, that distinction is implied in the description of first degree murder. Other states make premeditated murder in its own category."

I recalled one of the cold cases I had solved for Sam. "A boyfriend and girlfriend get into a fight. The girlfriend plans on throwing the boyfriend out of her house. They argue and he leaves. He gets a gun out of the glove compartment of his car, comes back into the house and shoots his girlfriend. He had time to cool down and decided to kill her."

"That would be a good example." Mansfield said with no emotion in his voice.

"I recently helped the medical examiner's office solve just such a cold case." I said, glancing at Judge Ford. She removed her reading glasses and frowned at me. A barely perceptible shake of her head warned me to back off. I glanced at Kosinski. Was this when she would ask to approach the bench and request I be removed? She merely looked away and sat back in her chair. For some reason, she actually WANTED me on the jury!

"I don't understand the heat of blood distinction." I said.

Judge Ford spoke up. "Let me explain. The idea of 'heat of blood' implies the sudden emotional state where murder is committed but never premeditated. If a person has time to cool down and consider the circumstances and then commit murder, then they are not operating under the onus of 'heat of blood'. Does that explain it?"

"Yes." I nodded. I had definitely felt "heat of blood" when I sat in the witness stand!

———

TWO HOURS later as the time reached 5:30 PM Mansfield finished discussing the fine details of types of murder and types of evidence and our job as a jury. Joe led us out into the hallway. We waited as everyone leaned against the wall. Not a person made eye contact or spoke. Bobble Head smiled once at me. "I like you." She whispered.

Joe gave us instructions to return the next morning at 830 AM unless we heard from him before then. Check your texts, he said. I raised my hand, and he sighed as he said, "Yes, Dr. Merchant?"

"Does this mean all fourteen of us are on the jury?"

"No, the attorneys will decide on the final fourteen after the next group has gone through what each of you just went through." He took business cards from his pocket with his cell phone number. "Hopefully much quicker since they've heard the murder speech. My number if you have any further questions."

Two officers met us outside the jury room and led us down a set of stairs. The main courthouse was now closed for the day, and we took a back stairway behind Judge Ford's office that emptied directly onto Main Street. The officers escorted us down the street toward our far distant, and presumably cheaper, parking lot. The sky had cleared, and the western sky burned with the dying sun. I shivered from more than just the cold!

Chapter 11

"Excuse me, uh, doctor?"

I paused in front of the Art Center on Main Street and turned. Who was asking for me? It was one of the women in my group. She hurried toward me along the cracked sidewalk, her once poofy hair now pulled back by a hairband. She paused before me and caught her breath after placing a hand on her chest. She wore a long, false fur coat over a pale blue double-knit polyester pant suit.

"Sorry. I'm not in good shape. Asthma." She smiled and adjusted her glasses. "Not to cat fur, thank goodness. But to dog dander. And mold spores. Live in Louisiana and allergic to mold spores! Lots of mold here in the rainy south."

"I'm sorry. What was your name?"

"Rhonda Fall." She smiled. "But my balance is pretty good. I haven't fallen. Lately, anyway. My late husband died from a fall, believe it or not. Off the side of a mountain. Snow skiing. I never skied, of course. I stayed in the room and sipped spiced apple cider and watched it snow. I'll never forget when they came and told me. I haven't been back to Colorado since. Reminds me of death."

Me, too! I thought. "Okay, Mrs. Fall. What can I do for you?"

"Oh! Yes!" She adjusted the hairband. "I thought I recognized you. I wanted to tell you that I will not hold it against you." Her bright green eyes widened, and she nodded as her hand fell across her chest again.

"You're husband dying?"

"No, not that."

"Hold what against me?"

"The trial. Your testimony." She said exasperated, as if I should know exactly what she was talking about. "I know what our lawyer was trying to do. She told us ahead of time she would try to implicate you in the death of our mother. But it turns out you were not the bad guy after all. The surgeon was. So, I hope you don't harbor any bad will against me because I don't hold anything against you."

I blinked and squinted at her as I thought. Where had we met? "Are you talking about the trial nine years ago? Your mother was Mrs. Dixon?"

"Yes. Actually, her name was Melody Chesterton Dixon. She always dreamed that her maiden name meant she was related to G. K. Chesterton. You know, the theologian and author? Father Brown mysteries and all?" She nodded as if I understood every word she was saying.

"I was against suing, but my two sisters insisted." She drew a deep breath and let it out in a wet steamy cloud. Moisture appeared at the corner of her crinkly eyes. "They are older and they've always looked down on me. Didn't think I could make a common sense decision! I tried to tell them the villain wasn't the doctor, it was whoever shot her!"

"After all we had been through, the last thing I wanted was a trial." She gasped for breath and opened her voluminous purse and rummaged inside. She withdrew an inhaler and placed it between her lips and inhaled and closed her eyes. "Better." She said hoarsely, and dropped the inhaler back into her purse.

"Mrs. Fall, I did everything I could to help your mother. Her injuries were just too serious." I felt the old guilt surface. Had I? Of course I had!

"I know that. But they never found the shooter. There was never a trial. No closure. My sisters said they wanted justice, so they went after Dr. Reynolds. Then, Dr. Reynolds died, and all that was left was the estate."

"I am so sorry." I didn't know what else to keep saying.

"The jury found in our favor, but by then, his estate was protected. His kids shifted money around and there was nothing left. And then, of course, there was the cap on malpractice awards in this state. That is why Ms. Kosinski wanted to pull you into the suit, too. More money." She raised an eyebrow and pushed her pale, blue eyes widened. "More money for her! We only got about forty percent of the settlement. And now, she's defending a murderer!"

I swallowed hard. How could this get any worse? I might be on a jury with a person who had tried to sue me. "Well, I am willing to put all of this behind us if you are, Mrs. Fall."

She nodded. "Yes. Behind us. I just want to know something." She paused and looked around, gathering her courage. She nodded after making some kind of decision and looked back at me. "Why did our mother die before she got to surgery?"

I cleared my throat. "Like I said, her injuries were too severe. I'm not sure there was anything that could have been done differently." I wasn't about to tell her about the delay. I reached out slowly and placed a hand on her arm. "Again, I am sorry for your loss."

Rhonda nodded and sniffed. "Thanks. I guess we get to spend the next few days together, so I'm going to put this behind me and move on." She straightened and nodded. "Yes, move on." She headed down the sidewalk toward the parking lot as the sky continued to grow darker.

—

"YOU'RE TELLING me the daughter of the murder victim you worked on ten years ago is on the jury with you?" Dr. Francisco said as she spooned gelatin into her mouth with her left hand. Her right arm was wrapped in a bandage.

I nodded. "Yes! What are the chances?"

"Want some pudding?" She motioned with her spoon to the table beside her bed. Her hair was still covered with a pale blue surgical cap.

"Not really. You need help with the gelatin?"

She held up her left hand. "No. I've got it down after two days! Going home soon. If they get my discharge papers done."

"Who is taking you home?"

"Missy." Missy was Sam's receptionist. "Maybe hoping you would serve on a jury was too much if you have to sit next to Rhonda Fall. There's no way I could have known she would be in the jury pool much less get called. The process is totally randomized."

I sat back and pushed my glasses back on my nose. "She told me they never found her mother's killer."

Sam shrugged. "I wasn't here when that happened, remember? I've only been medical examiner for a year."

"But you still have access to the case, right?"

Sam froze and eyed me with suspicion. "Why are you asking about this?"

"I will be on this jury for hopefully only a few days. But she will ask me all kinds of questions."

"Which you will not have to answer. You were part of a malpractice lawsuit, not the criminal investigation."

"Which never revealed the killer."

Sam placed her empty plastic gelatin cup on the table. She studied me through her purple and gold eyeglasses. "I am now officially intrigued. I got you into this mess, so I'll investigate it. But keep your mind on the trial. I want a full report on the proceedings. Tamika Ford is a new judge. I need to know how she thinks. I haven't had to appear in her court. Yet."

"Well, you might need to hurry with your review. We may be sequestered if this is a first-degree murder case."

Sam froze. "You don't know yet?"

"We only heard a preliminary overview of the case. The prosecutor lectured us on all the different forms of murder convictions. I'll know in the morning, assuming they complete the jury selection this evening."

Sam tapped the tabletop with a purple fingernail. "I'm the medical examiner. I can get a message to you anytime I like, as long as it doesn't involve this trial."

"I thought you didn't know Judge Ford?"

"I know the bailiff, Joe. He owes me one." She looked at me and put her left hand on my arm. "I heard last night was bad."

I blanched and got up and paced around the room. "I've never seen anything like that." I paused at the window and bit my thumb. "I don't think I can do this, Sam."

"I know." She said quietly. "My mistake for putting you in the field so soon."

I turned. "Why not get Dr. Wang to sign off on these dead bodies?"

"Because, Jack, he would start the autopsy before the crime investigators arrived."

My eyes widened. "What?"

"I'm joking, of course. But Dr. Wang sees only a puzzle to be solved. He doesn't see the person. It would take him forever to sign off on the decedent, Jack. In these cases, it is important for the medical examiner to make certain the person is dead and to do some preliminary tests that are very time sensitive, such as to determine approximate time of death. Then we get out of the way and let the crime investigators gather the evidence."

I slumped into the chair by her bed. "When I agreed to be your consultant, I thought I would be reviewing imaging studies only."

"Jack, once I get well, you won't have to go out again. I promise."

"And if I get a call tonight?"

She frowned. "You'll need to go. I'm sorry. I'll be home. Maybe! But I'll be on pain meds. By tomorrow night, I'll be fine enough to go. Promise. I have to get well enough to be queen, right?"

"Will you wear a crown?" I stood up trying to lighten the mood. I let the macabre memories of the last night fade away.

"Of course. Golden and shiny! Now get out of here and tell those nurses to get their rears in gear. I'm stripping out of this hospital gown to my birthday suit, and I'll parade down the hall until they let me go."

I didn't doubt her one bit! I was barely out of Sam's room when my phone rang. Not Trenda, thank goodness. But, Ron!

"How's it going?" I asked.

"Labor is progressing, but she's getting some elevation in her blood pressure, Jack. You've got my call covered, right? I'm not leaving her." Ron said with a desperate tone in his voice. For a moment, I felt the old sadness. Janice and I had tried to have children. Somewhere in a cryogenic unit were eggs she had harvested without my knowledge.

"Yes, Ron. I got it." I pushed the painful memory deeper into my mind.

"How was jury duty? Get off?"

"No. I'm pretty sure I'm definitely on the jury. I have to be back in the morning at 830 to find out." I glanced at my watch. 6:30 PM. Our virtual radiology coverage began at 6 PM so all emergency room studies were being interpreted by them and then called to the ERs. All I had to do was cover any simple procedure call. "Who's on for IR?"

"Rolly." Ronald said. "He already has a GI bleed at Central."

"That keeps me out of the loop for a bit." A GI bleed meant someone was bleeding from somewhere in their gastrointestinal tract, most likely from the colon. Rolly's job was to put a catheter in the arterial system and thread it out to the branches of the arteries supplying the colon. If he found an area where blood was leaking into the colon, he would inject tiny particles and "embolize" the bleeding branches. These particles blocked the tiny blood vessels allowing blood to leak into the colon and would stop the bleeding. But finding a tiny bleeding site was tedious. There was a lot of colon to look at! "The on call IR nurse and techs will be tied up with him so I won't have anyone to do a procedure with."

"Yeah, about that." Ron said ominously. "There's a patient at Fairmont East with a potassium of 8 needing a dialysis catheter. The ICU is begging me to put one in. I tried to tell them the IR team was tied up but they're afraid the patient will code if we don't start dialysis ASAP."

I sighed and leaned against a wall. Nurses and aids passed me by tending to patients on the floor. "I'm already at East. Checking on Dr. Francisco after her wrist surgery. But, Ron, I can't put in a catheter without a nurse or tech."

"Yeah, I know. Dr. Alexander in ICU said the patient's nurse will come down and help out and Tremayne in X-Ray is training to work in IR. He's agreed to scrub in with you. It's a slam dunk, Jack. Should only take you five minutes to put it in."

I closed my eyes and rubbed my temple. Headache coming on. What a day this was turning into. "Fine. I'll get Tremayne to set things up."

"You're the best, Jack." He ended the call.

"If I'm the best, then why did you almost have me fired?" I growled. Thankfully, he didn't hear me.

Chapter 12

Mr. Oliver Jackson weighed 450 pounds. Ron hadn't mentioned this inconvenient fact. No wonder the ICU doctor didn't want to try putting in a dialysis catheter at bedside! Jackson's bulk lapped off the angiogram suite table. Tremayne glanced up at me when I walked into the angiogram suite. He was scrubbed in wearing gown, gloves, and cap but his eyes spoke volumes. "Hey, Dr. Merchant. We may have bitten off more than we can chew."

My eyes widened at the sight of Mr. Jackson. I glared at his nurse standing over to the side, typing notes into a laptop computer on a rolling stand. She never made eye contact. I examined the patient's neck. The tissue from the top of his head to his shoulders flowed down in a mountain shaped mass of adipose tissue. Normally, I would find the jugular vein in the neck with ultrasound to make my initial needle stick.

"I don't think we have a needle long enough to reach his jugular vein." I said.

Mr. Jackson was totally unresponsive, and his respirations bordered on hyperventilation. I glanced at his nurse. "I don't guess Alexander wanted to try?"

She looked at me and nodded. "Sorry, Dr. Merchant. I'm

Pam, by the way. No matter what is happening, we need that catheter ASAP."

I shook my head and lifted a blanket over the patient's legs. His pendulous belly lapped over his legs. "Tremayne, we're going for a femoral approach. Far less dangerous than harpooning his neck and possibly hitting his carotid artery. Pam, I need you to pull his belly up and tape it out of the way. Tremayne is already scrubbed in and sterile, so he can't do that."

Pam nodded. "Of course. Anything I can do to help."

Well, she was being far too congenial for my bad attitude. Change course, Jack. I smiled at her. "Thanks for being here. Our usual nurse is tied up with a GI bleed."

Pam wore a blue surgical cap, and a mask hung from around her neck. Her dark hair was pulled up into the cap and her bright green eyes focused on me. "I know this is a challenge, Dr. Merchant. But I've heard good things about you from your technologists."

I merely nodded and got ready for the procedure. I put on my lead apron and then my surgical cap and mask. Tremayne cleaned and draped the patient's groin area after Pam taped his belly out of the way. I pulled on my sterile gown and Tremayne helped me with my gloves.

With an ultrasound probe, I identified an engorged vein in the man's groin crease. "Well, the femoral vein is huge. Shouldn't be hard to hit."

I deadened the skin over the vein and punctured the vein with a long needle. I fed a tiny wire through the needle and turned on the fluoroscopy to inspect the lower abdomen. The wire on the X-Ray had moved up into the position where the femoral vein fed into the iliac vein.

"We're in the vein." I released the fluoroscopy and easily went through the procedure of dilating the skin around the wire and then feeding the dialysis catheter up the vein to the level of the inferior vena cava just above where both iliac veins joined from the lower extremities. It took all of five minutes!

"Good work, Tremayne." I said, stepping back. "I'll let you suture the catheter in place."

Pam was already on the phone communicating with the dialysis unit. I pulled off my gown, gloves and mask and hung my heavy lead apron on the wall mounts.

Pam made some more notes on her laptop. She looked at me and smiled. "Thank you, again, Dr. Merchant. You saved this man's life."

"No, Pam. I'm leaving that up to you." My cell phone rang. The long-distance number again. It could be a doctor whose number was from another area code. I stepped into the hallway and answered the call.

"Dr. Merchant? This is Faye with Brogan and Quince attorneys. I've been trying to reach you all day. I am reminding you of the panel tomorrow night."

I froze and almost dropped the phone. "Panel?"

"Yes, the medical review panel. You signed for the records last week. We're meeting by phone call at 6 PM." She said cheerily.

"I'm on jury duty." I said with a sinking feeling in my heart. I had forgotten all about the medical panel. Whenever a doctor was sued for malpractice in the state of Louisiana, a "medical review panel" was convened with one physician chosen by the plaintiff and one by the defendant, and then those two physicians chose a third panel member. There was no choice in the matter. Barring near death, once you were chosen you had no choice. Worse than jury duty. At least with jury duty, there was a chance you may not be chosen.

The panel then would review all the medical records regarding a malpractice suit to determine if, in their opinion, the accused physician, nurse, hospital, etc. had fallen short of the "standard of care". The job was thankless and paid only a pittance. And, the panel decision was only an opinion and carried no legal standing. I had spent hours the week before going over the medical records on this case and had promptly forgotten all about it.

"I'm sorry to hear that, Dr. Merchant. Call the office tomorrow after 9 and we'll see if we can reschedule. But I doubt it. The time is running out for this panel, and we've been trying to convene it for two years. Have a good night." The line went dead. I held the phone uselessly at my ear in total, confounding disbelief. The records were at home, so I could at least look at them tonight. But calling the office in the morning would be problematic if I was seated on a jury with no access to a phone until lunch break! What else could happen? The phone rang in my ear, and I cursed, jerking it away to glanced at the caller ID. Fairmont East ER! What now?

"Hello?" I answered angrily, putting the phone to my other ear.

"Jack, this is Jacobs in the ER. Heard you were in the house."

"Yeah, unfortunately."

"Listen, we can't wait on your Virturad partners to look at an emergent CT. Someone with the police department coming in hot with head trauma and I need you to look at the CT ASAP. The last time that happened, it was your friend."

"Sanchez." I said, my heart rate quickening. Back in December Sanchez had been shot, and I had been in the hospital the night they brought her in. "We know who it is yet?"

"No. Just got a call from the dispatcher they are on their way."

"I'm just around the corner in Angio. I'll be right there." I hurried down the hall wondering if Sanchez, or worse, Langley, would show up on my CT table! I said a silent but desperate prayer, hoping God would listen to this fallen sinner.

THE WHIRLING BLUE, red, and white lights outside the ER doors filled the night with strobe. At least four police cars lined the drive through as the ambulance pulled up to the doors. The first person through the door was Jerry Langley followed by Gloria Sanchez.

Jerry's face was red with exertion or anger, I couldn't tell which. He saw me and made a bee line.

"Jack, thank God you're here."

"What's going on, Jerry?"

"Bad stuff." Sanchez joined us.

"Jean Planchett, head of our evidence room." Jerry said, huffing and puffing.

"It's bad, Merchant." Sanchez motioned over her shoulder.

"They cut her eyes out, Jack!" Jerry said.

"What?"

"Ya'll need to move your butts out of the way." An EMT said as he wheeled a stretcher toward the trauma room in the ER. The patient on the stretcher was strapped in and moaning in pain. Bandages covered her eyes, but blood soaked her dark, curly hair and her dark skin.

Jerry tried to follow, and Dr. Jacobs stepped in front of him. "No! Don't need you in the room."

"We're not leaving her unguarded." Sanchez said.

"Ma'am, no one here is going to hurt our patient. I need you two out of the way." Jacobs headed toward the trauma room. "And you need to get to CT, Jack." He shouted over his shoulder.

I put a hand on Jerry's shoulder. "Why don't the two of you wait over here in the hallway out of the way? You can keep an eye on the door to the room."

I escorted them to two chairs sitting in the hallway down from the trauma room. Sanchez sat, but Jerry paced. "She's been with the department for over twenty years. She was here when I was a rookie. Makes the best chocolate chip cookies." He paused, and I saw unshed tears in his eyes. "Someone cut out her eyes, Jack! Who does something like that?"

"Jerry, please sit down. I'm heading to CT so I can look at her scan when they bring her around. She's in good hands. Jacobs is the best." I looked past him. "Sanchez, can you?" I motioned to Jerry. She stood up and took him by the shoulder and turned him around.

"Sit. Gather your wits, Jer. I know this isn't a homicide and I hope it doesn't turn into one, but we will find the SOB that did this? We need to calm down and think. Okay?" She looked at me and I nodded.

"I've been there done that, Jer." She said quietly.

I left them and made my way back to Radiology. Jalayla, the CT technician's eyes widened as they rolled Jean Planchett into the room. She still had the bandages over her eyes, only she no longer moaned in pain.

"Dr. Merchant, they cut out her eyes?" Jalayla's eyes widened in horror, and she started to shake.

"I'll help you get her on the table, Jalayla. Let's just get this done, okay?"

She nodded mutely and I saw a tear run down her cheek. She swiped it away. I helped the nurse from the ER pull Planchett over onto the CT table. Her body undulated without muscle control as if she were dead. I got the shivers then! Jalayla positioned her head and squeaked when she pulled back a gloved hand covered in old blood. She retched and I pulled her away before she threw up. She nodded as she regained control.

"It ain't the blood. It's the idea they took her eyes." She whispered.

Five minutes later, the scan was finished, and they took Planchett back to the ER while I sat before the monitor. Nausea hit me as I scrolled through the images of her brain. The orbital sockets were empty of the normal eye globe and optic nerve. Air and blood filled both. The rectus muscles that moved the eye in all directions hung in the air and blood like those boneless, air-filled dummies that writhed in front of the latest tire sale.

I focused on the brain, the real question in this case. Surprisingly, no bleeding. And the bony sockets around the orbits were intact. Whoever had removed this woman's eyes had done so with precision. In fact, my mouth fell open as I realized the optic nerves had been severed cleanly, as if with a scalpel. Who was this monster?

I called Jacobs and filled him in on the findings and then left Jalayla crying in the control room of the CAT scanner. I wandered back to the ER. Jerry and Sanchez were sitting forlornly in their chairs.

"You look white as a ghost." Sanchez said, while chewing on her toothpick.

"It wasn't a pretty sight. Fortunately, no brain damage." I said and then groaned. "Sorry, that was too close to a tasteless pun. Any word?"

Jerry shook his head and his phone rang. He stepped to the far end of the corridor and took the call. Sanchez glanced at me and patted the chair beside her.

"Have a sit."

I sat beside her and put my face in my hands. "What a day."

Sanchez nodded and glanced at me; her lips pursed. She blinked a few times. "Okay, I've got to say this, so don't interrupt me."

"Say what?"

"You're doing it."

"Doing what?"

"Interrupting."

"Sorry."

She looked away. "Jack, I apologize for thinking you were

a killer. After this weekend, it seems Talako has the market cornered on murders. Two since Saturday morning and an attempted one tonight. Whoever did that is a monster. You're not."

I glanced at her. "Thanks. That's not like you."

"What's not like me?"

"To be apologetic? Introspective?"

"People can change. Unfortunately, I'm not usually one of them."

"You left Colorado Springs." I leaned back in the chair. "So, tell me. Why did you come to Talako?"

Sanchez pulled a toothpick out of her pocket. "Know what this is?"

"A toothpick?"

"Not just any toothpick. It's infused with cinnamon. My father got me hooked on these when I was young. I loved the taste of cinnamon. They're hard to find. Order them on the Internet. Keeps my breath fresh." She stuck it in her mouth. "I screwed up, Jack. I went off books looking into you as a murderer and my boss didn't like it."

"Not surprising. You are a jaguar, after all."

She punched my arm. "You called me that before."

"The waitress at the diner in Colorado called you that."

"Well, I don't like it."

"Let's see." I held up a finger. "One, you're a stalker. Two, once you sink your claws in, you don't let go." My forehead wrinkled in feign shock. "But you're not very stealthy. You don't sneak up on things."

"Ok, so I pounce."

"More like a feral cat than a jaguar."

Sanchez smiled, and I followed suit. It felt good to smile. "So, why were you and Jerry at the courthouse today?"

"Oh no!" She said. "We can't even be seen talking, Jack. One accusation of jury tampering and a mistrial can be declared and the perp walks. No, we are NOT talking about it."

"Chew on your toothpick, then." I looked up as Jerry returned.

"Let's go, Sanchez. The chief is letting us head up the investigation. We got leads to follow."

Sanchez stood up and put a hand on my shoulder. She smiled at me. "Hey, Jack, see you in court!" She winked, and they walked away.

Chapter 13

Mercifully, I received no further calls during the night. Before I went to bed, I tried to review the medical records for the panel, but my mind was so fuzzy, I couldn't concentrate. I never received a message from Joe. That meant I had to show up at 8:30, like he said.

I parked in the lot assigned for the jury and watched Gill climb out of his truck. I grabbed my phone and a sack lunch and waited while he walked over carrying a Lilo & Stitch lunchbox.

"Did you steal one of your girl's lunchboxes?"

Gill raised an eyebrow and put his hand to his chest. "I am hurt by your implications I would steal from my own child. This happens to be MY lunchbox given to me by Latoya, my oldest!"

"Then, this turn of events would indicate you were chosen for the jury." I said.

"Yep. Didn't get a text to the otherwise."

"Good morning, Dr. Merchant."

I turned as Rhonda Fall joined us. "Looks like all three of us made it onto the jury. Exciting, isn't it?"

Gill raised an eyebrow, and I introduced him. Rhonda shook his hand. "You know each other?"

"I work at the hospital with Dr. Merchant." Gill said. "I keep the machines running."

As we walked down the sidewalk toward the courthouse, I spied Bobble Head and Snarky ahead of me. We went through the arduous procedure of security check and made our way up to the hallway outside Courtroom 3. Joe waited for us and put us in a lineup. Once again, we leaned against the wall like first graders. He motioned across the hallway to a door.

"As I indicated yesterday, that room will be your jury room. It will be locked at all times. You must present a photo ID to get in. I want all of you to go into the room and leave your phones, purses, laptops, tablets, lunches."

The room was smaller than I anticipated. A long conference table filled most of the room with fourteen chairs around the table, leaving little room to maneuver around the perimeter. Stained blinds covered a grimy window that allowed little light to come in from outside. A door in the corner opened onto a small bathroom. A short hallway connected the room to the outside hallway with two love seats in the hallway and a table with a coffeepot and all the fixings. At least there would be room for a few of us to spread out. Once we left our belongings, Joe took us out into the hallway again and lined us up against the wall. He went to the far end of the line.

One by one, he called the name of the person standing in front of him and pronounced them "Juror number one" and so on until he came to me.

"Jack Merchant, you are juror number 13 and therefore the first alternate. Judge Ford will explain your duties once we get into the courtroom."

The 13th juror and an alternate? Good, that meant I didn't have to vote. But if I had to hang around for the entire trial, what difference would not voting make? Gill was the last in line.

"Virgil Brown, you are juror number 14 and the second alternate."

"Ditto to Dr. Merchant?" Gill said.

"Yep." Joe pointed to the doors. "We are ready now for the jury to enter. You will fill in the jury box in the order in which you are lined up with the first juror on the far end of the first row and the others to follow. Dr. Merchant and Mr. Brown will sit in the two chairs outside and beside the jury box." He looked over his shoulder at us. "Sorry, they're not nearly as comfortable as the regular chairs." He went to the door to the courtroom and opened them, motioning us to go in.

A different group of people from the prospective jurors sat in the rows as we entered. Police officers, firemen, parish deputies, and several people in white lab coats all sat on the far side of the courtroom. The nearest rows just inside held about two dozen people. Spectators? Family of the victim? Witnesses?

The attorneys stood at their tables, facing us as if at attention. The accused did not make eye contact with any of us. Gill and I settled into hard, wooden chairs while the rest of the jury filled the box sitting in padded chairs. After we sat down, Joe took his list to the clerk of court. Today, she wore a bright lime green blouse. Joe went to the door on the opposite side of the judge's desk.

"All rise for the Honorable Judge Tamika Ford."

Ford entered and hurried up to her desk. She sat down and we all followed suit. She referred to documents on her desk and a laptop beside.

"Clerk of the court, have we seated a jury?"

"Yes, your honor." The clerk said.

"Will you please swear in the jury?"

The clerk stood up and Joe said, "All rise."

Everyone stood as the clerk led us through an oath of the jury. "Raise your right hand. As members of the jury, do you solemnly swear or affirm that you will diligently inquire into and true presentment make of all indictable offenses triable within this parish which shall be given you in charge, or which shall otherwise come to your knowledge; that you will keep secret your own counsel and that of your fellows and of the state, and will not, except when authorized by law, disclose testimony of any witness examined before you, nor disclose anything which any grand juror may have said, or how any grand juror may have voted on any matter before you; that you will not indict any person through malice, hatred, or ill will, nor fail to indict any person through fear, favor, affection, or hope of reward or gain; but in all of your indictments you will present the truth, according to the best of your skill and understanding?"

Ford turned to face us. "If you agree to this oath, then say, 'I do'." Thank goodness we didn't have to repeat it. We all said, "I do."

"You may be seated. I will now address the jury with instructions, so please pay close attention." She said to us. "First, there are two alternates, Jack Merchant and Virgil Gill. You will conduct yourself as if you are a member of this jury. If, for some reason, someone becomes incapacitated during the trial, you will replace that person as a voting member of the jury. During deliberations, if you remain an alternate, you will not attend the final process, nor will you have a vote in the final verdict. Do the two of you understand?"

"Yes." I said.

"Yes, ma'am. And I go by Gill." Gill said. Ford fought back a smile.

"Duly note, Mr. Brown." She turned her attention to all of us.

"Now that you have been sworn in, I will give you some preliminary instructions to guide you in your participation in the trial. It is the duty of the jury to find from the evidence what the facts are. You and you alone will be the judges of the facts. You will then have to apply to those facts the law as the court will give it to you. You must follow that law whether you agree with it or not."

"Nothing the court may say or do during the course of the trial is intended to indicate, or should be taken by you as indicating, what your verdict should be. The state has already instructed you as to the types of evidence that will be presented for your consideration. As you know, this is a criminal case."

"There are three basic rules about a criminal case that you must keep in mind. First, the defendant is presumed innocent until proven guilty. The indictment brought by the government against the defendant is only an accusation, nothing more. It is not proof of guilt or anything else. The defendant therefore starts out with a clean slate."

"Second, the burden of proof is on the government until the very end of the case. The defendant has no burden to prove his or her innocence, or to present any evidence, or to testify. Since the defendant has the right to remain silent, the law prohibits you from arriving at your verdict by considering that the defendant may not have testified."

"Third, the government must prove the defendant's guilt beyond a reasonable doubt. I will give you further instructions on this point later but bear in mind that in this respect, a criminal case is different from a civil case."

"I will give you a summary of applicable law. In this case the defendant is charged with second degree murder. I will give you detailed instructions on the law at the end of the case, and those instructions will control your deliberations and decision."

I let out my breath. Second degree murder meant we would not be sequestered!

"Now, as to the conduct of the jury. During the course of

the trial, do not speak with any witness, or with the defendant, or with any of the lawyers in the case. Please do not talk with them about any subject at all. You may be unaware of the identity of everyone connected with the case. Therefore, in order to avoid even the appearance of impropriety, do not engage in any conversation with anyone in or about the court-room or courthouse. Try and remain in the jury room during breaks in the trial and do not linger in the hall. To that end, the bailiff will secure you in the jury room during the course of the trial. He will give you instructions regarding eating, using the bathroom, etc."

"In addition, during the course of the trial, do not talk about the trial with anyone else—not your family, not your friends, not the people with whom you work. Also, do not discuss this case among yourselves until I have instructed you on the law and you have gone to the jury room to make your decision at the end of the trial. Otherwise, without realizing it, you may start forming opinions before the trial is over. It is important that you wait until all the evidence is received and you have heard my instructions on rules of law before you deliberate among yourselves."

"Let me add that during the course of the trial, you will receive all the evidence you properly may consider to decide the case. Please do not try to find out information from any source outside the confines of this courtroom. Do not seek or receive any outside information on your own which you think might be helpful. Do not engage in any outside reading about this case or the law involved. Do not attempt to visit any places mentioned in the case, whether in person or via maps or online resources. You must not read about it in any publica-tions or watch or listen to television or radio reports of what is happening here. Do not use the Internet or any other form of electronic communication to obtain or provide information to another, whether on a phone, computer, or other device. This includes, but is not limited to, the use of websites and search engines, or other online resource or publication for the use of sending or receiving information on the case. Do not attempt to learn about the parties, the witnesses, the lawyers, or me. Do not send or receive emails or text messages relating to the case or your involvement. Do not read or post information on Facebook, or any other blog or social networking site."

"The reason for these rules, as I am certain you will understand, is that your decision in this case must be made solely on the evidence presented at the trial."

Ford said all this without missing a word. She had done this many times! She drew a deep breath and continued. "Since this trial is for second degree murder, you will not be sequestered and you may go home at the end of the day's presentations. The trial will now begin. First, the government will make an opening statement, which is simply an outline to help you understand the evidence as it is admitted. Next, the defendant's attorney may, but does not have to, make an opening statement. Opening statements are neither evidence nor arguments. The government will then present its witnesses, and counsel for the defendant may cross-examine them. Following the government's case, the defendant may, if he wishes, present witnesses whom the government may cross-examine. If the defendant decides to present evidence, the government may introduce rebuttal evidence."

"After all the evidence is in, the attorneys will present their closing arguments to summarize and interpret the evidence for you, and the court will instruct you on the law. After that, you will retire to deliberate on your verdict."

Chapter 14

I glanced at my watch. We had arrived at 8:30 AM and waited in the hall for a half an hour. It was now after 9:30 and we hadn't even started the trial. I had tried to call the attorney's office for the panel, but they did not open until 10 A.M. Maybe I could get in touch over lunch. I poured over the medical panel case in my mind, trying to remember the particulars of that case as the clerk of court read the indictment. But, for now, another legal case was before me. Ford motioned to the court clerk.

"The court clerk will now read the indictment." Ford said.

Lime blouse stood up and read from a document. "On or about February 14, in Choctaw Parish, Louisiana, the defendant, Rex Eagleson, committed the offense of Second Degree Murder In that he, in committing or attempting to commit a forcible felony with an independent felonious purpose - namely, stealing a valuable artifact from Paloma Preston and aggravated battery knowingly made physical contact of an insulting or provoking nature, inflicting multiple punches to the head and face rendering the victim unconscious. He subsequently shot the victim with a crossbow inflicting mortal wounds from which the victim succumbed in route to the hospital. As second-degree murder, the sentence is life imprisonment at hard labor without chance for parole."

I winced, glancing at Rex Eagleson. Stoney faced, he stared straight ahead at nothing. For a second his gaze cut to meet mine and I could swear there was a smile on his lips. I looked away as the clerk of court sat down.

"I will now call the state to deliver an opening statement." Ford said.

Mr. Mansfield took the podium and shuffled papers. Were we in for another boring information dump? He paused and took off his glasses and rubbed his eyes. He walked away from the podium and stopped in front of the jury box.

"Ladies and gentlemen of the jury, I want to thank you for your service today. You have a very important job. It is simply to make sure that Paloma Preston gets the justice she and her family deserve." He gestured to people sitting on the left side of the courtroom. Men and women glared at the defendant. Some wiped tears from their eyes.

"Our contention is that the accused became obsessed with the victim, Paloma Preston after meeting her at a local bookstore and discovering she had an artifact of great value he wanted. On the evening of February 14th, witnesses will be presented who will testify Mrs. Preston and Rex Eagleson had an argument at the bookstore. She followed him out into the parking lot and the two continued to argue. Witnesses will testify he struck her in the head with his fist and then put her in the van and drove away."

"It is our contention Rex Eagleson took Mrs. Preston to her house in order to locate and take the artifact. They were heard arguing once again. He then left her alone in her living room and retrieved a crossbow and arrows from his van. He threatened her with the crossbow and then shot her in the chest."

"A UPS driver arrived next door and heard her scream. He ran back to his UPS truck and called 911. Rex Eagleson ran from the house, got into his van, and drove away. When the UPS driver returned to the house to help Mrs. Preston, smoke began to pour from her house. Rex Eagleson had set the house on fire to cover the evidence of his murder."

Mansfield paused and drew a deep breath. "We request that you, the members of this jury, find Rex Eagleson guilty of second-degree murder where he will be automatically sentenced to life imprisonment with hard labor with no chance of parole. At least behind bars, Rex Eagleson will be unable to stalk other innocent women and deprive them of a life well lived."

Mansfield returned to his seat and Kosinski stood up. She wore a simple white dress with no sleeves tied at the neck with a light blue silk sash. She moved gracefully to the podium without the swagger I was used to. She smiled at us.

"Members of the jury, I want to thank you for your time. I know you have very important tasks and concerns, and this duty has pulled you from them. But being a member of a jury is the most important civil duty one can perform. For you see, any one of you, or even I, for that matter, could be sitting in the accused chair looking at a lifelong commitment to prison for something we did not do. My client, Rex Eagleson, is a blue-collar worker in the sports department at a local Super-Mart. He has dedicated his life to community service. In fact, Rex frequently visited the Christian Life Book Store to meet with a group of parents of home-schooled children. His purpose was to start an archery class for those students as part of their physical education module. The assertions of the prosecution portray him as a stalker. Nothing could be farther from the truth. The defense will present you with corroborating evidence Rex was not the man seen arguing with the deceased and later arriving at her home. Rather, he was across town at his favorite diner."

She paused and moved away from the podium to stand before the jury box. For a moment, her gaze fixed on mine and then away. "We have heard accusations of lying and deceit, but I will show you the truth about Rex Eagleson. And when you see the truth, and not a host of fabrications and wrong assertions, you will find Mr. Eagleson not guilty. Again, thank you for your kind consideration and your precious time. One day, you may sit in that chair falsely accused of a crime and you will want a concerned and dedicated jury to carefully consider all evidence. I am sure that you will."

Kosinski glanced once at me as she made her way back to her seat and smiled. I averted my gaze. I knew it was wrong, but the mere fact she was defending Rex Eagleson was enough to convince me the man was most probably guilty.

"Thank you, counselors, for your opening statements. The state may proceed with its case." Ford said tapping her gavel on the desk.

Zuniga took the podium. Her hair was pulled back in a tight coil on the back of her head and she wore a dark brown pant suit with a light green blouse. She appeared all business and no nonsense as she activated the large screen monitor. The smiling face of a woman most likely in her forties appeared on the screen. She had dark skin and black hair hinting at perhaps a Hispanic heritage.

"I would like to introduce you to Paloma Rodriquez Preston." Zuniga said. "Mrs. Preston was forty-two years old, a widow, and taught a kindergarten class to home schoolers. Mrs. Preston spent two days a week with kindergarten students in a classroom in the back of the Christian Life Book Store in Talako, Louisiana." Another photograph appeared with several children gathered around her in a park setting. "The parents of these children gave me permission to show this photograph. Mrs. Preston was beloved by her students and their parents. She is a naturalized citizen from Matamoros, Mexico." Another photograph showed a younger version of Mrs. Preston surrounded by a rag tag group of children standing in the middle of what appeared to be a rundown down village.

"Miss Paloma Rodriquez was an orphan raised in an orphanage in Matamoros, Mexico, just across the Mexican border from Brownsville, Texas. Paloma Rodriquez was adopted by an American couple who founded and ran the orphanage." Another photo showed a young adult Paloma standing with an older couple in front of a church. "She became a citizen of the United States when she was twenty-one years old. She attended college and graduated with a degree in special education. She met her future husband, Benjamin Preston, in college." In the next photo, Paloma wore a wedding dress and stood next to a tall, handsome man with light blonde hair wearing a tuxedo.

"Unfortunately, Paloma Preston and Benjamin never had children even though they desperately tried. It turns out Paloma suffered physical trauma as a young teenager at the hands of traffickers and this trauma produced irreversible bodily damage preventing her from having children. The couple were about to adopt a child when tragedy struck."

The next photo showed Paloma standing before a gravestone. "Benjamin was killed in a convenience store robbery. He was a random customer who stopped to buy gas at the wrong time and the wrong place. Devastated by her loss, Paloma never remarried. She never adopted a child. Instead, she dedicated her life to teaching children and giving them opportunities she never had."

The next screen showed a list of names. "The prosecution will call these witnesses to the stand to demonstrate the evidence we believe will convince you that Mrs. Paloma Preston was stalked and murdered by Rex Eagleson after he could not locate a treasured artifact belonging to Paloma Preston."

Zuniga returned to the table and Mansfield stood up.

"Your honor we would like to call our first witness, Ruby Bamburg."

A heavy-set woman with long, salt and pepper hair stood up from the first row of the courtroom and made her way slowly to the witness stand. Her eyes were rimmed in red, and she sniffed as she stepped into the stand. The clerk of court swore her in, and she sat down. She wore a loose flowered dress and a large, pale blue rimmed set of glasses. Mansfield walked to the stand and stood only feet away from the jury box.

"Mrs. Bamburg, do you know Paloma Preston?"

Bamburg nodded. Mansfield pointed to the court reporter. "Mrs. Bamburg, I know this is difficult for you, but would you please answer verbally for the sake of our court record?"

"I'm sorry." Bamburg stuttered. "This is just so hard."

Mansfield turned back to his end of the table and retrieved a box of tissues. He offered the box, and Bamburg took one and placed it up to her nose. "I know," she gulped, "I mean I *knew* Paloma. She was my best friend."

"I know this is difficult, Mrs. Bamburg, but please be patient with us. How long have you known Mrs. Preston?"

"Since college. We were roommates in college. I was her maid of honor at her and Ben's wedding." She dabbed away tears with the tissue. "I miss her so much."

Mansfield paused, to let that sink in. I glanced at Kosinski. She looked like she had swallowed a toad. Eagleson just stared straight ahead, his features unreadable. Once again, a wave of oppression seemed to wash over me. How cruel was it that this woman would have to relive the murder of her best friend? For that matter, why had God allowed Paloma to die? Or, Janice for that matter? I closed my eyes and fought back memories of Janice on her own death bed, charred and burned beyond recognition. Nausea took me and I broke out in a sweat. I felt a hand on my arm and looked up into the eyes of Gill.

"It's okay, Doc." He whispered. "I'm praying for you."

No one heard him as Mrs. Bamburg's sobs filled the courtroom. She finally stopped and Mansfield returned to his questioning. "Mrs. Bamburg, where do you work?"

"At Christian Life Bookstore. I've been working there for, gosh, fifteen years. I was the person who suggested Paloma teach home schooled children in one of our conference rooms." Bamburg sniffed. "She was such a good teacher. Loved those kids so much."

Kosinski tensed and I knew she wanted to object or something, or anything to stop the portrayal of Mrs. Preston as anything resembling a saint. But I realized if she did, the jury, including me, would see her as badgering a sad, mourning friend of the deceased. Sam wanted me to observe what it was like in this courtroom. I never knew it could be so emotionally trying for the family and friends of the victim. I leaned forward so I could see Rhonda Fall sitting in the middle of the front row. She had her hand pressed to her lips and her eyes glistened with tears.

Mansfield retrieved a document from his table and returned to the witness stand. "Mrs. Bamburg, do you recognize this document?"

She studied it and nodded. "Yes."

Mansfield walked over to the clerk of court. "Your honor, the state would like to enter this document into evidence."

The clerk took the document and stamped it with a hand stamp and wrote something on the paper. Mansfield took the document and handed it to the judge. "Your honor, this is a police report of a formal complaint registered by Mrs. Bamburg on February first of the year in question."

"I will allow it." The judge said. The clerk took the document and carried it to Kosinski. Kosinski glanced at it briefly and shrugged. "We have no objections, you honor."

Mansfield returned to the witness stand. "Mrs. Bamburg did you file that police report?"

"Yes." Bamburg stiffened. "I had to."

"And can you tell the court the substance of your complaint?"

"It was about that man." She pointed to Rex Eagleson.

"Objection, your honor." Kosinski stood up. "The witness has not established the facts of this report to our satisfaction before falsely identifying the accused."

"Sustained." Ford tapped her gavel. She turned to Mrs. Bamburg. "Mrs. Bamburg, please confine your comments and answers to the substance of the questions only, please."

Bamburg frowned and anger twisted her face. She took off her glasses and rubbed her eyes. "Yes, Ma'am."

Mansfield seemed unfazed. "Mrs. Bamburg, why did you file this police report?"

"I saw a man wandering around the bookstore. He seemed to be following Paloma around the store. He was glancing at her and everywhere she went, he was a few yards behind. When she went into the conference room to teach, he left and went out to a white van and got in. But he didn't drive away. He just sat there." Bamburg nodded. "And it wasn't the first time. I saw him in the store at least three times the month before. Every time, he was following Paloma from a distance."

"And why did you consider this worrisome enough to contact the police?"

"Well, it was her history." Bamburg nodded and glanced at us. "She was abducted as a teenager and horrible things were done to her and it affected her whole life and here was another person possibly stalking her, maybe to abduct her." She pointed to Eagleson. "He was going to kidnap her. I knew it and sure enough he did!"

"Objection, your honor." Kosinski shot up from her chair.

"Sustained." Ford said before Kosinski could give the reason why. A smile crossed Eagleson's face, and he turned his gaze in my direction. I looked away.

"Mrs. Bamburg, once again control your responses. The

jury is to ignore those last remarks. Mr. Mansfield, I am also issuing a warning to you." She tapped her gavel.

"Mrs. Bamburg, I think we understand you were worried for Mrs. Preston's safety. Would you tell us what happened on February 14?"

"Well, it was Valentine's Day, and the children exchanged valentine cards in their classroom and Paloma let them have a little party. Some of the moms were there to help. She came out of the classroom and bumped into," she paused and glanced at Eagleson and then at Ford, "a man. They had words. I'm not sure what was said, but you could tell Paloma wasn't happy."

Bamburg paused and took another tissue from the box and dabbed her eyes. "The man marched out of the store, and she followed him. They ended up out in the parking lot and I could tell they were arguing. I couldn't hear what they said," she glared at Kosinski as if anticipating an objection, "but he grabbed her and hit her up side the head. She sort of slumped, and then he slid open the side door of his van and threw her inside. Before I could react, he hopped in his van and drove off with her." Bamburg groaned and began to sob. "I called the police, but it was too late. They were gone. Just like that, Paloma had been kidnapped again!"

Mansfield paused and let the sobs fill the courtroom. It took a few minutes for Bamburg to recover. He stepped closer to her. "Mrs. Bamburg, can you identity the man who kidnapped your friend?"

"Yes, I can." Bamburg said. "He is sitting right there at the end of that table." She pointed to Eagleson.

"Let the record show Mrs. Bamburg has identified the assailant as the accused, Mr. Eagleson. Now, Mrs. Bamburg, how can you be so sure the accused is the same person?"

"Look at his eyes."

Everyone in the jury turned their attention to Eagleson. Mansfield pressed the remote control, and the booking photograph of Rex Eagleson appeared on the screen. "Your honor, since this booking photograph is already a part of the formal arrest record, we merely want to show it to Mrs. Bamburg."

Rex Eagleson glared at the camera, his long dark hair carelessly hanging to his shoulders. Each eye was a different color.

"Mrs. Bamburg is this photograph of the same man you saw in the store that day?"

"Yes. Look at his eyes. They are of different colors! How could you miss that? It's creepy."

"Objection, your honor. The witness is disparaging my client."

"Mrs. Bamburg, please refrain from maligning the accused." Ford said.

"Well, it's true." She pointed to Eagleson. "His eyes are different colors. How could anyone miss that?"

"Thank you, Mrs. Bamburg. I have no further questions."

Mansfield returned to his table. Kosinski leaned over to her associate and they whispered for a moment. I noted she never once even looked at Eagleson. Xavier stood up and buttoned his coat. His dark skin and almost white hair were very striking and exuded an air of quiet confidence. He walked languidly to the podium with a sure cadence to his step. He paused behind the podium.

"Mrs. Bamburg, I am Robert Xavier and along with Ms. Kosinski we represent Mr. Eagleson. I am so sorry for the loss of your best friend." His voice was deep and soothing like the voice of Mufasa from the Lion King. "I just have a few clarifying questions for you. Do you mind if we continue? Or do you need a short break?"

Bamburg glared at him and glanced up at Ford. "No. Let's get this over with."

"Thank you." Xavier touched the remote control on the podium and brought up a video on the television. "Your honor we would like to place this video as our exhibit for the defense."

Mansfield stood up. "We object, your honor. The prosecution was not advised of any video footage."

"Your honor," Xavier said quietly. "We only obtained this video footage this morning. I beg you consider the importance of this evidence and allow it to be introduced to the court."

Ford took off her reading glasses and held them in her hands as she looked back and forth between the two men. "I will allow it, Mr. Xavier. But no more last-minute information. Do you understand?"

"Thank you, your honor." Xavier turned to the video footage. "As I said we would like to introduce this video into evidence as surveillance footage from the parking lot outside Christian Life Bookstore." He walked away from the podium with a document and handed it to the clerk. "Along with this affidavit from the shopping center security center asserting this is from video footage obtained on the afternoon of February 14 in front of Christian Life Bookstore."

Mansfield leaned over and whispered to Zuniga. Gill leaned toward me. "I don't like these kinds of surprises, Doc."

Xavier returned to the podium and touched the remote control. No sound came from the television set as a man come out through the front doors of the bookstore followed by Paloma Preston. The man paused just before exiting the frame and looked up at the camera. He wore a dark cap and sunglasses. He walked out of the frame. Paloma Preston followed him and disappeared from the frame. Xavier rewound the footage and paused the video with a clear image of the man wearing sunglasses.

"Mrs. Bamburg, can you identify the man in this video?"

Bamburg's mouth was open, and she nodded. "Yes."

"Was he the man you saw in the store?"

"Yes, he was."

"Are you sure?"

"Yes."

"Mrs. Bamburg, the man running out of the store is the same man you saw stalking Mrs. Preston on February first?"

"Yes." Bamburg said, and I had to admit, smugly.

"But this man has on sunglasses. Did he have on sunglasses while he was in the store on February 14?"

Bamburg froze and put her hands to her mouth. "Well, uh, I don't know."

"You don't know?" Xavier moved toward the witness stand. "If you don't know, how can you be sure the man you saw in the store that day is the accused?"

Bamburg look over at Eagleson. "Well, it was him. I know it."

"You know it?" Xavier said quietly. "Mrs. Bamburg you may be accusing an innocent man of kidnapping your best friend based on superficial appearances alone if you cannot corroborate the color of his eyes."

"Objection, you honor." Mansfield said. "Counsel is badgering the witness."

Ford paused and shook her head. "No, I'll allow it. Mr. Xavier, ask an objective question, please."

"Of course, your honor." He said. "Mrs. Bamburg, you recognize Mr. Eagleson as the man you saw in the store on February first because you saw he had two different color eyes, as you have testified. Is that true?"

"Yes." Bamburg said meekly.

"So, I will ask you something very simply. Can you be absolutely certain that the man we see in that video, wearing sunglasses, was the same man you saw on February first?"

Bamburg looked at us with deep desperate eyes. Tears filled them and she looked down at her lap. "No, I can't be certain."

"Thank you, Mrs. Bamburg. I know that was difficult. Your honor we have no further questions."

Mrs. Bamburg stood up and shook her head violently.

"But it was him. I tell you it had to be him. Who else could it have been?"

Ford pounded her gavel. "Mrs. Bamburg, stop talking and leave the witness stand.

"He did it, I tell you. He killed my best friend. I know he did." Mrs. Bamburg began to sob.

Ford pounded her gavel again. "Bailiff, please assist Mrs. Bamburg from the courtroom."

Joe came over and gently took Mrs. Bamburg by the elbow and helped her out of the stand. Her sobs echoed throughout the room as she left through the double doors. Ford looked at us.

"The jury will disregard those last remarks as someone in deep emotional pain. Remember, your job is to consider only the evidence and not the opinion of this witness."

Zuniga came to the podium. "Your honor, it will take a few minutes to get our next witness on the monitor via video chat."

Ford nodded. "Seeing as how it is now 11:30, I will recess this court until 1 PM."

Joe had returned and said, "All rise."

Judge Ford stood up as we did, and Joe motioned for us to follow him. I glanced once more at Eagleson and the gleam in his eyes and the wicked smile on his face were unmistakable!

Chapter 15

Joe led us back to the jury room, where we milled about in the cramped space until everyone settled into a seat. I immediately grabbed my cell phone to check for messages. I had to get out of the medical review panel that evening. Gill sat beside me.

Joe stood in the door leading to the small foyer room with the couch. "Ladies and gentlemen of the jury. You may use your tablets, laptops, or phones. Just remember what Judge Ford said. No seeking information on this trial and no talking among yourselves about the trial. I will have sodas and water brought in here in a moment, along with several pizzas. If any of you have special dietary needs, I hope you brought a suitable lunch because we have limited food choices here in the courthouse. I'll be back in a minute."

Bobblehead lifted her hand. "Can we at least get out of this room for a moment?"

"When I return with the pizza, I'll take you across the hall to an empty courtroom where you can spread out while you eat. You can come and go between there and the jury room as long as you don't go down the hall."

"I'll save my peanut butter and jelly sandwich for later." Gill patted his lunchbox. "What'd you bring?"

I looked up from my phone. "Why, you want to trade? Like in grade school?"

Gill frowned. "Doc, I didn't have much to trade in school. I was on the special food program. Got free breakfast and lunch and I ate everything. Nothing left to trade. They were the best meals I had all day. I have six brothers and two sisters. Not much on the table at home!"

"Nine of you?"

"Yep! Now, what did you bring?"

"Frozen lasagna meal. Probably over a year old." I picked up my sack lunch and tossed it into a nearby trash can.

I found a voicemail and listened to it. "Dr. Merchant, we're sorry, but we cannot postpone the panel. We look forward to hearing from you this evening and we will call you on your cell phone."

I tossed my phone on the table. Gill put a hand on my shoulder. "Hey, Doc, pizza ain't that bad."

"It's not pizza I'm upset about. I have another legal quagmire this evening. I'm surrounded by lawyers."

"What was that joke you told me once? Let's see. Why didn't the great white shark eat the lawyer who fell overboard?"

I rolled my eyes. "Professional courtesy."

Bobblehead laughed from across the table. "Good one, Dr. Merchant. Don't mind if I call you that, do you? Latonya Washington and I'm a ward clerk at St. Alexander. Work on the pediatrics floor."

I smiled. "Nice to meet you, Latonya. This is my friend Gill Brown."

She raised an eyebrow. "Oh, I know all about Mr. Gill."

I glanced at Gill, and he sighed. "We used to go to church together."

"Until he runs his happy rear end off down to the boats

and the riverfront." She snapped, pushing her huge glasses back on her face. "What got into you? The devil?"

"I teach the Bible, Latonya, to the homeless down on the river front." Gill said.

"Don't forsake the gathering together, Gill. You belong in church with your wife," Latonya said. She crossed her arms over her considerable bosom. "What that woman has to put up with!"

"Did you say something about the devil?" An older African American woman said from across the table. I recognized her as one of the five who tried to get out duty. "I can't see that man too well with my poor eyesight, but I could feel it."

"Feel what?" I said.

"The demon in that man." She pointed a crooked finger at me and I noticed a white scale covered one of her eyes.

I sat back and glanced at Gill. Nobody objected at my end of the table. "Demon?"

"My name is Dianne Tucker and I'm a retired pastor from Fuller Life Tabernacle over in Bayou City." She leaned toward me. "I may not see too well with these old eyes, but the Holy Spirit within me has given me the gift of discernment. That man is pure evil."

"Just a minute!" A tall man in a tightly pressed button shirt stood up. His hair was shot through with streaks of gray. His face was clean and lean. "I'm Henry Crenshaw and the judge said we shouldn't be discussing this case."

Another man sitting next to him merely nodded. He was shorter, with a military cut and a definite military air about him. "Mr. Crenshaw is correct." He looked at my end of the table with a steady gaze. "If anyone finds out we have violated the rules, the chance is very high for throwing the indictment out the window."

"That's right." Henry said. "Probabilities are very high, judging from what we just witnessed. I suggest that we keep our conversations about things other than the trial." He sat back down.

"Did you say probabilities?" The Snarky Blonde said from the far end of the table. "Are you an accountant?"

"Retired computer programmer. And your name?" Henry said.

"Zenia Ricketts. I'm an insurance adjuster." She said and turned her attention back to her phone.

The tattooed lady stood up and headed to the foyer with the love seat. "I can't stand sitting in this room. I'm claustrophobic." She paused and looked at me. "Wouldn't have any Xanax on you, Dr. Merchant?"

"I'm a radiologist. I don't write prescriptions routinely." I said.

"Consuela Giddens, social worker. I should have brought some from home." She began pacing around the foyer.

"We are just one happy little bunch of coconuts, aren't we?" A young white woman said to my left. "I'm Autumn Coleman, college student. And I am loving this! I mean, a real murder trial!" She smiled and Latonya groaned across from me.

"Jesus, take me away, please." She mumbled under her breath.

A man in a button down shirt to my right chimed in. "Aaron Fields. Engineer with Masterson Petroleum."

Next to him Rhonda Fall gave her name. Sitting next to her a well dressed woman nodded. "Sybil Shepherd. No relation to the actress."

An African American man in a bow tie and jacket at the end of the table smiled. "Dante Marshall, bank executive."

A woman with muddy hair wearing a teal "Super-Mart" vest sat in the corner. We looked at her expectantly. "What?" She said. "I'm Mrs. Lucy Kosack. I work at Super-Mart."

"Do you think wearing that vest is wise." Henry said.

"I'm cold. It keeps me warm. And, I have to go to work right after this confounded trial!"

"My name is Rocky." The military guy said. "Where's the pizza?"

Just then, Joe returned with the drinks and led us across the hallway to a much smaller, but empty courtroom. Pizza had been spread out on the attorney's table. Autumn squealed when she saw the judge's desk and ran up on the raised platform. She collapsed into the chair.

"All rise for the honorable Judge Autumn Coleman." She said in a low voice. We ignored her.

Gill and I took our pizza and sodas back to the jury room along with two other people, Dante and Rhonda. She smiled and waved at me as she sat down and awkwardly picked at her pizza. I tried to ignore her. There was so much I could tell her about her mother's care. But to what end? It would only create unnecessary anxiety.

"Doc, is it true?" Gill mumbled through his pizza.

"Is what true?"

"Dr. Lamb has bought Bayou City Medical Center?"

I paused and tried to put on my best game face. Gill laughed.

"Hey, I already know. Murray had us go over to check out the equipment a month ago. I just couldn't tell anyone." Murray Washington held the position of administrator for the radiology departments in the Fairmont system.

"Was he guzzling antacid?" I chewed on the tough pizza. Maybe I needed some antacid.

"He's pretty twitchy about it." Gill said. "Doc, we got an old hospital filled with outdated equipment. It's gonna cost and arm and a leg to update the radiology department over there."

"And Murray hates to spend money!"

"Well, from what I understand, the docs over there wanted to be a part of Fairmont."

"That's what I understand. If that's so, then Lamb will find the funds."

"Want to bet he'll funnel them from the current Fairmont hospitals? I mean you can't get blood from a turnip."

Rhonda Fall moved over to sit beside me, and my heart raced. What was she going to ask me?

"I haven't met you." She put her hand toward Gill. "Rhonda Fall. Dr. Merchant took care of my deceased mother years ago. Isn't it a small world? And I guess the two of you know each other? An even smaller world!"

Gill glanced at me and took her hand. "Gill Brown. I work with Dr. Merchant at our hospital. I keep all the machines running."

"Oh, I get it!" She shook his hand. "You're Scotty to his Doctor McCoy! You know, like on the Enterprise!"

Gill merely smiled. "Something like that, Miss Rhonda."

Rhonda blushed and laughed. "Miss Rhonda? Oh, I like that!"

Dante Marshall scooted down to our end of the table. He was a bit on the portly side with chubby cheeks. He ate his pizza with delicate bites. "I couldn't help but overhear. The Fairmont Medical Systems is buying out Bayou City Medical?"

I glanced at Gill and swallowed. Gill shrugged. "I guess the cat is out of the bag."

Marshall smiled. "The bank has some office property in the downtown area of Bayou City that badly needs leasing. This means doctor's offices moving into the area, doesn't it?"

I shook my head. "I don't know, Mr. Marshall. I'm a radiologist, a hospital-based physician. I wouldn't know about leasing offices and all that. And this isn't official yet. I'm sure you know how deals go. It could fall through just as easily as a rumor gets started."

Marshall nodded. "Yeah, right! I know how the game is played." He took his phone out into the foyer.

"I hope that don't get me fired." Gill said.

"I wouldn't worry about it, Gill. I'm sure Dr. Lamb has already tipped off his investors."

The other members of the jury trickled in, and I checked my email on my phone to see if it was possible the panel might have been rescheduled at the last minute. No such luck. But I saw a text from Sam. She asked that I give her a call after my jury duty today. She ended the text with enigmatic phrase, "I need to see you about a dead man."

Chapter 16

We marched back into the courtroom. I glanced over at
Eagleson. His gaze was focused on documents in front of him.
What had Dianne Tucker said about demons? Did the devil
make him do it? That wave of oppression that came over me,
what was that? What had she said? Something about a "spirit"
of discernment?

Zuniga stood up and motioned to the monitor. "Your
honor, we were unable to connect with our next witness due to
power outages in the witness' area. We will postpone that testimony until later in the trial."

"Any objections from the defense?" Ford said to Kosinski.

"No."

Mansfield walked to the podium. "The prosecution calls
Dr. Fidenzio Fernandez to the stand."

Dr. Fernandez wore a dark red wool sweater over a white
shirt and black bowtie. He walked with a loose, lanky gait to
the witness stand. His black hair hung down to his ears and a
sharply demarcated beard cut close to the skin framed his
deeply tanned face. He wore a black rimmed pair of glasses.
The court clerk swore him in, and Mansfield began questioning.

"Dr. Fernandez, what is your profession?"

"I am a professor of Meso-American archeology and history at LSU in Baton Rouge." He said in crisp tones.

"And how would you describe your area of expertise?"

"I study the archeology and history of Mexico and Central America and portions of South America."

"Your honor, we have already entered into evidence the following photographs supplied by Dr. Fernandez." Mansfield motioned to the monitor. A photograph of Paloma Preston standing next to Dr. Fernandez filled the screen. Her smiling, beaming features radiated joy. My heart sank at the sight of her. She held a golden disc in her hands.

"Dr. Fernandez, who is the person with you in this photograph?"

"Mrs. Paloma Preston."

"Would you tell the court about your visit with Mrs. Preston that led to this photograph."

"Certainly." He turned to face the jury. He had been well rehearsed. "I received a call from Mrs. Preston in December of year before last. I believe this would place her call and subsequent visit weeks before her death. Mrs. Preston has an interesting heritage. She shared with me how she was left on the doorstep of an orphanage in Matamoros, Mexico. The orphanage raised her until she became a naturalized United States citizen at age twenty one and moved to northern Louisiana."

"Mrs. Preston claimed to have an artifact that might be of interest to me. I arranged a visit, and she traveled to Baton Rouge and met with me on December 27. At our visit, she showed me an object. I believe you can see the photograph of this object? Yes?" He glanced at Mansfield.

Mansfield touched the remote and the next photograph revealed a golden disc. A gruesome image had been carved into the disc. "As you can see, this disc would be of great interest to any archeologist. The disc itself is about four inches wide and one inch thick. It is quite heavy, and metal analysis revealed a composition of 70% pure gold beneath an outward bronze/brass veneer."

"Dr. Fernandez, would you describe the image on the disc?" Mansfield said.

"The image represents the myth of Coatlique. In brief, this is an Aztec myth. This image is of Coyolxauhqui, the sister of Huitzilopochtli. Legend has it that Coatlicue became pregnant after giving birth to the moon and four hundred stars. This followed a vow of chastity, and Coyolxauhqui was so angry she killed her mother and the unborn child. But the unborn child sprang forth from his mother's womb and cut the vengeful Coyolxauhqui into pieces, throwing all but her head down the side of a mountain. Thus was born the god Huitzilopochtli and the ritual of human sacrifices of the Aztecs." I studied the gruesome image of a dismembered woman on the disk and I closed my eyes as the image of the woman at the Tiger's Tail filled my mind.

"The next photo shows a closeup of the other side of the disk. As you can see, there are two parallel bars along one side of the oval rendition of a person's head. The bars represent the number ten. The three dots across the upper bar represent the number three. This is the Aztec symbol for the number thirteen. The more ornamental face shaped object beside it is of unknown origin. The closest image I have come across would show this is a designation for an evil spirit. Therefore, this image on the disk would refer to a 'thirteenth' evil spirit. Such an entity is unknown to the Aztec mythology. And that is why I told Mrs. Preston this disk was a fake."

I glanced at Gill, and he shrugged. Why were we seeing all this? Thirteenth evil spirit? My head was spinning with these images, and I needed some fresh air.

Mansfield must have read our minds. "I know the court is probably wondering why we are spending time on this. But I ask for patience as this disk helps to understand motive for the murder of Paloma Preston."

"Proceed, Mr. Mansfield." Ford said.

"What do you mean by referring to this disk as a fake?"

"The Aztec empire had plentiful gold until the Spanish conquistadors arrived. In the decades afterwards, gold was extracted and sent back to Spain. Somewhere on the bottom of the Atlantic Ocean are Spanish ships filled with precious Aztec gold jewelry. Disks such as the one depicted in the photograph would have been very rare. And very valuable. However, metallurgical analysis of scrapings from this disk reveals metallic contents not native to the Aztec region. I believe this disk was manufactured in the early 1800's in order to appear to be an Aztec artifact."

Kosinksi stood up. "Your honor, this is all fascinating. But, would counsel please come to the point?"

"I agree with the defense. Can we get to your point, Mr. Mansfield?" Ford said.

"Certainly. Dr. Fernandez, what is this disk worth?"

"If it were genuine, priceless. Even as a fake composed of mostly pure gold it has an estimated value of a half million dollars."

Muttering and murmuring filled the courtroom. Even I managed to gasp in shock. Judge Ford tapped her gavel. "Silence in the courtroom please."

Dr. Fernandez leaned forward and looked up at Judge Ford. "I do not want to waste the court's time, your honor, but the possible history of this disk is germane to the death of Mrs. Preston."

Ford tilted her head as she looked down on Fernandez. "Very well, Dr. Fernandez. We will be patient for a little while longer."

Fernandez pointed at the photograph with a long finger. "I believe an explorer from the early 1800s by the name of Silas Stoneheart used this disk to dupe his investors. At the time this disk was made, Mr. Stoneheart had a reputation, not necessarily legal, of acquiring artifacts from Mexico and South America to sell to interested buyers. He approached such an interested group in New Orleans, sometime after the Louisiana purchase, and used this disk to fool them into investing funds so he could travel to Mexico for more of these 'Aztec' disks. The group was indeed fooled, and money flowed into Stoneheart's coffers. However, he never arrived in Mexico and disappeared with his ship and all his men. Rumor has it he sailed to the Amazon area instead of Mexico. The disk went with him. And surfaced in the possession of a poor orphan from Matamoros, Mexico named Paloma Rodriguez. Now, I assured Mrs. Preston I could place the item up for auction to several museums so it would be placed where it could be studied. She said she would get back to me. And this is where it gets interesting." He sat back. "She told me there was a man who had been harassing her about the disk. He claimed it belonged to him, and he wanted it back. She came to me for confirmation of authenticity."

"So there was a man Mrs. Preston claimed harassed her and wanted the disk, correct?"

"Yes."

"Did she give you any information about this man or his motive?"

"She did. Mrs. Preston mentioned a man by the name of Rex Eagleson. She said this man had approached her many times at her home and at her place of work, a Christian bookstore claiming the disk belonged to him."

I glanced at Eagleson and his gaze was fixed on the table before him. "Did Mrs. Preston characterize these instances where she was approached at the bookstore?" Mansfield asked.

"Objection." Kosinski didn't even stand. "Hearsay."

"Sustained."

"Dr. Fernandez, did Mrs. Preston share with you the

reason she believed another person might be interested in acquiring the disk?"

"Yes. She said the person who contacted her on multiple occasions believed the disk was associated with an entity the person called 'the thirteenth demon' and believed this demonic being was connected to end time prophecies from the book of Revelation."

Mansfield held up his hand to quiet the murmuring before Ford could tap her gavel. "Besides Mrs. Preston, Dr. Fernandez, were you approached by anyone else about the disk?"

Dr. Fernandez nodded. "Yes. The day I met with Mrs. Preston, we had coffee in my office and I then escorted her to her vehicle. She became very agitated when she saw a white panel van parked nearby. She refused to tell me why she was agitated and quickly got into her car and drove away. Intrigued, I approached the van, and a man got out. He asked me about my visit with Mrs. Preston. I, of course, told him our conversation was confidential. But then, he surprised me by asking specifically about the disk. He claimed the disk belonged to him and he said, and I quote because I will not forget it, 'I will do whatever it takes to get that disk.' He got back into the van and drove away."

"Did this person identify themself?"

"No. But I would know him if I ever met them again. The man had very distinctive eyes, each of differing colors. And he is sitting right over there." Dr. Fernandez pointed at Rex Eagleson.

The moment was electric and my skin crawled. Eagleson looked up at Fernandez and something dark and deadly filled his eyes, twisting his features into a sneer that lasted for mere seconds.

"Let the record show Dr. Fernandez has identified the accused, Rex Eagleson. No further questions." Mansfield said.

Kosinski tapped on the keyboard for her tablet and stood up. "I have a couple of questions. Dr. Fernandez, in order to put an object up for auction don't you have to present verification of the object's origin?"

"Yes."

"Did Mrs. Preston present you with such, I believe it is called, provenance?"

"No."

"You just took her word this precious gold disk has been in her possession since the day she was placed at the orphanage?"

"I had no reason to disbelieve her."

"But isn't it possible she may have acquired this disk in other, let's say, illegal ways?"

"Objection, your honor." Mansfield said.

"Sustained. No more speculation, Ms. Kosinski." Ford said tersely.

"I'm sorry, your honor. I'm just trying to find out if it is possible Mrs. Preston may have acquired this disk in some other way. Without paperwork, we can't be certain where it came from? Can we, Dr. Fernandez?"

"This is correct." Fernandez said quickly. "But Mr. Eagleson didn't have paperwork, either."

Ford tapped her gavel. "That last statement went beyond the scope of questioning and the jury will disregard it."

I didn't see how in the world I was supposed to do that. But Kosinski had made her point. Tit for tat, back and forth, certainty and speculation—all part of this complex game. Now I saw why Sam had wanted me to be on a jury.

"I have an additional question that just came to mind, Dr. Fernandez." Kosinski said. This time, she approached the witness stand. "You claim to have met Mr. Eagleson in the parking lot on the day in question. What was he wearing?"

"A black cap, black leather jacket and jeans."

"And his eyes? You claim to have seen his eyes?"

"Yes. Two different colored eyes."

"He wasn't wearing sunglasses?"

"How would I have seen his eyes?"

"Dr. Fernandez, have you at any time accessed information regarding this case after Mr. Eagleson's arrest for murder?" Kosinski asked.

Fernandez touched his mustache. "I must admit, I saw the news on television. And I read about it on the Internet."

"Have you ever seen Mr. Eagleson's photographs on the Internet or news?"

"Yes." Fernandez said quietly.

"Was his eye malady obvious on these photographs?"

"I did notice it, yes."

"So, I ask you again, are you absolutely certain the man you met in the parking lot did not wear sunglasses?"

Fernandez looked at the jury in desperation. He blinked. "I must admit, I cannot be certain."

"No further questions." Kosinski smiled as she walked away.

Over the next hour, four witnesses took the stand. Each had been in the parking lot when the altercation between Eagleson and Preston had taken place. Each person talked about a man in a black cap and a white van. Each time, Kosinski skewered their testimony by referring to the sunglasses.

But Mansfield and Zuniga did not seem affected by the cross-examination testimony. Neither did I. Just because Eagleson had worn sunglasses didn't mean he wasn't the man in the van. My watch told me it was 2 P.M. and Judge Ford called for a thirty-minute break.

I headed to the jury room and the one bathroom. Afterwards, I sat by Gill silently and checked my email. Nothing from the law firm! I stepped into the foyer and called Sam.

"Sam, how are you feeling?"

"Hurting, Jack. I've got metal in my bones."

"Which you asked for."

"I know!" She said. "Listen, I just wanted to give you a

follow-up. I know you can't talk about your case, but I looked into that other murder case we talked about. I'm getting the evidence box delivered from lock up and I'm going over the autopsy report this afternoon."

"Thanks, Sam. Mrs. Dixon's daughter is sitting right near me in the jury room."

"Has she asked anymore about her mother's case?"

"Not yet. But she did cozy up to me at lunch. I know it's coming."

"Just tell her you don't know anything."

"Any more news on Dr. McVay?"

"Your friend, Sanchez, thinks it might be related to a satanic ritual. Nothing concrete." Sam coughed and winced in pain. "Dang it! That hurt. Every twitch and movement hurts."

"Going to toss beads, huh?" I smiled.

"Shut up!" I heard a beeping in the background. "Yes! Time for my next pain pill. Call me tonight, Jack." And she was gone.

I stared at the blank screen on my phone. Satanic ritual? Evil spirits? What world I had stepped into when I took on the consultant job? Scientific or supernatural? And now, even on this jury, the devil kept poking his head up where all could see.

Chapter 17

We took our seats in the jury box once more and the afternoon wore on with a couple more witnesses who had seen Eagleson at the store prior to the 14th.

Zuniga came to the podium. "Your honor, I would like to call Miriam Waters to the stand."

An elderly woman with a walker made her way to the witness stand. She had short, gray hair and a pale face coated with powder. She actually wore a tiny hat on the top of her head. Her plain beige dress hung loosely on her frame. She had to be helped into the witness stand by Joe and, breathing heavily, she finally settled into the chair.

The clerk swore her in, and Zuniga began questioning. "Mrs. Waters, are you okay?"

"Just short of breath, honey. Should have given up cigars a bit earlier than I did. I thought those skinny ones would be healthier, you know. But I guess not. I'll be okay in a bit. I'm about to catch my breath." She fanned her face with a bony hand and finally drew a deep breath and blew it out. "I'm ready, dear."

"Mrs. Waters do you live across the street from Paloma Preston?"

"Sure do, honey. Been living there, oh, for about forty years. Of course, Paloma didn't live there that long. She was probably in diapers when Shelly and I built that house. I remember when she moved in, oh, about five years ago. That was after her Ben died, of course. She couldn't afford the house they had been living in and had to downsize. I took her one of my cherry pies to welcome her to the neighborhood. Sweet girl, she was." She sat forward. "I would take her a pie about once a month, and we would sit in her living room and have pie and coffee and she would tell me all about her horrible childhood in Mexico. So tragic. But she was a brave one to overcome her past." Waters looked over at Eagleson. "Only to be killed by that one over there!"

"Objection!" Kosinski shot to her feet.

"Sustained." Ford tapped her gavel. "Mrs. Waters, please confine your remarks to the answers to counsel's questions only."

Waters turned a wary gaze in Ford's direction. "I suppose I will, then." She looked back at Zuniga. "What else did you want to know, honey?"

Zuniga seemed to have the patience of Job. "Can you tell me where you were on the afternoon of February 14?"

"Well, I had made a strawberry shortcake. It was always Shelly's favorite treat on Valentine's Day. He's been gone now, oh, about three years. But I still make it in memory of him. He was such a good husband. Took good care of me and the children. We had five, you know. And fifteen grandchildren. Too bad they all live somewhere in Texas!" She frowned. "No one to take care of me after an entire life spent raising them."

"Mrs. Waters, back to the question. Where were you the afternoon of February 14?" Zuniga's voice sounded strained.

"I took a piece of my strawberry shortcake and got it ready to take over to Paloma. I knew she would get home from the classroom about 4 o'clock. So, I was going to go sit on the front porch and wait for her. But it was too cold for me!

I don't have much fat on these bones, you know. And it can get real cold in February. So, I sat in my living room and opened the blinds so I could see across the street when she got home."

"You said it was before four?"

"Yeah, right at 3:45 PM. I know cause I checked my clock. Shelly built me a grandfather clock, you know. Beautiful woodwork and painting. I wind it up every night when I go to bed. Hasn't had the wrong time in years." Waters nodded as if that was all that needed to be said and sat back in her chair.

"Mrs. Waters, when you looked across the street at Paloma Preston's house, what did you see?" Zuniga said calmly, although I could see the muscle clench in her jaw.

"Well, there was this white van sitting in her driveway. I kind of wondered what sort of problem she might have. Her central air has been acting up. I told her she should have gotten a gas system and not a heat pump. Gas is so much more efficient. At least that is what Shelly told me. But we still put in a fireplace when we built the house. I love my fireplace. Keeps these old bones warm." She hugged herself. "Why y'all keep it so cold in here?"

Zuniga swallowed and came toward the witness stand. "Mrs. Waters, did this van have any kind of markings? Any indication of what kind of service Mrs. Preston was receiving?"

"Well, come to think of it, no! Just a plain old white van. Funny thing is, I noticed I couldn't read the license plate very well. Had mud smeared all over it. But the van itself was spotless. The sun reflected off the windows right into my eyes." She nodded. "Yep, spotless."

"Did anyone come out of Paloma's house around that time?"

"Yes, this man came out to his van and opened the side door, the one I couldn't see, and got something out and went back in." Mrs. Waters said.

"What did that man look like?"

Waters leaned forward and looked at Eagleson. "Like him."

"Let the record show that Mrs. Waters is pointing at Mr. Eagleson." Zuniga said. She paused as if waiting for Kosinski to object. Kosinski's attention was focused on her laptop. Zuniga continued.

"Mrs. Waters, did you see anyone else other than this man around this time?"

"Yes, this UPS truck pulled up next door and a young man took a package up to the front door of the house next door. That would be Metilda Mertz's house. You know, Mertz like Ethel in I Love Lucy?" She smiled and tapped her chin. "Anyway, he was cute! I just love those tight shorts they wear. Shelly used to be on the swim team in high school. My, but he looked good in those speedos!"

"Uh, Mrs. Waters, can we stick to the facts, please?." Zuniga said. "What did the UPS man do after he delivered the package next door to Mrs. Preston's house?"

"Why he went back to his truck and then he stopped and looked right at Paloma's front door like he heard something. Now, my hearing isn't that good, and I never heard a thing. But he must have, cause he ran across Paloma's yard to the front door. Then, he banged on the front door and tried to open it and then ran back to his truck." Her breath quickened, and she sat forward. "Oh, my, it was so disturbing! I stood up and walked to the window and that man came running out of Paloma's house carrying something. He jumped into his van and tore out of that driveway like the devil himself was chasing him."

Mrs. Waters gasped for breath and fanned her face. "I'm sorry. It's so upsetting what happened next." Zuniga stood patiently at the witness stand.

"Take your time, Mrs. Waters. Take some deep breaths and try to relax."

Waters nodded and soon breathed more normally. She

reached for a tissue and wiped her eyes. "That UPS man came running to the door and opened it and smoke came boiling out. That's when I came to myself and realized I had to do something. I grabbed my land line phone and called 911. Shelly always told me that no matter what happened, don't ever get rid of that land line. I told them there was a fire across the street. It wasn't five minutes, and the fire truck arrived. The station is just down the street about two blocks. And they all swarmed in and started working on the fire."

"That will be all of my questions right now, Mrs. Waters."

"But there's so much more that happened! The police came and then they took out Paloma's body in a body bag. A body bag! I had to get my oxygen and put it on I was so upset." Mrs. Waters gripped the front of the witness stand with pale fingers.

"Mrs. Waters, you don't have to go on." Zuniga said. "Just try and calm down. I have no further questions." She looked up at Ford.

"Let's give Mrs. Waters a moment to compose herself." Ford said to Kosinski.

Kosinski looked up from her laptop and rose from her seat. "Actually, I have just one question for Mrs. Waters, if she is ready."

Mrs. Waters slowed her breathing. "Fine. Get on with it."

"Mrs. Waters, was the man who came out of the house wearing sunglasses?"

Waters paused and mopped some more at her face. "Why, he was. I remembered thinking when I saw him the first time about why he would be wearing sunglasses inside."

"Anything he might have been wearing that you could remember?"

"He had on a black jacket and a cap." Waters said.

Kosinski stepped away from her table toward the court-room rows. She nodded and three men stood up in the second row. Each man had on a black jacket, a black cap and sunglasses. "Did they look like any of these men?"

"Objection, your honor." Mansfield stood up, anger filling his voice. "This is a cheap trick."

"Your honor, I'd like to make a point that the witness only saw a man in dark clothing and cap and sunglasses. There doesn't appear to be any specific detail that clearly implicates Mr. Eagleson." Kosinski said innocently.

Ford sighed and put her reading glasses up on her head. "Ms. Kosinski, this is a rather dubious stunt."

"But she's right." Mrs. Waters said. We all turned our attention to Waters, now standing in the witness stand. Her hand was pressed to her temples and face was a white as milk. "Oh, my goodness. Shelly told me to never lie. Never, he said. After all, Satan is the father of lies. I have to admit anyone of those men looks like the fellow I saw. Oh my! What have I done?" She collapsed into the chair and looked up at the ceiling. "Paloma, I am so sorry, honey. I tried my best."

Before Ford could say anything else, Kosinski spoke up. "I have no further questions of this witness."

Chapter 18

"OMG, that was like in a television show. Or a movie!" Autumn said around the granola bar. We had been taken back to the jury room for an afternoon break and found a basket of snacks on the table with cold bottles of water.

I settled into my seat and once again, in vain, checked my email. Henry Crenshaw closed his eyes in irritation. "We can't talk about this, Miss Coleson."

"It's Coleman." She glared at him. She pulled her knees up to her chest and continued to eat her snack.

Gill leaned over to me. "Any luck on your email, brother?"

"No. Looks like I'll go from one legal argument to another." I put down my phone and thought about Dr. McVay. "I'm thinking about another crime."

"And what would that be? Paying us only thirty-five dollars a day for this?" Gill said.

"No, that body the police found on the river front Saturday."

"Doc, you said you couldn't talk about it." Gill whispered. "Like our jury stuff. Unless you realize that what we talk about is privileged info, right? Doctor patient confidentiality?"

"Yeah, but *you* were the doctor, and I was the patient."

While I had been suffering through my maladies before Christmas, thanks to tampering with my body by Dr. Korskin, Gill had been there along the way to steer me in the right direction.

"I got it from the Great Physician." Gill smiled. "You don't have to tell me anything. Unless it helps to talk about it to somebody. You know I'll keep quiet about it."

"He was an old professor of mine, Dr. McVay."

"The transplant surgeon?" Gill asked.

I turned my chair to face him. "You knew him?"

"Yeah, he worked at Fairmont Central. That must have been before you got there." Gill looked off into the distance as he thought. "Yep, he was still at the medical center teaching off and on. I know this because I had to go to the OR and babysit his heart-lung machine."

"He did heart transplants at Fairmont?"

"For a couple of years only. Hearts, lungs, kidneys. Even had some surgery residents following him around. He was a nice man. Very friendly. Very kind. Unlike most surgeons I worked with back then." Gill looked back at me. "Why would anyone want to kill him?"

"I don't know. But they cut out his kidneys and left him on a bench by the riverfront along the jogging path."

"Cut out his kidneys?" Gill said. "He had to be north of eighty years old. Why would anyone want his kidneys? It's not like you can give them to someone else."

"Exactly." I said. "There's a theory it may be related to some kind of satanic ritual or something."

Gill sighed. "Lots of crazies in this world. But we know for certain it wasn't Rex Eagleson. He was in jail."

I threw a look at Gill. Was Rex Eagleson a psycho? Was that question purely rhetorical? I never had a chance to think any more about it. We had to go back to the courtroom.

THE REASON for the break became apparent when we arrived back in the courtroom. The television had been moved directly in front of the jury box. On the screen was a video chat window with the word "Paused" filling the screen. Mansfield took his place at the podium and tapped on a tablet in front of him.

"Members of the jury, we have a witness who has been sworn in and will be testifying by video chat. The witness you are about to hear from is NOT the same person we tried to reach this morning. This is a different witness and the video interview has been approved by Judge Ford and by the defense. You will see and hear our witness, and I will be asking the questions. I am sharing my screen with you on the monitor." He tapped the tablet again, and a man appeared in the image. He was small framed with dark skin and straight black hair.

"Mr. Patel, this is Mr. Mansfield with the prosecution. Thank you for agreeing to speak with us today via a live video chat. Could you introduce yourself to the courtroom and tell us where you are at the moment?"

The man nodded and wiped sweat from his brow. "My name is Prima Patel and I am currently working for UPS in Seattle, Washington." His voice cracked a little and his hands shook.

"You sound a bit apprehensive, Mr. Patel." Mansfield said.

"I thought I had put all of that behind me." Patel said, looking away. He crossed his arms and sat back in his desk chair.

"Mr. Patel, do you recall where you were about 3:45 PM on February 14 of the year in question?"

"Yes. I was delivering a package to Mrs. Daisy Ledbetter at 805 Sunflower Lane in Talako, Louisiana." He paused.

"And what happened during that delivery?"

Patel cleared his throat and sat forward nervously. "I heard a woman screaming. It came from next door at 807 Sunflower

Lane. When I heard her scream, I ran across the yard to the front door." He hyperventilated and swallowed heard. "Give me just a minute. Just a minute."

"Take your time, Mr. Patel. Just tell us what you heard and what you saw."

"I came to the front door, and I heard more screaming from within from a woman's voice. I heard a man's voice say something like, 'Shut up!' So, I pounded on the door and tried to open it. But it was locked. I didn't know what to do, so I ran back to my truck and found my cell phone and called the police."

Patel stood up and paced around his chair desk. His head moved out of the frame of view.

"Mr. Patel, we need you to sit down so we can see your face, please." Mansfield said.

Patel paused behind his desk chair. He gripped the top of the chair with his hands, and he froze. Was he going to run out of the room? He finally turned the chair toward him, sat down, and turned around to face his camera. "I, uh, ran back to the door. I figured if someone was hurt and there was a fight or something, then maybe I should do something about it. I'm not a fighter, you know. I don't weigh more than ninety kilos." He wiped his mouth, his eyes focusing on the camera. "But it was the right thing to do. I kicked open the door, and a man ran out, shoving me to the ground. I rolled around until I heard his van start up and peeled out of the driveway. Smoke and flames were coming out through the front door."

Patel stood up again and walked out of the frame. "Just a minute. Give me just a minute!" He said from a distance. He returned to his chair and sat down.

"Sorry. It's so hard to recall all of this. I had to leave Louisiana. I moved as far away as I could because of what I saw when I ran into that house."

"What did you see, Mr. Patel?"

We sat silently in anticipation. Patel nodded slowly. "She

was in the middle of the living room on fire. Fire and smoke all around her and I couldn't do anything! I choked on the smoke, and I had to run back out and leave her on fire."

Patel put his hands to his face and sobbed. "Oh God! The smell! I can still smell smoke and burning flesh and I can't do this anymore. I can't."

"Mr. Patel." Mansfield said. "We thank you for your time, but please don't sign off just yet." He looked up at Ford. "We have no further questions."

Mr. Xavier came to the podium, buttoning his coat. He spoke in that soothing voice. "Mr. Patel, my name is Robert Xavier and I know this is difficult, but it is almost over. I want to ask you just one more question, if I could. Would you be willing to answer one more question?"

Patel's sobbing slowed and his gaze was fixed on a pool of tears on the desk before him. "Okay."

"The man you saw running from the house, did you notice the color of his eyes?"

Patel slowly looked up from the desk, blinking away tears. "The color of his eyes? No! He had on sunglasses, and it was so fast and then I was down and then he was gone! Just like that!" He snapped his fingers. "That fast and he was gone, leaving me to save that woman. And I couldn't. I couldn't. I just sat in the yard until the fire truck pulled up."

"I have no further questions." Xavier said, and before anyone could move, he touched the tablet, and the connection closed.

Judge Ford tapped her gavel. "It is now 5:30 P.M." She turned her attention to the jury box. "I would remind members of the jury not to discuss the details of this trial with each other or anyone else outside this courtroom. Again, do not attempt to access any additional information. Remember that doing so could result in a mistrial. Please be here tomorrow at 8:30 AM as we continue the presentation of the state's case."

"All rise." Joe said. We stood up and this time, everyone remained in place until the jury left the courtroom. I cast one last glance at Eagleson. His two different colored eyes focused on me.

Joe led us out the back entrance once again and out onto the street. Gill walked with me down the sidewalk. The sun sat low on the horizon and a chill filled the air. Music thumped somewhere behind us.

"Mardi Gras parade on the riverfront." Gill said. "Doc, if you don't mind, I'm heading toward the river front instead of the parking lot. My wife and kids are meeting there to see the parade."

"I didn't know you like parades." I paused

"I don't. But she do." He grinned at me and headed off toward the riverfront. I sighed and exhaled steam into the cold air. What a day.

Chapter 19

The call came the minute I got in my car. I glanced at the time. 6 P.M. Time for the medical panel to convene. I put the car in gear and headed for my apartment and answered the call.

"Hey, this is Dr. Merchant. I just left the parking lot at the courthouse. You can go ahead and do your due diligence while I'm driving home. I have the medical records on my laptop at home and the images are pulled up on my home reading station ready for me to review." I almost ran a red light and lurched as I threw on the brakes.

"Very well, Dr. Merchant. My name is Todd Quince, the attorney managing this session. I believe we have met before."

"Yes, on too many past panels." I said as the light changed to green.

"I have on the phone Dr. Melody Evers and Dr. Tyrone Peterson."

I greeted them. "Dr. Peterson is a general surgeon in Baton Rouge and Dr. Evers is a radiologist from Monroe. Before we get started, I'll allow the attorneys to introduce themselves." Quince said.

"I am Montgomery Majors representing Dr. Henderson." A man said.

"I'm Patrice Reynolds representing Dr. Grant and the staff of Kennington Memorial Hospital." A woman said.

"And, I am Madeline Kosinski, representing the family of the child, Monique Dupont in this travesty of justice."

I almost ran off the road. Kosinski was representing the person suing Dr. Henderson, Dr. Grant, and the hospital where they worked! Her introduction was laced with a snarky attitude. It was her all right! How had she joined this panel so quickly? Probably from her car just like me.

"Thank you. I will remind the attorneys I will allow them to call back in to this conference after our deliberations, and they will have the chance to ask any questions." Quince said.

"I'm looking forward to that." Kosinski said. "I can't wait to hear what your panel has to say. Especially Dr. Merchant."

Before I could comment, I heard the unmistakable beep as Quince severed the attorney's calls. I had arrived at my apartment.

"All three of you have been on medical panels before. I will read for you the definition of malpractice and the decision you must make." Quince said.

"The Louisiana Medical Malpractice Act, which governs the duties of the providers on the Medical Review Panel, calls for one of the following findings based upon the evidence. One, the defendant breached the standard of care. Two, the defendant did not breach the standard of care. Or, three, there is a material issue of fact, not requiring expert opinion, bearing on liability, which the court must consider."

As Quince went through the definition of malpractice and the responsibility of the panel, I made me way to my apartment and sat before my computer. I hardly heard a word they said. Kosinski! Why! God, what did I do to deserve this?

"More specifically, the panel must determine whether or not the health care professionals breached the standard of care. If the panel finds that there was a breach of the standard of care, then the Panel must also decide whether such breach caused or contributed to the plaintiff's alleged injuries." Quince continued.

"I'll read for you the charge against Dr. Henderson, Dr. Grant and Kennington Memorial Hospital." Quince droned on as I followed along on my printed copy of the charge.

"On May 15th of last year, ten-year-old Monique Dupont presented to the emergency room of Kennington Memorial Hospital with abdominal pain and fever. The emergency room physician ordered laboratory tests and an abdominal and pelvic CAT scan. This study revealed, and I quote 'An enlarged, edematous and gangrenous appendix with significant surrounding inflammation and fluid.' The emergency room physician consulted the surgeon on call, Dr. Mitchell Grant. Dr. Grant agreed to operate, and the patient was taken to the operating room on Sunday evening. At the end of the surgery, a discrepancy in the sponge count was noted. An X-Ray was taken and reviewed by Dr. Grant. He determined no retained sponge was present. The following day, Dr. May Henderson arrived to provide radiology services. Dr. Henderson interpreted the X-Ray of the abdomen taken the evening before and mentioned a 'radiopaque foreign body projected over the abdomen' and signed the report. On Tuesday, Monique developed sudden abdominal pain and vomiting. She also demonstrated signs of intra-abdominal bleeding. A CAT scan was performed and interpreted by an outside radiology group. The CAT scan revealed intra-abdominal bleeding and a large, retained hemostat left in the abdomen during surgery from Sunday evening. Dr. Frank Sutton was taking weekday surgery call for the hospital and arrived soon after. Monique was taken to surgery, and a large hemostat was found in the abdominal cavity along with significant loops of dead small bowel. The bowel was resected, and Monique received blood transfusions and was transferred to a pediatric center in Lake Charles. Monique spent two weeks in rehabilitation and has significant complications from the surgery including short small bowel syndrome, malrotation, abdominal wall scarring, and mental and physical distress."

Quince went on reading what was surely Kosinski's manifest against medicine implicating the hospital, all nursing staff, and both doctors. He finished and I heard all three of us sigh in exasperation.

"We will address at first, the charge of a violation of the standard of care by the nursing staff and general staff of the hospital's emergency room. Dr. Peterson, you're the surgeon. What is your opinion of the care rendered by the staff?"

"I don't see any failure on the staff's part to render care." She said.

"Dr. Evers?"

"I agree."

"Dr. Merchant?"

"Only question I would have is why wasn't the count for equipment off? The surgery staff noticed a missing sponge according to their records. No one mentioned a missing hemostat. I would think missing a hemostat would be a significant error."

Silence from Peterson and Evers. Peterson cleared his throat. "Well, it is the responsibility of the surgical assistant to keep track of all equipment used in the case."

"And obviously someone missed the hemostat." Evers said.

"Then wouldn't that constitute a violation of the standard of care?" I said.

"Silence again. I cleared my throat and continued. "Dr. Peterson, I know you don't want to throw the surgical staff under the bus, but someone dropped the ball on this one. I mean, Dr. Peterson, if this was you who would you blame? If the surgical staff missed the count, I know you're the 'captain of the ship' but wouldn't it be the fault of the counting person?"

"Yes, it would, Jack." Peterson said reluctantly. "I agree."

"Me, too." Evers said.

"Very well, if you will give me a moment, I have written out a statement to that effect while you were talking. It will go into the final decision document. Let me read it for you." Quince said. He read the sentence, and we all agreed on its accuracy. Ultimately, the panel would find the surgical staff culpable in the case. We would decide later if that capability resulted in injury to the patient, which obviously it had.

"Now, let's move on to Dr. Grant. Dr. Peterson?"

"Dr. Grant was totally dependent on the counting staff to keep track of equipment. Even if you evoke the 'captain of the ship' idea, he can't be accountable for leaving something behind when he was never notified the count was off."

"But he looked at the X-Ray." Evers said. "And he told his PA to close. I'm no surgeon but I would think a hemostat the size of garden shears would be easy to see on an X-Ray."

"You're a radiologist." Peterson said. "Of course you would notice it."

"And a surgeon wouldn't?" Evers said.

"Look, Grant said in his deposition the X-Ray was on a small monitor, and he glanced at it looking for a sponge, not a hemostat. He's not trained to read X-Rays and he shouldn't be held accountable for missing something. He probably thought the hemostat was lying on the patient's exterior." Peterson said.

"But he didn't say that." I said. "I'm looking at his surgery note and all he said was 'no sponge seen. Instructed PA to close.' If he saw the hemostat he should have mentioned it, even if he thought it was on the surface."

"Not necessarily, Jack." Peterson said. "Your radiologist missed it, too."

"No, Henderson mentioned the hemostat." Evers said.

"Yeah, PROJECTED over the abdomen. What does that

mean? Sounds like a dodge to me. Isn't the national flower of the radiologist the hedge?" Peterson said hotly.

"Can we dial it down a bit?" Quince interrupted. "Let's get back to Grant. Sounds to me like there is a conflict between what he said in his deposition and what he wrote in his note."

"Exactly." Peterson said. "It was the radiologist's job to notify him the minute he saw a retained hemostat and if she had, then they would have taken the patient back to surgery sooner. I don't think she is responsible for what happened."

"Let's do this." Quince said. "Let's talk about Dr. Henderson."

"I know for a fact, that hospital uses a virtual radiology group at night and on two days out of the week." Evers said. "Dr. Henderson belongs to one of these large corporate radiology groups like the one that tried to take over our practice. They send them all over the state to fill in on select days of the week. The corporation signs a contract with the hospital for coverage and the radiology gets a salary and is told what to do. Dr. Henderson said in her deposition she only works where she is sent, and Kennington has a radiologist on site Monday and Thursday to read up studies and to do any procedures."

"Your point?" Peterson said.

"My point is this. How can you develop a rapport with the ordering physicians when you're only around two half days a week? Dr. Henderson has to come and go quickly and does not have the kind of rapport with Dr. Grant that we have in our practices."

"And that is supposed to allow her to get away with crappy work?" Peterson said.

"No." I interrupted as the tension built again. "But, Melody, look at the report. Dr. Henderson said the 'hemostat is projected over the abdomen' and probably she thought it was lying on the patient's skin. She said as much in her deposition. But she didn't mention that in the report. You and I both know she should have at least questioned the location of the hemostat. And, regardless of her rapport with the ordering physicians, she should have called someone about the hemostat, even if it was the nurse taking care of the patient."

"So, we are throwing her under the bus and letting Grant off?" Evers said hotly. "Jack, the American College of Radiology has established that the ordering physician is equally responsible for reading the final report as the radiologist is for communicating the findings. Grant was satisfied with a quick glance at a monitor and assumed he knew enough about X-Rays that he didn't need a radiologist to tell him if a sponge was present. And I know him. He's an older surgeon and he has only one good eye."

"Hey!" I shouted. "I'm currently on a jury in a murder trial and I have been listening to this kind of back and forth all day. Can we stick to the facts and not disparage the doctors and nurses?"

"Thank you, Dr. Merchant." Quince said. "We have established the breach of a standard of care in the operating room at the hands of the hospital personnel. So, can we make a decision on the physicians?"

"I propose Dr. Henderson breached the standard of care by not mentioning the hemostat could possibly in INSIDE the patient and not contacting the surgeon at the time she saw it. Isn't the communication of significant results required by your college?" Peterson said.

"It is." I said. "I agree. You are correct. Dr. Henderson should have mentioned the possibility the hemostat could have been left at surgery and should have called someone immediately and then documented that call in the report."

"I'll agree to that on one condition." Evers said.

"What's that?" Peterson said.

"That we at least acknowledge the confusion between Grant's surgery note and his assertion he was not responsible for looking at the X-Ray. We can, and I'm looking at the guidelines, say there is a *material issue of fact, not requiring expert opinion, bearing on liability, which the court must consider.*"

"That means Grant will be taken to court!" Peterson growled.

"Oh, this will go to court." Quince said. "I can guarantee it. Even though the malpractice cap for all damages cannot exceed $500,000 in Louisiana, the attorneys will go for future medical expenses which is not covered under that cap. This is going to court no matter what we say."

"And there won't be any magical flow chart Grant will be able to pull from his pocket. Right, Jack?" Peterson said sarcastically.

"What does that mean?" I said.

"We all know what happened ten years ago." Peterson said.

"How?"

"He's right, Jack." Quince said. "In our circles, you're Darth Vader."

"And, in our circles, you're a legend." Evers said.

"I don't want to be either of those!" I growled. "Look, a ten-year-old kid had routine appendix surgery, and someone left a hemostat in her belly. That is wrong and we all know it. We can't reverse what happened. But we can make sure she gets some kind of settlement for her future. And, just maybe, have an impact on the doctors involved so this won't happen again with them. So, can we get on with this?"

I heard silence punctuated by occasional deep breath. Finally, Peterson spoke.

"I'll agree to the material fact clause. Grant is getting up there in years, but he is a far better surgeon with just one eye than most of the younger surgeons coming out of residency."

One eye? My thoughts instantly went to Eagleson. I closed my eyes and drew a deep breath. One good eye. One bad eye. It was coming down to the eyes, wasn't it?

Then I thought of Kosinski representing the family. The question of "material fact" would be enough to take the case to trial. And I knew Kosinski. She would put Henderson on the stand and skewer her with questions and damage her self confidence forever. But the facts could not be ignored. The evidence spoke for itself. We had to decide based on the evidence, not our emotional commitment to our individual practices. That fact came home to me harder than ever before in light of my jury duty.

Quince went through the process of writing up the final document after we agreed that harm had resulted from the breach. I had been on a dozen of these panels and only about a third of them resulted in the panel finding for the plaintiff. Most malpractices were sad cases where, instead of mistakes, it was the natural progression of disease that caused the perception of malpractice. No one wanted to experience pain. Everyone expected doctors to work miracles.

Against the sound of Quince tapping on his laptop, I listened as Evers and Peterson talked about their practices. Their sudden animosity vanished. Finally, after we agreed on the wording of the final document, Quince got both attorneys back on the phone. He read them our final decision.

Majors spoke up. "Thank you for the decision." He sounded less than truly grateful.

Reynolds echoed the sentiment.

Kosinski sighed. "I guess what you're telling me is that Dr. Grant lied in his statement of fact." She said tersely. "I guess we'll see everyone in court. That's the only way we'll get to the truth!"

Quince disconnected the attorneys, and my heart finally calmed down. My face burned with anger at Kosinski. I heard nothing else Quince said as he went through the final instructions about signing the decision.

At least the family would have a chance to recover future medical costs. Monique would have a lifetime of physical distress!

My mind drifted to Rhonda Fall and her questions about her mother. She did not know about the delay in getting her mother to surgery. No one could have predicted that delay would cost her mother's life. What had Saul's medical panel concluded? As the other two doctors said their goodbye I spoke up, my voice shaky.

"Mr. Quince, can I have a private conversation with you after this is over?"

"Sure, Dr. Merchant. Let me make sure no one else is on the conference line. No, we're good. How can I help you?"

"You've been doing these panels for a long while, right?"

"Fifteen years."

"Were you involved in the medical panel for Dr. Saul Reynolds?"

Quince was quiet for a moment. "I was in charge of that panel. How could I forget it?"

I tensed and leaned toward the phone. "Ms. Kosinski represented the family and put me on the stand. She tried to implicate me in her client's death."

"Uh huh." Quince said noncommittally. "And you pulled out the magic flow sheet."

"Granted! I'm a legend."

"More like a pariah."

"Okay, can you talk about what went on during that panel?"

"Dr. Merchant, I have every panel's conclusion on file. While the cases have statutes of limitations, there are none on criminal activity resulting in a person's death. I am required by law to keep a record. Just in case." He cleared his throat. "Now that you mention it, I recall a rather contentious discussion from the panel members regarding the absence of records during the arteriogram you performed."

"Yes, those records were part of the PACS system, not the general medical records. Kosinski never subpoenaed those records."

"And you skewered her from the stand, Jack. You made a very long lasting and powerful enemy. How many panels have you been on?"

I thought for a moment. "At least six in the last ten years. Why?"

"Let's just say I have a problem with the ethical behavior of Ms. Kosinski, and we did not have this conversation. By suggesting your name, I've kept you involved in panels and Kosinski has left you alone. There is a tight circle of attorneys working malpractice and you are known as a good panelist. You've been kept off Kosinski's radar thanks to attorneys like me. Every panel you've been on has shown me how fair you are to the plaintiff and the defendant. Most doctors have a knee jerk tendency to clear their colleagues. It seems your experience in the court room with attorneys like Kosinski has given you a better point of view." Quince cleared his throat again. "But you've damaged your reputation the past year or so."

"My wife died. She was murdered." I said.

"So, I have learned. You're fair game, Jack. I would say anticipate some litigation coming at you in the near future."

"Great! More fodder to make my already terrible day even worse." I paused. "Can I see the panel results?"

Quince was silent for a moment. "It is highly irregular. Panel conclusions are for the attorneys only."

"I'm on a jury right now. Turns out one of the members is the daughter of the woman who died. I told her I would try and find out more about the criminal side of things. They never caught the killer."

"And how does information from the panel help with that?"

"It doesn't. But let's just say it will keep me feeling guilty. Guilt is a powerful motivator in my case."

"I'll email you the documents. But I can tell you the

discussion about you was only addressing the lack of records. You weren't being sued."

"By the way, who were the panelists?"

"I only recall one. Dr. Robert Lamb."

"Fairmont Medical's administrator?" I said in incredulously.

"He still had a license, and all licensed physicians are subject to being put on a panel."

What had Lamb said about me? Ten years ago, did he even know who I was as the newest member of the radiology group? Lamb's reputation as a surgeon would make him perfect for a panel convened against a surgeon. But it was highly unusual for a physician familiar with the defendant to be put on a panel. How had he managed that? Probably through his many nefarious connections! "How did he end up on a panel for one of his hospital's doctors? Isn't that a conflict of interest?"

"It can happen." Quince said. "Highly unusual. The panel concluded Reynolds did not violate the standard of care. If Kosinski had known about Dr. Lamb on the panel, she could have contested it. As it is, she had planned on taking the case to court no matter what the panel decided."

"No doubt to go after me."

"I think you are correct, Jack."

"Mr. Quince, thank you for helping out. I hope the panel conclusion holds out." I said with genuine emotion.

"I wouldn't count on NOT being subpoenaed, Jack. Kosinski will drag all three of you into court to find out why you reached that conclusion. Take care." He hung up.

I stumbled from my little bedroom office into the living room. I was hungry and thirsty and tired and filled with anger. Turmoil filled my mind!

The constant jockeying to put the blame on someone else wasn't confined to our panel. The sifting of truth claims in court and the shifting of blame to some nebulous person wearing sunglasses was just as bad. There had to be objective truth somewhere! Why did we have to play these games? Mistakes were made and a child had suffered. Doctors are only human and when we make mistakes people suffer. In court, the stakes weren't as high. Were they? If Eagleson was innocent, and Kosinski was successful in shifting the blame to some other unknown assailant what would happen if Eagleson WAS guilty? Would a murderer walk free? But also, an innocent man could pay with his life for the wrongdoing of someone else. No system was ever perfect. Law or medicine, we did the best we could. Maybe I should give Kosinski the benefit of the doubt.

I went to my bathroom and looked at myself in the mirror. "What about it, Jack? Could Kosinski be right?" I raised an eyebrow and shook my head. "I hope not!"

My mind whirled with facts and innuendos and half truths and turf battles. I had to do something! I looked at my reflection in the mirror and licked my lips. I could taste the cold liquid on my tongue. I heard the strident beeping of the slot machines. The only thing that would assuage these feelings sat towering over Choctaw River. It was time to go to the boat!

Chapter 20

I could taste the crab cakes! Of course, I would wash it down with iced tea, not beer. I had not been back to the casino since before Christmas. This would be a test, I reasoned. I can certainly go to one of my favorite restaurants at Paradise Cay without drinking alcohol. Or gambling! Right? I was in the car, about to start the ignition, when my cell phone rang. I glanced at the caller ID. Sam!

"Hey, Sam." I answered.

"How did it go today?"

I started the car and waited for the phone to switch over to the speaker. "Long, grueling, and not something I want to do again."

"Where are you?"

"I'm in the car."

"You're just now getting home?"

I paused. "No. I had a medical review panel call meeting that lasted about an hour, and now I'm starving."

"Good. Meet me at Strong's." The line went dead. I just stared through the windshield at my apartment door. A Talako establishment, Strong's served blue plate diner specials. The food was excellent, including their world famous strawberry pies. No beer. No alcohol. Plenty of iced tea. I glanced up through my moon roof at the clear, cold February sky.

"Very funny, God."

An old building sat across the street from Continental College, one of the oldest colleges in the south. No parking spaces remained in the small front parking lot so I parked in the back of the brick building and made my way up a rickety set of metal stairs to the back entrance. I had to walk through a hallway stacked with boxes of food and supplies to the main dining room. Old Formica tables and booths filled the interior. Sam sat at a table near the back. The room was almost full.

I sat down and slipped off my jacket in the warm air and inhaled the fragrance of pancakes and burgers. Sam looked up from her menu. Her two-tone hair had been restored to its former luster and her glasses glittered in the harsh fluorescent light. She wore her eggplant-colored scrubs. A heavy bandage encircled her right wrist.

"I could eat the south end of a cow headed north." She said. Gold, green, and purple beads hung around her neck.

"You went to the parade?"

"I did. One of many y'all have in Talako. Wasn't half bad. Not New Orleans level, of course. I scoped out the parade route for my debut as queen on Friday." She laid the menu on the table. "Saw your friend Gill. Told me about your day. Nothing about the trial, of course."

"He did?"

Sam frowned and put her left hand on my arm. "Said you had a rough time but wouldn't tell me why."

I looked away and nodded. "The victim had a similar fate to Janice, I'll say."

"Oh!" She patted my arm. "Time to stress eat! What will you have?"

"Burger and hash browns. The chunky ones cooked on the grill." I said. So much for crab cakes and a beer. "And iced tea."

She nodded and called over a server. She ordered pancakes, scrambled eggs, bacon, and the same hash browns. I placed my order.

"Now," she waited until the server poured her a cup of coffee. "I'm starving. Opiates do that to me. I wanted to talk to you about the other case."

"Dr. McVay?" My tea arrived. I sipped it. No alcohol. But lots of sugar. Sam could use it for pancake syrup.

"No, Mrs. Dixon. Her daughter, you said, was a jury member?"

"Yes. Asked a lot of questions."

Sam reached down with her right hand, winced, and then retrieved a folder from her purse. She placed it in front of me. "I have a lot of questions, too. Here's the police report. I'm asking for the evidence box and that should be in my office by tomorrow morning." She sat back as her food arrived on three plates!

My burger sat amidst the brown, crispy fragrant hash browns. They weren't really hash browns. They were more like the smothered potatoes my grandmother used to make. I bit into the burger and sighed in satisfaction. Made from a secret recipe, Strong's burgers were heavenly. Not too thick, on a small bun with all the trimmings. Not fancy. Just delicious. I ate some hash browns and the flavor of paprika and pepper and salt titillated my taste buds.

"You okay?" Sam said.

"I'm starving." I said. "We had some cold pizza. I might as well have eaten the box it came in because I couldn't tell the difference."

"Take something to lunch tomorrow. Should have told you about that." She ate some of her pancake.

"I did. Didn't have much at home to take. Now, about Mrs. Dixon?"

"Big problem, Jack. The autopsy on Mrs. Dixon is not just poor, it's criminal. My predecessor should go to jail for his negligence. What a sloppy beast he was!" She ate more pancake and chewed noisily. She looked at me. "I ought to exhume the body and take a second look."

"It's been ten years. What good would it do?"

"Jack, an autopsy on a ten-year-old body would be more accurate than any drivel Dr. McCorkin put in his reports." She drank her coffee and shook her head. "I'd heard rumors he was corrupt. But the more I dig through old cases, the more I'm seeing something else going on."

"Like what?"

"It's Louisiana, Jack. The old politicians didn't just have skeletons in their closets. They had the authorities put them there and then put the authorities in the closets with them!"

"I'm sorry I brought all this up." I finished my burger.

"It would have come to the surface sooner or later. Which is another reason I need you, Jack. More cases for you to review. Money in the bank for you." She finished her meal and wiped her mouth. "Now, aren't you glad you didn't go to Paradise Cay?"

I froze. "What?"

"Oh, come on, Jack. I saw it all over your face on the river front. The last two months have been tough on you. And now, on a jury and a medical panel review in one day! That would drive anybody to drink." She leaned toward me and smiled. "There's more than one reason I asked you to meet me for dinner, Jack. I'm trying to help you stay out of trouble." She motioned to the server.

"Now, a piece of their strawberry pie. Join me?"

I smiled. "Why not?"

I WAS EXHAUSTED by the time I drove home. I sat before my radiology computer to close down the studies I had uploaded from a DVD for the panel discussion. I glanced at the list of current studies waiting for my group to interpret. Should I? Now, what was Mrs. Dixon's name? There shouldn't be that many people with Dixon for a last name. But her name was something strange, something ethereal, maybe?

I opened a search window and typed in several name combinations and got nowhere. I closed my eyes and picture Kosinski stalking me on the stand. I had the flow sheet from the procedure on my phone. My eyes flew open! I had taken a screen capture and saved it under my photos. Would it still be there from ten years ago? Probably.

I opened my photo program on my iPad and went back to the year and month in question. Yes! It was still there. Eartha Mae Dixon. Yeah, that was ethereal, all right. I clicked on her name and pulled up her image file. I had made sure we never erased her files, even though after ten years, inactive patients were purged from the system.

I pulled up her angiogram and reviewed it. I hadn't missed anything. The damage to the inferior vena cava was there. And the partial tear in the aorta was what probably led to her death. She had bled from the two largest blood vessels in her body!

I looked through her list of images. When she arrived in the ER, the ER physician had ordered X-rays and a CAT scan of her abdomen and pelvis. I opened the CAT scan and waited for the images to pull from the archive. It took about five minutes to find all the images and load them into my viewing program. First, I checked the report. The study had been interpreted by a name I did not recognize, one of our VirtuRad partners.

I scrolled through the images. Sure enough, the lower chest was filled with dense fluid, bleeding from the vessel damage. The blood had compressed the lung. I scrolled down through the upper abdomen cuts and paused. I glanced at the report.

The VirtuRad radiologist had mentioned a track of air

through the liver extending into the lower chest area. That was probably the bullet path. What we did not have ten years before was the advanced software we now had. Our images back then were collected in a "slab" meaning the entire bulk of tissue in one block of images.

This meant I could now, using improved software, do reconstructions of the slab as if I was making slices from right to left and front to back.

I brought up the reconstructed images in two other windows. That way, I could look at the anatomy in all three dimensions at one time. Ah, there was the air track leading from an open wound on the front of the body through the edge of the liver, behind the stomach barely missing the spleen and through the back of the left lung.

I paused and scrolled again. What was this? A second track of air seemed to branch off the main track of air at a shallow angle. The second track was not as big as the main track and it passed close to the tip of the spleen ending at a rib.

I magnified the image and examined the rib. Using "bone" windows I changed the settings, sort of like changing brightness and contrast, to accentuate the bone over the soft tissues. Sure enough, there was a "divot" along the inside curve of the tenth rib in the back of the chest. Not only that, tiny fragments of white scattered away from the rib like they had splashed out of the divot.

I pulled up a measuring circle and calculated the "CT" number. Each type of tissue had a definite level of "brightness" with air being the lowest and metal the highest. These tiny fragments should register as bone. Perhaps a fragment of the bullet had broken off the main bullet and hit the rib. But if so, where was the fragment? These tiny white flecks were far too small to be from a bullet.

I looked at the number that appeared from the measurement. The number was too low to be the typical metal from a bullet. But too high to be the calcium from a bone fracture. I sat back in total confusion. What was I looking at? If the bullet had fragmented, there should have been more fragments along the track and a bullet would have to hit bone to fragment. The main air track led through soft tissue, the liver.

Could there have been two shots to the victim's abdomen? I placed the police report on the desk in front of my radiology computer. I read the main report of the incident and there was no mention of two entry wounds. No photographs were included. They were in the evidence box. This was just a summary.

I closed the folder and studied the constellation of tiny metallic fragments next to Eartha Dixon's tenth rib.

"What happened to you, Mrs. Dixon?" I typed up my summary in an email attachment and sent it to Sam. Maybe after we reviewed the contents of the evidence box, we might know more. I paused. I was excited. My heart raced. My brain tumbled. In fact, I felt more alive than ever in the last few weeks. And I had typed "we" in the message to Sam. Funny how quickly the thoughts of Paradise Cay had crumbled away!

Chapter 21

The next morning, after meeting Gill at the parking lot, we talked as we walked through the cold morning air toward the courthouse.

"How was the parade last night?"

Gill laughed. "I got beads out the wazoo! My wife loved it! The kiddos loved it! My little flock of homeless didn't mind picking up leftover snacks, either! You should have come. It would have done you good to laugh and smile, Jack. I saw Dr. Francisco."

I hugged my jacket tighter around me. "I almost went to Paradise Cay last night."

Gill stopped and grabbed my shoulder. We halted right in front of the art center. "Jack! I told you to call me when you feel like that. Man, you really ought to go to something like Gambler's Anonymous or something. You need a sponsor who understands what you're going through."

I looked up at the big man and his deep, brown eyes. "Gill, no one knows what I've been through."

"Jesus does." Gill said quietly. "And before you ignore that thought, he was betrayed. His friends turned against him. He lost his best friend, Lazarus. And he suffered the worst type of torture and execution man ever came up with. He knows what you're going through. And, in a program, they talk about a higher power. You know that Higher Power, Jack. I know you do."

I nodded and continued down the sidewalk. "I'm working on it, Gill. I'm going to church with Jerry. He's trying to get me into his men's Bible study class." I paused and turned to face Gill. "And get this. Sanchez was at church Sunday!"

"Get out of here!" Gill grinned. He slapped me on the shoulder, and I almost fell over. "See, if it works for her, brother, it will work for you. Just give it time." He took my shoulders in his big hands and turned me to face him. "Now, repeat after me."

"Repeat after me." I said trying not to grin.

"I, say your name."

"I, Jack Merchant. You know what I could have said there."

"Take this seriously, Jack. I, Jack Merchant, promise God right now that I will call Gill if I ever feel the urge."

I looked into his eyes. "I, Jack Merchant, promise God right now that I will call you if I ever feel the urge."

"Or, Gill will whoop my butt."

"Or, Gill will whoop my butt!" I finished with a laugh.

Gill turned me toward the courthouse and put his arm around my shoulder. "Doc, everything is going to work out. Be patient. God is not finished with either one of us yet."

"Sam called me. I'm pretty sure she's looking out for me, too. We ended up eating strawberry pie at Strong's."

"My wife's pie is better." Gill said. "But it's hard to beat their hash browns. Only thing better is hot, fresh Southern Maid donuts." He stopped and moaned. I joined him.

"I agree with you, there. Manna from heaven!"

"And the devil is sitting on your shoulder tempting you to eat the whole dozen." Gill said. He glanced at me. "What? You've never eaten a whole box?"

I just shook my head because the mention of the devil chased away the good thoughts of eating a hot, Southern Maid donut. "Gill, do you think Rex Eagleson is evil? I mean that whole thing with the disk and the thirteenth evil spirit or whatever. Maybe he wants that disk for more than its gold content. The man gives me the creeps!"

Gill never missed a step. "No doubt about it, Doc. I feel the evil pour off him like bad B.O. from Frankie down at the riverfront."

"Frankie?"

"Yeah. Says he's allergic to soap. Never bathes. He stinks like Lazarus after three days!"

WHEN WE ARRIVED at the jury room, Joe was waiting with a basket of pastries and a fresh pot of coffee. Instead of donuts, which I had a huge hankering for, a large cardboard box held a King cake, the default sweet cake of Mardi Gras. We sat down at the table and Joe looked at me.

"Notice anything different, Dr. Merchant?" Joe said.

"Me?" I looked around at the table. "Pastries? A King cake?"

"No, Mrs. Lucy Kosack is not here. She had a heart attack last night and is in the hospital."

Everyone groaned. I tried to picture her and remembered a middle-aged woman who said she was a greeter at the Super-Mart. Then it hit me.

"That means?"

"You're no longer an alternate. You're not the thirteenth juror. You are now a member of the jury." Joe said.

I shrugged. "Only difference is I get to vote." And then the number thirteen resonated with me and I shuddered. Thirteenth juror no more in a trial with the thirteenth evil spirit.

We were ushered into the courtroom and I left Gill alone

in the alternate seats and took Mrs. Kosack's empty chair. Sitting on the front row on the prosecutor's side were more, I assumed, family members. One elderly lady with gray hair pulled up into a bun on the top of her head sat at the middle end of the left sided pews with tissues pressed to her face. She sniffled and seemed to be crying. What caught my attention, however, was Jerry Langley and Sanchez on the front row next to a half dozen official looking individuals. That meant today was all about the evidence.

Mansfield welcomed us and called a witness to the stand, Fireman Robert Orville. Orville was tall and could have easily been Mr. July in a fireman calendar. I definitely needed to start working out again. He looked to be about thirty and was dressed smartly in a formal fire department uniform. The clerk of court swore him in.

In my new seat on the front row, I had a much better view of Rex Eagleson and Kosinski. I refused to look at the man much less Kosinski.

"Fireman Orville, will you tell me about the call you received on February 14?"

"Yes, sir. At about 3:45 P.M. we received notification from the 911 operator of a fire at 807 Sunflower Lane. My crew loaded up quickly. The address was only two blocks down from the station and we were there within five minutes."

"Do you wear body cameras?"

"Only the lead fireman wears a body cam and on this day, that would have been me."

"Ladies and gentlemen of the jury, I am about to play a recording from that body camera and I will introduce it into evidence." He carried a USB drive and handed it to the clerk.

Back at the podium, he pressed the play button on his remote. My heart raced and my spit dried up. Jerky images came from the camera on Orville's chest as he ran to the front door. Smoke poured from the open door, and he ran into the smoke.

Through smoke, we saw flames coming from something in the center of the room. Muffled voices shouted for help from Orville. He waved the smoke away with his hands and the source of the flames appeared illuminated by light coming through the open door.

I gasped and leaned forward in my chair as panic gripped me. Mrs. Preston's body lay in the center of a living room, her skin blackened by smoke. A mist poured over her and put out the flame. The rest of the living was not on fire, just her.

The view from the body camera moved closer as Orville bent over to examine her body. Something warped and red protruded from her chest. Melted feathers? No, it was plastic fins on the end of an arrow. But the view shifted closer, focusing on her empty, lifeless eyes. I groaned again as memories of Janice's burned body filled my mind. I closed my eyes and prayed for stability. I couldn't hurl right here in the courtroom. I was not the only one disturbed. Bobble Head, Latonya, cursed behind me. Others moaned in disgust.

Mansfield paused the video with Paloma Preston's eyes centered in the video window. He turned off the monitor and mercifully, it went blank. "I would play more of this, but I think we'll let Fireman Orville give us the details." He made no comment on our discomfort. I sat back slowly, breathing deeply in and out, and looked up at Ford. She sat forward at her desk, her gaze fixed on me. I nodded slowly, as if to say I was all right, but I wasn't.

"Fireman Orville, I have in my possession your written report of the events that day." Mansfield held up a document. "And I would like to introduce this into evidence." He handed the document to the clerk.

"Now, would you tell us what you found when you entered the house?"

Orville pulled a folder from under his right arm. He opened it and sat it on the railing of the witness stand. "If you don't mind, I'd like to refer to my copy of that report."

"Objection." Kosinski stood up. "The details are in the document and counselor has asked for Fireman Orville's personal recollections."

"Sustained." Ford said. "Fireman Orville, give us your personal account of what happened. If you need to refer to the record for details, we will cross that bridge when we get there."

Orville calmly closed the folder. I could tell he had done this many times, but it had been a year since the murder. However, I don't think I would forget what I just saw on the monitor. How could he?

"I entered the house, and it was filled with smoke. Flames were coming from a source in the center of a living room. On closer inspection, the object on fire was a human being. Lefty, that is Fireman Leftbridge, extinguished the fire with a fire extinguisher. The rest of the room was not on fire. Only the body."

He looked at us. "I examined the body and noted the person had considerable third-degree burns all over the visualized body. And I noted that a rodlike structure protruded from the chest. I checked for a pulse and found none. The rest of my men checked the remainder of the house to make sure no other fires were in place."

"Lt. Orville, after the body was removed, isn't it standard procedure to have a fire inspector determine the cause and source of a fire? Particularly if a death occurs?" Mansfield asked.

"Yes. I am also the regional inspector. After the body was removed, I performed a brief examination and returned the next day for a formal investigation. My results are included in my written report."

Mansfield retrieved the document from the clerk and took it to Orville. "Just so we will have crossed all our tees and dotted our 'I's would you refer to page twelve of the submitted written report and read the final conclusion?"

Orville took the document. "After careful investigation, it has been determined the fire resulted from the accelerant, lighter fluid, placed on the body of the victim."

Mansfield nodded and retrieved the document. "No further questions."

I exhaled unaware I had been holding my breath. Kosinski came to the podium. Today, she wore a teal green blouse and matching skirt. For a moment, her eyes flicked in my direction. Did she just now realize I was a voting member of jury? She looked back at Orville. "Just a couple of questions. Did you see anyone leaving the house when you arrived?"

"No."

"You said the time between your call and arrival was about 5 minutes?"

"Yes."

"Earlier testimony from the neighbor across the street claimed a man ran out of the house, got in a white van and drove down the street. Did you see a man driving a white van?"

"I did not. But I was not looking down the street from the station."

Kosinski nodded and seemed to be deep in thought. "Well, it's just that a prior witness said between the time the man got into a van and drove off and the firetruck appeared were almost simultaneous. Can you explain why you didn't see this supposed white van?"

"Objection, your honor." Zuniga said. "Asking the witness to speculate."

"Sustained."

"I'll withdraw the question." Kosinski said. "I'm just trying to clear up some confusion on my part. Fireman Orville, it is your testimony you never saw a man driving a white van pass you as you came to Paloma Preston's house?"

"Yes." Orville said quietly with a frown on his face.

"No further questions." Kosinski returned to her seat.

What was she up to? Trying to discredit Mrs. Waters' and Mr. Patel's testimony. Why? What did it matter in the timeline? I studied Kosinski's face as she whispered to Xavier.

What followed was more testimony from a police officer responding to Mrs. Patel's call and more body camera footage. By then, I was numb and struggling to hold back bile and anger.

"We will convene for thirty minutes to give our jury members a break." Judge Ford stood and we marched back to the jury room. The atmosphere was gloomy and subdued. All except Autumn who seemed excited and hyper! She drank coffee and chowed down on a chocolate bar while the rest of us avoided making eye contact.

"Doc, you okay?" Gill said.

I shook my head. "Not in the least."

"What's wrong, Dr. Merchant?" Latonya said.

"His wife was murdered, and her body was burned." Gill said loudly, looking around the room defiantly as if to warn anyone to ask any further questions.

"Sorry for your loss." Latonya reached over and patted my hand. The gesture brought tears to my eyes.

"I don't think we should discuss this any further." Henry, the computer programmer said tersely. "Too close to the facts of the case." He paused and glanced at me. "But I am sorry for your loss."

Before anyone could say another word, a scream filled the room. Dianne Tucker, the woman with the bad eye stood up at the end of the table. She held a piece of king cake in one hand and the other was pressed to her mouth. King cakes were popular leading up to Mardi Gras. The ring like cake covered with icing and gold, green, and purple sugar crystals was a heavenly delight. But hidden within the cake was a tiny plastic baby representing the Christ child. The king cakes honored the visit of the Magi to the Christ child. If you got the piece with the baby in it, it would be your turn to buy the next cake.

Mrs. Tucker pulled her hand away from her mouth holding the plastic baby and blood poured down her chin. "I broke a tooth." She said and blood sprayed across the table. We all moved back as she coughed our more blood.

"I'm on blood thinner." She looked at me. "Help me!"

I ran around the table and grabbed a handful of napkins and shoved them into her mouth. "Breathe through your nose and I'll try and stop the bleeding."

Her eyes widened in panic, and she grabbed my hand and tried to pull it away. She coughed and blood shot out of her nose into my face covering my glasses in a red dots. Joe appeared in the foyer doorway.

"What the heck is going on here?" He looked at the blood on the table.

"He's trying to kill me!" Tucker jerked out of my grasp and fell backwards over her chair. We all heard the thump as her head hit the wall.

Suffice it to say, Joe called 911 and took the rest of the jury to the small courtroom. He directed me to an employee's bathroom off to the side. I tried to clean up the blood from my hands and my face. I looked at my reflection in the mirror above the sink. My hair was stiff with clotted blood and tiny wrinkles around my eyes carried red trickles of blood.

"You look like hell." I said. "After this morning, who can blame you for looking like that?"

We sat in the smaller courtroom and Joe appeared. "It is now 10:30 A.M. Judge Ford will allow you to go home and get cleaned up and be back in the jury room by 1 P.M. Mr. Gill, you are no longer an alternate. Let's try not to lose anyone else, shall we? And no more king cake!"

Chapter 22

Instead of heading home, I drove to the medical examiner's office on Grim Drive. That's right! The medical examiner's office was on Grim Drive! Sam wouldn't have had it any other way.

Missy sat up from behind her desk when I walked in. "Dr. Merchant! Either you need an ER or you're the walking dead."

"I need to talk to Sam. Is she here?"

"She's in her office. I'll warn her of the zombie apocalypse."

Sam met me in the hallway and gasped. "What happened to you?"

"King cake." I said.

"Come again."

"One of the jurors bit into the baby in a king cake and broke her tooth. She was on blood thinners and sprayed me with her blood when I tried to help, and I need to take a quick shower. You have scrubs here, I take it?"

"Of course. I ordered some in your size to keep in stock." She led me back through the main morgue room to a locker room. The main locker room had once been labeled "MEN" and now was labeled WO"MEN", since more women were in the building than men. Gone were the days when the men far outnumbered the women. The women's locker room had the "wo" marked out. I went inside and stripped off my clothes and stepped into the shower. I scrubbed for over ten minutes to get the blood out of my hair.

When I finished, I stood in front of the mirror and wiped away the steam. I had worn my glasses in the shower to clean them, and I was quite the sight! My hair stood on end and dark rings surrounded my eyes. I pulled off my glasses, and the reflection blurred.

"That's better!" And then I laughed. And laughed. And laughed until my sides hurt. "A king cake!"

My underwear was fine but my pants, shirt and socks were soaked. I threw them away in the contaminated red barrel. I looked through lockers until I found one with a pair of socks. I noted the name and promised I would bring "Hector" a new pair of socks. Bright red socks had an emblem from his favorite soccer team. My leather dress shoes cleaned up fairly well. I combed my hair and decided to go commando on the deodorant. I glanced at my watch. I had forty-five minutes to talk to Sam before driving back to the courthouse.

Sam sat behind her desk once again piled with folders. She sipped on a purple hued drink.

"What happened to the green one?" I asked.

She looked up. "Had to go. Put some prune juice in and it's drinkable."

I grimaced. "My mother drank prune juice to loosen her bowels. Constipated?"

"Pain meds will do that to you." She scowled at me.

I sat in front of the desk. "Can you get access to Fairmont's PACS system?"

"Of course I can." She pointed to two monitors on the side wall. "Just open the icon for Fairmont and put in your credentials. Only thing is, the monitors aren't 5K so I can't rely on X-rays of the chest or abdomen or mammograms."

"I need to pull up a CAT scan." I tapped on the keyboard, put in my sign in and brought up the PACS program. I searched for Mrs. Dixon's studies. "I need to show you something."

Sam rolled over in her chair and sucked on the prune juice concoction. My nose wrinkled at the smell. "Oh, that brings back memories."

"Did your mother make you drink castor oil?" Sam grinned.

I tried to ignore her, but the memories just wouldn't go away. "Let's just sat I had a hard time letting go." I cleared my throat. "Sam, this is the CAT scan of Mrs. Dixon."

"From ten years ago?"

"Yes. Now, look. Right here are two air filled tracts through the liver. They start out as one and then diverge. The largest tract exits the chest wall. But the smaller tract ends at the tenth rib." I pointed to the findings with my mouse arrow. I moved the pointer to the tiny metal fragments. "See these high-density flecks?"

"Yeah, looks more dense than bone."

"Exactly. Whatever hit the rib wasn't hard enough to fracture the rib, but it left these traces of some kind of metal." I looked at Sam's brightly colored eyeglasses and saw the squinting, focused look, meaning she was intrigued.

"No mention in the police report of any bullets found at the scene. And the gun was never found. Meaning two shots could have been fired." Sam slurped the last of her concoction and rolled back to her desk. A tower of folders toppled, and she let them slide to the floor, pulling a folder out. She rolled back over to me groaning in pain. "Keep forgetting about my bad wrist. Here." I took the folder and opened it on the desk before us.

"Now, look on page three." She said.

I leafed through the pages. She pointed with her good hand. "Right there. The autopsy report mentions something very strange. Stippling and gunpowder residue *beneath* the entry site. You would expect stippling from a close-range gunshot or one pressed against the skin but on the surface." She turned to the next page filled with photos.

"Now, look at the entry wound. See any burn marks on the skin?"

"No." By now, I had seen enough bodies in the ME's office to recognize such a thing. "How did the residue get *inside* the skin?"

"What if there is a hole in the skin and the perp sticks the gun into the hole and then pulls the trigger?" Sam said. "I've been wracking my brain to figure out how that could happen."

"So, what? She was stabbed first and then he shot her, too?" I said.

"I've seen weirder things. Maybe he was trying to cover up the tract of the first weapon." Sam shrugged.

"But, why?" I said.

"Only thing I can figure out is whatever made that second tract was most likely the first object shoved into her. And, whatever it was left a tract very distinctive of such a weapon."

"And it left some kind of metallic residue when it hit the rib?"

"Exactly! The perp stabbed her with something, then pulled it out and then shot her hoping to cover up the first tract."

I tapped the monitor before me. "But his aim was off. The first tract was left intact. Did the ME mention any of this?"

"Of course he didn't!" Sam cursed and swore more when she hit her wrist on the desk.

"Any tissue samples left over of that area?" I pointed to the rib.

"No!" Sam massaged her chin with her good hand. "I need a report of what you see."

"I sent it in an email."

"Good. Based on that analysis I can reopen this case. It's a cold case after all." She looked at me with those penetrating eyes almost the color of the green in her hair. "You realize what this means?"

"No!"

"We need to exhume the body." Sam stood up and crossed to a shelf. She examined stacks of papers and pulled one off. "Yep!" She held up the paper. "Get her daughter to sign this release and we can exhume the body."

I gasped. "What? No! I can't do that! I mean, she's got two sisters who are mad at her. And they'll be ticked off."

Sam fed the form into the laser printer and tapped on her laptop. The paper sucked in and slid out with all the information filled in. She handed it to me. "You said she wanted to find out more. Tell her the medical examiner has new information."

"But then she'll know I work for you. And then everyone will know. And then they'll start asking questions. And, why don't we wait until this is over?"

Sam raised an eyebrow and sighed. "Yeah, you're probably right. This trial isn't going to go past the weekend. But the minute you're done with deliberations, get her to sign that release. In the meantime, I will go over McGoober's autopsy records and see if, by some divine miracle, he managed to stumble into the truth."

I glanced at my watch. "Crap! I'm going to be late!"

Chapter 23

I made it back just in time. I collapsed in my chair next to Gill.

"Doc, you go to work?" He pointed to my scrubs.

"I didn't have time to go home. Showered and changed in the locker room at the M.E.'s office."

Sitting across the table, Rhonda Fall froze in her examination of her cell phone. She glanced at me. Had she heard us talking? If so, now she knew I worked for the ME!

Joe took us in, and the trial resumed with Zuniga calling Hector Alba to the stand. Hector worked with the crime investigation division of the ME's office, and I often saw him in the hallways. Fortunately, he couldn't see my socks! Or, rather *his* socks. The clerk swore him in, and Zuniga had him relate his identity and his profession. He avoided looking in my direction, thank goodness.

"Mr. Alba, you oversaw the processing of the crime scene for the death of Paloma Preston on February 14, correct?

"Yes."

"I have entered your report into evidence, but can you review your findings?"

Hector droned on about blood spatter and fire damage

and partial fingerprints. No DNA was recovered from the body because of the fire.

"You said you recovered a partial fingerprint?"

"Yes." Zuniga handed him the remote control and he pulled up an image on the monitor. "There are twelve points of correlation with a known person in our database."

"Is that degree of correlation significant?"

"It indicates a greater than 75% probability the partial matches the full fingerprint of the person."

"And who is that person?"

"Rex Eagleson." Hector said.

"Any other significant finding?"

"Yes." Hector moved to the next photograph showing a warped red plastic cylinder. "This is an arrow removed from the victim's body. We matched it with a Hyperspeed 371 arrow used with crossbows."

"That is interesting." Zuniga turned her gaze toward us. "A crossbow?"

"Yes. It is a common arrow used by hunters for small game."

"Where can you find such an arrow?"

"A sports store or Super-Mart."

"No further questions." Zuniga took a seat.

Kosinski bypassed the podium and stood directly before the witness stand. "You said there was 75% probability of a match with Mr. Eagleson's fingerprints. Where did you get Mr. Eagleson's fingerprints?"

"From our database." Hector said.

"And how did his fingerprints end up in the database?" Kosinski tilted her head.

"When he was booked, the police routinely collect fingerprints."

"So, Mr. Eagleson's fingerprints were not already in the database?"

Hector blinked. "Well, I don't really know."

"Mr. Alba, you are an expert on fingerprint analysis, correct?"

"Yes." He said through tight lips.

"You would know if Mr. Eagleson was, say, a repeat offender because his fingerprints would have already been in the system?"

"Yes, that's true."

"So, in the system there is a 25% likelihood his fingerprints would match with someone else? Did they?"

Hector glanced down at his report. He squirmed.

"Don't look at your report, Mr. Alba." Kosinski said. "Answer the question, please."

"There were some fingerprints that did match." Hector said quietly.

Kosinski moved closer. "I didn't hear you, Mr. Alba. And I want to make sure the jury hears you. Were there other matches to the fingerprints?"

"There were at least six with less than 15% correlation." Hector pointed with his hand at the monitor and brought the other image back up. "But this low value is the threshold we use for definite identification."

"I didn't ask you for commentary, Mr. Alba. You just told me there were other matching fingerprints other than Mr. Eagleson that were already in the criminal database. That is all we need to know. No further questions."

Hector looked right at me with that desperate help me look on his face. He sighed and left the witness stand. Kosinski skewers another one!

———

JERRY LANGLEY TOOK the stand next. After being sworn in, Mansfield took to the podium.

"Mr. Langley, can you tell the court of your initial involvement in this case?"

"I was called to the murder scene as part of the homicide division. I observed the victim's body and assessed the crime scene. We put out an APB for the white van."

"And was it located?"

"No."

"I understand the Bayou City Police contacted you later that day regarding a suspect?"

"Yes." Jerry nodded. "A man walking along the highway was sideswiped by a moving vehicle. Fortunately for the man on the street, the driver of that vehicle slowed to about ten miles per hour and only grazed the man when he stumbled into the car's path. The police arrived to find Rex Eagleson in the ditch with a broken ankle from the fall in the ditch. When he was taken to the hospital, the patrol officer smelled smoke and had seen our APB. He alerted us and we arrived shortly after the ER visit to interview Mr. Eagleson."

"So, at that point, he was merely a person of interest?"

"Yes, because of the smell of smoke and the presence of burns on his hands and his clothing observed by the Bayou City Police patrolman. We also recovered his clothing from the hospital and had it tested by the crime investigation division."

"Ladies and gentlemen of the jury, I direct your attention to the monitor. What the jury is about to witness is the footage captured on Lt. Langley's body camera during an interview of Rex Eagleson. We will play it in its entirety so you will see there are no edits." Mansfield pressed the play button.

Chapter 24

Detectives Gerry Langley and Ruth Beasley entered and sat at a table. Lt. Langley placed his body camera pointing toward the other side of the table. Rex Eagleson was brought into the room in a wheelchair. He sat at the table.

"Mr. Eagleson, I am Lieutenant Jerry Langley with the Talako Police Department. This is Detective Ruth Beasley. We would like to ask you some questions."

"Can we make it snappy. I'm headed for surgery to take care of my broken ankle. It hurts like hell." Mr. Eagleson leaned forward over the table and grimaced. His two-tone colored eyes were obvious in the bright light.

I listened half-heartedly as Jerry asked Rex about his injury. Rex answered the questions with minimal words such as "yes" and "no" and "fine".

"Mr. Eagleson, you say you fell into a ditch when a car sideswiped you. Why were you walking down a country road in the middle of nowhere at sunset?"

"I often go for a walk."

"The nearest building is an abandoned strip mall five miles away. Were you at the strip mall?"

"No."

"How did you get so far away from any building or structure."

"My girlfriend dropped me off."

"Who is your girlfriend?"

"Lydia Smalley."

"Why did she drop you off in the middle of nowhere?"

"We had a fight."

"About?"

"She was supposed to meet me for dinner at the diner and she never showed on time."

"What diner?"

"Ducks and Decoys diner on highway 80."

"You were at the diner?"

"Yes."

"What time were you at the diner?"

"I arrived there around 3 o'clock and waited until 5:30 before she answered my calls."

"And did she tell you why she was late?"

"She said she had a flat. I know it was because of Dennis."

"Dennis?"

"Her other boyfriend."

I noted the cold, unemotional tone of Eagleson's voice. If he was mad and his girlfriend had another boyfriend, he didn't seem upset about it.

"When did you leave the diner?"

"She showed before 6 and we left in her car. We argued and she dumped me out in the middle of nowhere."

"Mr. Eagleson, the doctor testified you smelled of smoke and fire when you arrived at the emergency room. Why was that?"

"Someone had been burning trash in the ditch I fell in. I rolled around in the ashes and soot. Some of it was still on fire." He raised his bandaged hands. "Burned my hands."

"Who brought you to the hospital?"

"The old man who almost killed me. He stopped and pulled me out of the ditch and helped me to his car."

"Were you mad at him?"

"Yes."

"How did you react to being in his car?"

"I bit my tongue. He was old. Dementia. I had to show him how to get me to the hospital."

"Mr. Eagleson, were you anywhere near Sunflower Lane today?"

"No."

"Do you own a white panel van?"

"I did until last week."

"What happened last week?"

"Lydia borrowed it."

"Did she return it?"

"No."

"Do you have another vehicle?"

"I have a truck. It's at the diner."

"Mr. Eagleson have you ever visited Christian Life Bookstore?"

Silence. Eagleson looked away and fidgeted. "Did she tell you that?"

"Who?"

"Paloma Preston."

"Why would Mrs. Preston tell us you were at the bookstore?"

"Because we had an argument."

"When was this?"

"Around the first of February."

"Can you tell us what the argument was about?"

"The white horseman." Eagleson looked back at Jerry.

"The white horseman?"

"In Revelation. One of the four horses of the apocalypse."

"Why were you arguing about the white horseman?"

"We disagreed on eschatology."

"I'm not familiar with that term."

"The end times."

"I see. And what was the substance of this argument?"

"She saw the white horseman as the Anti-Christ. I see the white horseman as a *TYPE* of an anti-Christ."

"I'm not sure I understand the distinction."

"I don't expect you to. You're not a theologian."

"And you are?"

"I took some online courses."

"Perhaps you can explain to us why this distinction is so important?"

Eagleson sighed and gestured with his bandaged hands and his voice filled with excitement. "Jesus will return as a warrior with a sword coming out of his mouth. And the sword is considered to be the Word of God. The white horseman carries a bow, a much smaller and less formidable weapon. This is why he is a TYPE of anti-Christ and not the true anti-Christ who will fool the nations after the rapture."

"I see."

"Paloma is a pre-millennialist. I'm a reconstructionist post-millennialist. Rushdoony advocates a return to the Mosaic laws. The white horseman will, therefore, be an instrument of justice until the return of Christ and his Sword. True justice. Eye for an eye."

"In your opinion, who is the white horseman?"

Silence and Eagleson leaned forward. "It could be you. It could be me. It can't be Lt. Beasley because she is a woman."

"What happened during the argument?"

Eagleson sat back. "I left the store after she cussed me out. Imagine a woman of God using such language."

"And what did you do once you left?"

"Got into my van and drove to the diner."

"Did you meet anyone?"

"Lydia."

"Mr. Eagleson were you at the bookstore on February 14th?"

"No."

"We have video footage showing you at the bookstore."

"Well, whoever you're seeing in that video it wasn't me. I didn't go there all day. I wasn't going back and get treated the way I had been treated."

"At 3:45 PM on February 14th where were you?"

"At the diner. Waiting for Lydia."

"Were there other patrons there?"

"Yes. I spoke to my favorite waitress, Mrs. Atkins. She always brings me fresh, hot apple pie."

"Where do you work?"

"I work in the sports and hunting section of the Super-Mart on I-20."

"Are you familiar with crossbows?"

"Yes."

"In what way?"

"I hunt with them. Mostly small game for sport like squirrels, possums, and the like. I sell them at the Super-Mart."

"When is the last time you shot a crossbow?"

"Yesterday morning during a demonstration at the store."

"Do you own a gun?"

"I own a 20 gauge shotgun."

"Pistol?"

"No."

"Mr. Eagleson, did you see Mrs. Paloma Preston after your fight on February 1?"

"No."

"Had you ever visited the store before February 1?"

"Many times. They have a nice section on eschatology. Not as diverse as I would wish."

"When you visit the bookstore what do you do?"

"Browse. Sometimes, I sit down and read passages from a

book to decide if I want to buy it. Lately, I have met with homeschooling parents to start an archery class for the kids."

"Mr. Eagleson, would you object to a search of your home?"

"No. I have nothing to hide."

So smug, no emotion, no reaction. Who was this guy?

"Do you wear sunglasses?"

"Yes. As you can tell I have unusual eyes. Sometimes I am light sensitive even inside."

"Mr. Eagleson, where are the clothes you wore when you came in?"

"I don't know. They took them off me for my X-rays. And then I went back to the ER. I have my wallet and that is all."

"Where are the keys to your van?"

"Lydia has them."

"You said earlier she picked you up in her car before you had the fight. Did she say where your van was?"

"No."

"Did you ask?"

"Yes. She wouldn't tell me."

THE VIDEO PAUSED and Mansfield turned to face Jerry. "Lt. Langley did you collect any evidence from the hospital?"

"We found his clothes discarded in a dumpster behind the emergency room. The hospital personnel said they had no idea how they got to the dumpster."

"Were you able to locate Lydia Smalley?"

"We found her address but when we arrived, we discovered her apartment was empty. The landlord said she had been gone for a couple of weeks."

"Did you ever recover the white van Mr. Eagleson claims was taken by Lydia Smalley?"

"No."

"Was a vehicle registered in Mr. Eagleson's name with the DVM?"

"A truck, but no van."

"Did you interview any of the patrons at the diner?"

"Yes. None of them recalled Mr. Eagleson being there the afternoon of February 14."

"Including this waitress Mr. Eagleson mentioned?"

"We were unable to locate her. She quit the day before and did not leave any forwarding information."

I sat back mulling over these chains of events. Everything seemed so convenient. The van was missing. Lydia was missing. The waitress was missing.

"I have no further questions for Lt. Langley."

Kosinski stood up. "Your honor I understand the crime investigators will provide more information and we reserve the right to recall Lt. Langley to the stand after that testimony."

"No objection." Mansfield said.

Jerry left the witness stand and avoided my gaze. He sat on the front row with Sanchez. I almost gasped when I saw the woman who came through the doors. Trenda Gayle from the medical examiner's office sat beside Langley.

"Will Trenda Gayle come to the witness stand please?" Zuniga stood up and traded places with Mansfield.

Trenda carried a folder and glanced once at me and then settled into the witness stand. The clerk swore her in, and Zuniga motioned to the monitor.

"Ms. Gayle, I have photographs taken by the crime investigators at the hospital. Were these photographs taken by you?"

"Yes."

"What are we looking at?"

"If you'll cycle through the first six photos you will see a pair of jeans, underwear, socks, flannel shirt and a New Orleans Saints jacket along with a black baseball cap."

The photos cycled and Zuniga continue to talk. "And these belonged to Mr. Eagleson?"

"Objection." Kosinski said. "A random set of clothing?"

"If the defense will be patient, we will establish the fact these clothes belonged to Mr. Eagleson." Zuniga said.

"Let's do that first, counselor." Ford said.

"Very well." Zuniga put the remote back on the podium. "Ms. Gayle did you test the clothing for DNA?"

"Yes. The DNA on the clothing matched the DNA of Rex Eagleson."

"And how did you obtain DNA from Mr. Eagleson to perform the test?" Zuniga glanced at Kosinski expecting an objection.

"He supplied a DNA sample at the Bayou City Police department."

"Did you do any other testing on the clothing?"

"Yes." She opened her folder. "If no one objects, I would like to refer to my report which has already been entered into the record. I wouldn't want to get any values wrong." She glared at Kosinski.

"No objection."

"We detected ash and soot from a fire. The soot contained chemicals from incinerated plastic. The profile of that plastic was compared to arrows obtained from Super-Mart and the profile was a match, specifically the Hyperspeed 371 crossbow arrow. We also detected lighter fluid residue. Also, fibers of burned carpet were found imbedded in the melted portions of the polyester jacket. These carpet fibers matched a brand commonly used in vehicles such as commercial vans. I have all the specifics of each test available for the jury to review."

"Which we will at the end of the state's presentation. No further questions." Zuniga returned to her seat.

Xavier took the podium. "Ms. Gayle, was Mr. Eagleson's DNA the only DNA found on the clothing?"

"No." Gayle said, raising her chin in defiance. "There were a dozen other contributors. However, the DNA matching

Mr. Eagleson constituted more than 32%. The other samples fell below 10%."

"I see. Now, you are an expert on DNA, correct?"

"Yes. My credentials are available to anyone who asks."

"Can you state, without any reservation, that the 32% DNA found on the clothing indicates the clothing could only have been worn by the contributor of that DNA? What I am asking is, do you think it is possible this clothing could have been worn by any one of those contributors?"

"It is possible. But unlikely."

"But, still possible? Just answer the question."

"Yes." Trenda said with clenched jaws.

"Now, as to the carpet fibers. Were they specific for a given brand of vehicle?"

"No."

"So, they could have come from any location, such as a car Mr. Eagleson may have ridden in."

I waited for Mansfield to object. He kept his mouth closed. I was beginning to get the rhythm of the court. Sam had been right. I needed to experience this.

"That carpet was of a particular grade used in commercial vehicles, not personal vehicles."

"Did you compare the carpet fibers to the carpet in Lydia Smalley's car?"

"We did not locate her car."

"I see. Your honor, we would like to enter into evidence an affidavit from Response Industries local representative." Xavier handed a document to the clerk. "This affidavit is from Jock Young, a local salesman for arrows and crossbows. Ms. Gayle, you said the plastic matched that used in arrows sold at Super-Mart, correct?"

"Yes."

Xavier approached the bench. "Here is a copy of the document I supplied to the court. Will you read the first three paragraphs and then summarize them for the jury?"

Trenda regarded the document with wary eyes and then took it from Xavier's hands. She scanned the document. "Well, Mr. Young claims the plastic analysis from our lab matches the exact type of arrow we suggested."

"Good. Now would you read the next two paragraphs out loud for the jury?"

Trenda looked up at me with desperation in her eyes. She drew a deep breath. "As representative of the manufacturer and seller of these arrows, I can testify there are over ten thousand such arrows sold throughout the region of Talako and Bayou City in at least twelve different stores. In fact, throughout northern Louisiana, we sell approximately 100,000 units per annum to various sports and hunting stores. Also, our sales online are almost double that amount throughout Louisiana and southern Arkansas."

Trenda looked up and glared at Xavier. He calmly took the document. "Let me ask you again, Ms. Gayle. Is there any evidence you collected that shows definitively that the arrow was purchased at the Super-Mart where Mr. Eagleson worked?"

"No." She said quietly.

Xavier returned to the podium. "I have no further questions. I now would like for Lt. Langley to return to the stand for our belated cross."

Trenda stormed away from the witness stand and plopped down beside Sanchez. Jerry sat in the witness stand again.

"Lt. Langley, Mr. Eagleson claimed he fell into a ditch filled with burned trash. Did you examine the site where Mr. Eagleson fell?"

"Yes, we located the site where Mr. Eagleson allegedly fell."

"And what was in the ditch?"

"Burned brush, papers, food containers, and other objects."

"Do you have a theory of how that burned trash ended up in the ditch?

Langley shrugged. "Not really. That stretch of highway is outside the city limits and burning trash is permitted. It might have fallen off a truck."

"I see. Did you test that trash?"

"Pardon me?"

"Did you test the trash for the same chemicals and residues found on Mr. Eagleson's clothing?"

Langley's face reddened and he glanced once at me. "No. We didn't think it was necessary."

"I see." Xavier retrieved a document from his end of the table. "We would like to enter this into evidence for the defense." He handed a copy to Lt. Langley.

"Lt. Langley, would you take a look at this list of items? We had our own independent lab analyze the items in the ditch. We wanted to save the court some time by presenting this now and not during our portion of the trial. I thought it would be easier. Can you read the list of ingredients found in the ditch for the jury?"

"There's no need. They're almost identical to those found on Mr. Eagleson's clothing." Langley slapped the document on the railing. "But if he did indeed roll around in this trash, he could have transferred those same chemicals from his clothing to the trash."

"Ah, but Lt. Langley, you are not a crime investigator. If you would read aloud the last paragraph." Xavier said calmly.

Langley gritted his teeth and read out loud. "It is our conclusion the quantities of these substances were far too high in the trash to have been transferred from an individual's clothing based on the analysis of the quantities of these chemicals in the samples tested by the crime lab. Therefore, we believe the chemicals on Mr. Eagleson's clothing came from the trash alone."

"Objection, your honor." Mansfield stood up and his

usually calm voice cracked with anger. "This is a stunt pulled by the defense. This evidence should have been presented during their portion of the trial so the state could counter with a cross examination."

"Sustained." Ford tapped her gavel. "Mr. Xavier, you will reserve the presentation of this evidence for your portion of this trial and I expect you to produce the witnesses to corroborate this report. I agree this is a stunt. I will not put up with any more of these stunts."

"Understood. We withdraw the evidence for now." Xavier said far too calmly. I realized he had planned the whole thing! "But I do have one more question for Lt. Langley."

"Proceed."

"Lt. Langley, did you search the dumpster where Mr. Eagleson's clothing was found for any other clothing?"

"Yes. There were other pieces of clothing present. Scrubs, hospital gowns, and the like."

"Isn't it unusual for a hospital to discard clothing in a dumpster?"

"I supposed. I'm not an expert on that."

"You're right. I would like to enter into evidence a statement by the hospital administration on the policy for handling of patients' belongings." He handed a document to the clerk. "It clearly states that no hospital employee can dispose of a patient's belongings without consulting the patient. So, Lt. Langley, did you ask the hospital employees in the emergency room how Mr. Eagleson's clothing could have gotten into that dumpster?"

"Now you're saying they are his clothing!" Langley said hotly.

"Uh, you know, Lt. Langley, I misspoke. As was clearly stated by Ms. Gayle, there were other DNA contributors to that clothing. Thank you for bringing that up again. Mr. Eagleson denies these clothing items belonged to him. In fact,

Lt. Langley, didn't you speak to a homeless man out by the dumpster at the time of your search?"

Langley's face reddened and he gritted his teeth. "Yes."

"And what did this homeless man tell you?"

"I asked him if he had seen anyone around the dumpster. He said he hadn't."

"What was he wearing at the time you asked him that question?"

Langley closed his eyes. "A New Orleans Saints jacket."

"I see. Now, we could enter into evidence video surveillance footage of you talking to the homeless man in the alleyway. Unfortunately, the point of view did not include the dumpster. But it clearly shows you talking rather animatedly to the man. Would you care to tell us more?"

Langley blinked several times. "He said he got the jacket out of the dumpster. He never saw anyone throw the clothes in. But he was cold. He took the jacket and put it on."

"Did you test his DNA?"

"No. He disappeared before we could."

"But you took the jacket from him and assumed it belonged to Mr. Eagleson?"

"Yes."

"Well, we can't expect our police force to be perfect all the time."

"Objection!" Mansfield shouted.

"Withdrawn. I have no further questions."

Judge Ford tapped her gavel. "Seeing as how it is now 5 P.M. and we had a shortened day, we will reconvene in the morning at 830 A.M."

Chapter 25

I hurried after Rhonda Fall and caught up with her at the next intersection. She glanced at me over her shoulder. "Oh, It's you."

"Hey, I was wondering if we could talk."

She turned to fully face me, and her eyes filled with anger. "Why didn't you tell me you worked for the medical examiner's office? Is that how you managed to get out of the malpractice suit? Inside connections?"

"No. I'm only a medical consultant and I started back in December for the first time." I pointed to a coffee shop on the next corner. "Can I buy you a cup of coffee?"

She regarded me warily. "Yes, and a sandwich. I'm hungry."

We crossed the intersection and stepped into the warm coffee shop redolent with the fragrance of coffee and pastries. Rhonda placed her order and found a table. I ordered my coffee and paid. How was I going to handle this?

I sat at the table with her. "You asked me about your mother's murder."

"Yes." Rhonda said quietly. Then her eyes widened.

"Wait! You're working with the ME's office? Did you find out something?" Her anger vanished in a wave of curiosity.

The server brought our coffee and a grilled cheese sandwich for Rhonda. "I did."

Rhonda bit into the sandwich and moaned with ecstasy. "Oh, this has always been my favorite sandwich. My mother used to make it and serve it with tomato soup on a cold day like today." She pressed her hand to her mouth as she chewed, and her eyes filled with tears. "It's been ten years, and I still miss her."

I thought about my parents for the first time in a long time. I felt the old guilt and pain inside. "I still miss my parents."

"Dr. Merchant, I'm so scared I'm going to forget her face. I can't see her like I used to be able to." She finished half of her sandwich and wiped tears from her cheeks with a napkin. "She was so kind to everyone even to the people who crashed into Dad's truck and put him in a coma. He lasted two weeks before Mom decided to pull the plug." She gasped and pressed the napkin to her lips. "I'm so sorry. This trial is stirring all kinds of memories and feelings, Dr. Merchant."

"I know."

She paused and her eyes widened. She blinked. "That's right. You said your wife had been murdered and set on fire, just like Mrs. Preston. This must be very hard for you." She looked down at her sandwich. "Now you know how I felt at that trial."

I sipped my coffee and pushed my thoughts of my parents and now, Janice away. "As I was telling you, I sat down and pulled up your mother's radiology studies the day she came to the emergency room. I may have found something."

"Found something?" Her excitement turned to suspicion. "Wait a minute. Are you saying there was something on those studies that you didn't see the first time?"

"Well, that's not what I mean. I never saw her CAT scan after they brought her into the emergency room."

"But you did her arteriogram!" She said tersely.

"That's true. It's just that our group uses a nighttime radiology service to review all of our emergency studies from the ER after 6 P.M. The CAT scan was read by one of those radiologists."

"But you had access to it, right?"

"Yes."

"Why didn't you look at it?"

I opened and closed my mouth. This was not going well. "Rhonda, I probably did look at it. I just don't remember the details."

"So why didn't one of these other radiologists do the arteriogram?" Rhonda pushed her sandwich away, leaned back and crossed her arms.

"They are not on site. They interpret studies from afar. We call it teleradiology. But I was on call for procedures. There is always a radiologist on call 24/7 for procedures. Back then, we didn't have an IR in the group, and, well I was new and had good training in IR." I paused as confusion and anger fought each other in her expression.

"What's IR?"

"Interventional radiology. Now, we have two members of our group who are experts on doing radiology procedures such as arteriograms."

"And you're tell me you're not one of these fellows? And yet, you did an arteriogram on my mother?"

"Rhonda, I have adequate training for basic arteriograms. The procedure your mother had was pretty simple."

"Simple, but deadly?" She said.

"Okay, we know she was fine when I sent her to the operating room."

"Then, what happened along the way?" She leaned

toward me. "You know, don't you? But you're not going to tell me so you can protect your precious medical partners."

"Okay, Rhonda, I did find out why there was a delay."

"Oh, good! More lies."

"No lies. I looked into the circumstances around her treatment, just as you said, and it turns out the elevator from radiology directly to surgery was out of order. They had to wheel your mother around and down another hallway and it took about five more minutes than it should have." I exhaled and my heart raced.

Rhonda opened her mouth to speak and then slumped back in her chair. "A faulty elevator?"

"Rhonda, listen to me. Your mother's injuries were too severe. Even surgery could not have saved her. She had two holes in her liver and blood in her chest and abdomen. She was bleeding too fast for any surgeon to have saved her. It's a wonder she even made it alive to the emergency room to begin with."

Rhonda sobbed quietly and dabbed tears with her napkin. "My mother said if it weren't for bad luck, we'd have no luck at all. She loved to watch Hee Haw reruns."

I had no idea what she was talking about. But at least her focus wasn't on me anymore. "Rhonda, after looking at her medical records I am convinced we did everything possible to save her life."

"Then why did God let that elevator break? Huh?" Rhonda threw the napkin down on the table. "I've been so mad at Him for ten years now. Why didn't He protect her? Why did He let this fiend attack and kill her? And who is that devil anyway?"

I reached across the table and tried to pat her hand. She jerked it back and hugged herself. "Rhonda, I reviewed her CAT scan and found something I think no one saw. It only makes sense afterwards. Hindsight is always 20/20. We're only human and we do the best we can."

Rhonda nodded and took my napkin and blew her nose noisily. "Fine. What did you find when you looked at something you should have looked at to begin with?"

"Rhonda, when Dr. Francisco, the medical examiner, hired me as a consultant the experience changed how I look at imaging studies. I have a different perspective. I'm more like a detective, you might say. There was a second track through your mother's liver. The police report and the autopsy report only talk about one gunshot. But I see two tracks. She was shot twice and there are some metallic residue next to a rib that might help us identify the gun or bullet that was used. Dr. Francisco wants to reopen the case and take a fresh look at everything."

Rhonda blinked her wet eyes at me. "So, we might get some answers as to who did this?"

"It's possible. I'm not making any promises, but this might bring justice to your mother and give you and your sisters some peace."

Rhonda nodded. "Okay. Then what's stopping you?"

I pulled the folded document out of my jacket pocket. "I was going to wait until after the trial, but since we are talking about your mother. Well, we will need to exhume your mother's body." I unfolded the document and placed it on the table before her. Rhonda pressed her hands to her mouth.

"Oh, my Lord in heaven!" She sobbed again. "I can't do this!"

"I understand how you feel, Rhonda." I wet my lips. "Just two months ago, I signed just such a document to have my wife's body exhumed. She was murdered and a second look helped us find the cause of her death. And her killer." Who Sanchez killed with an exploding MRI machine! Justice indeed!

Rhonda's eyes widened. "They had to dig up your wife? Oh, my! What will my sisters think?"

"It's up to you whether or not to contact them."

"Clotille lives in Oregon. Maisey lives in New Jersey. I hardly talk to them anymore. They get so sick and tired of me asking these questions. 'Just put it behind you, Rhonda.' 'Mom's gone, accept it.' They say." She picked up the paper and scanned it. "Do you have a pen?"

I pulled one from my shirt pocket and handed it to her. "Yes."

She signed her name. "When will you know something?"

"Probably after the trial is over. But I will let you know personally, Rhonda. I promise." I put the document back in my pocket after signing in witness blank.

Rhonda gulped the last of her coffee and nodded. "I'm tired. I'm going home."

"I'll see you tomorrow."

She left the coffee shop without a word just as my phone rang. I looked at the caller ID. Gill Brown.

Chapter 26

"Gill? What's up?" I left the shop and headed toward my car. Already the sun had set, and the sky was a dark blue gray.

"Well, Doc, I'm at Central. I'm on call tonight and I already had a call when I turned my phone back on. There's a broken portable X-Ray unit in the CCU. Guess who is a patient up here?"

"I really don't know." I climbed into my car.

"Mrs. Kosack? The jury member who had a heart attack? Remember her?"

"How could I forget." I started the car and waited until my phone switched to the speaker. "She's why I'm on the jury and not an alternate."

"Well, she wants to speak with you. Now."

"What?"

"Doc, she's pretty agitated and she said would talk to you and you alone about something to do with the jury." Gill said.

I glanced at my watch. I hadn't eaten anything and had only coffee. "Okay, fine. I'll be there in a few minutes."

"Better hurry. She's pretty uptight, Doc."

I parked at Central and took my white coat out of the trunk. I kept it for the times I might have to go up on the floor at the hospital. It helped grease the wheels when people saw I was a doctor. I walked into CCU and Mrs. Kosack's room was the first one. Gill waited outside the room.

"Hey, Doc, she's kind of excited."

"I'll say she is." Pam came into the room.

"Pam?" Pam wore a pink set of scrubs and a white coat.

"Yes, Dr. Merchant. I'm Mrs. Kosack's nurse. She's been asking for you for hours. I can't seem to get her to calm down."

"How's her heart?"

"She's fine. Funny thing is, she came in with typical anginal chest pain and they took her straight to the Cath lab. Her coronaries were fine. Normal. Dr. Davis thinks she might have had coronary spasm from too much excitement."

"Being on a jury during a murder trial can do that." I said.

"I gave her something to relax her. As far as Dr. Davis is concerned, she can go home. But she refuses to leave until after the trial is over." Pam put a hand on her forehead. Her dark hair was pulled back in a ponytail and her bangs hung to just above her eyebrows. She pushed them back and sighed. "Maybe you can talk some sense into her."

"If it's about the trial, we're not supposed to discuss anything."

"Doc, I think that ship has sailed with Mrs. Kosack. She's not on the jury anymore." Gill said.

Mrs. Kosack sat up in bed when I walked into the room. She reached both hands toward me. "Dr. Merchant! You've got to help me. Please."

I took her hands, and she focused her muddy brown eyes on my face. She had an oxygen tube under her nose and an I.V. running in her left arm. "They tell me you're with the police."

"Well, not exactly. I am a consultant with the medical examiner's office."

"Close enough." She glanced over at Gill and Pam. "I need to talk to you in private."

"That's fine, Mrs. Kosack." Pam pushed Gill gently from the room. He raised an eyebrow, and the door closed.

Mrs. Kosack looked past me to make sure the room was empty. "Well, he was at the Super-Mart the night I had my heart attack. They made me work from 6 to 10 even though I was on the jury. I couldn't refuse. They pay my insurance supplement for Medicare. I can't say no. I was standing at the door doing my greeting as usual and Bob walked up. He's real nice to me. I think he's sweet on me but he's ten years older! I told him all about the trial. I know I wasn't supposed to talk about it. I told him about Rex Eagleson and he looked over my shoulder at a man who had come in. That man heard everything I said"

"What man?"

"That man in the video. The one from the bookstore. You saw him in the video, remember?"

"Yes, I did."

"He had come in the door with his black cap on and black jacket and sunglasses and it was the same man, I tell you. He heard me talking about Rex Eagleson and that I was on the jury!"

I shook my head in confusion. "The man in the first video?"

"Yep. It was him."

"But that man supposedly is Rex Eagleson. He's in jail. He couldn't have been at the Super-Mart. You saw someone who looked like him."

"No!" Her hands squeezed tightly on mine. I winced in pain. "He took his sunglasses off right after he came in and I saw his eyes. Two different colors! I saw him and he recognized me. How did he recognize me? He looked surprised I was there and went over to the snack bar. I didn't know what to do. My heart started racing and I was hyperventilating so much I couldn't say, 'Welcome to Super-Mart'." She started breathing quickly and slumped back in the bed pulling me toward her. I finally extracted myself from her grip.

"He brought me a cup of coffee. Said I was doing a good job and then went back out of the store. I never should have drunk that coffee. Three sips and my heart started racing even more and I had this pain unlike anything I've ever felt. I dropped the coffee and passed out right at Bob's feet. Next thing I know, I'm in the hospital and they're telling me I'm having a heart attack."

She slowed her breathing. "Dr. Merchant, I've never had any problem with heart. I walk four miles every day. My cholesterol is 86!" She sat forward. "But I read a lot and I know there is a chemical or a drug or something than can make someone have a heart attack. That coffee tasted funny. That man put something in my coffee! He didn't want me to tell them I had seen him that night!"

"Mrs. Kosack, this all seems absurd. How could Rex Eagleson be in two places at once?"

"Evil twin! I tell you this man was the same in the video and he looked just like Rex Eagleson. They did it together. Rex had an accomplice, and it was his evil twin brother!" She said, nodding. "Just like that show on the Mystery channel."

"That's a little hard to believe." As if anyone should believe anything from a show on that channel!

"Well, go ask your police friends. See if he has a brother."

"Mrs. Kosack, I'm still on the jury. You shouldn't even be telling me this. If Ms. Kosinski found out about this conversation, she could move for a mistrial and Eagleson would walk."

"They don't have to know until after the trial. But I'm afraid for my life. That man is still out there and if he knows I'm alive, he's going to try to kill me again." She held out her arm. "Take my blood. Take it to the your coroner's lab and test it for that drug. I'm telling you it's there."

I rolled my eyes and stepped back. "Mrs. Kosack, why don't you just tell the police?"

"You don't even believe me. What makes you think they will? You've seen the video. You know who I'm talking about. Mr. Eagleson has an accomplice of some kind, I'm telling you. And, if I die in the next three days, it's because I'm telling the truth." She put a hand to her face in deep thought. "Wait! If I tell the police, it messes with the trial, right? Eagleson walks free. No! We have to do it this way. Please, Dr. Merchant."

I paced around the room. "I can take a couple of vials of blood. I'll have to stick you in the other arm. Don't want the sample to be contaminated by the intravenous fluid you're receiving."

Before she could say anything, I went out to the nurse's station. I realized I couldn't just order a blood test and get it back in time. But I could draw the sample myself and take it to Sam. If what she suspected was true, we would need that sample to prove there was another murderer helping Rex Eagleson. How absurd was that? An evil twin? Really? Mrs. Kosack probably saw a man with similar features and had a panic attack leading to chest pain mimicking a heart attack. Yes, that was MY diagnosis!

I bypassed the nurse's station and went into the supply room. Phlebotomists drew blood samples and arrived with their own pushcart of supplies. However, blood drawing supplies were also available to nurses in case of an emergency. I grabbed two vials for blood, a tourniquet, and a needle sheath. I turned around and Pam stood in the doorway.

"What are you doing, Dr. Merchant?"

I put the supplies in my coat pocket. "I need some blood for the medical examiner's office."

Pam lifted an eyebrow. "What?"

"You know I work there, right? You told Mrs. Kosack."

"Gill told Mrs. Kosack. I overhead. You can't take blood without a court order or warrant or whatever. Can you?"

"Pam, Mrs. Kosack believes someone spiked her coffee and made her have a heart attack. You said her coronary arteries were clean. There may be some truth to her story. I'm merely drawing blood and taking it to the coroner with her story. If we wait, any drug may no longer be in her system. It may not be there now. Time is of the essence. I don't need a warrant if the patient requests to be tested."

Pam pursed her lips. "Give them to me."

"What?"

"The supplies. Now."

I sheepishly took them out of my pocket and handed them to her. "Come on. You probably haven't drawn blood in years. I'll get you the samples."

Pam went to Kosack's room and drew two vials of blood. She peeled labels with Kosack's information and stuck them to the vials. She handed them to me.

"Now, you need to leave before anyone else finds out we did this."

"I don't want to get you in trouble."

Pam pushed me gently out the door. The touch of her hand on my chest sent chills down my spine. I looked into her intense gaze. "Dr. Merchant, you're a good doctor and I sense a good man. Truth is, I kind of believe Mrs. Kosack. There were some other anomalies in her blood tests that don't make a lot of sense. She might be telling the truth. Go find out."

"Pam, you're special."

"I bet you tell that to all the girls. If so, you need a better pick-up line."

I cleared my throat. It had been years since I had thought about pick up lines. Since before Janice. "I, uh, thank you. Listen, she's scared about going home until after the trial is over. We should be done by Friday afternoon."

Pam nodded. "I can put down some of her complaints and convince them to at least move her to a step-down unit until Saturday. How's that?"

"Good. Thanks again."

"Your friend, Mr. Brown left. Said to tell you to get some sleep. He said tomorrow will be a doozy!"

"Indeed, it will." I said as I placed the blood vials in my coat pocket.

Chapter 27

I took the vials to the coroner's office. I knew the reception room was locked after hours so I went to the rear employee's entrance. I pressed the button and smiled for the surveillance camera. The door opened and Trenda let me in.

"Can you believe it? The way she treated me?" Trenda said as she led me into the depths of the building.

"Yes, I can. I've been on the receiving end of her crafty ways, Trenda."

We arrived at Sam's office and Trenda paused. "I've been on the stand many times, Jack. But, never with her."

I took the blood vials out of my pocket. "Can you run these blood samples for drugs or illicit chemicals?"

Trenda took the vials and read the name. "That name is familiar."

"She was on the jury until she had a heart attack. She thinks she was poisoned." I paused as Sam's door opened and Sam looked out at me. "And I think she might be right."

"Say no more. Don't want to risk a mistrial." Trenda walked away.

"Jack? What are you doing here?"

"Dropping off some blood samples for screening. Can I come in?"

"Sure." Sam moved back behind her desk. "I'm just trying to get more paperwork out of the way so there will be no delay in my trip to New Orleans."

"How's the wrist?"

"Hurts like all get out. What's with the blood samples?"

I told her about my encounter at the hospital and she laughed. "Evil twin? Want to know how many times that has been used as an alibi?"

"Stuff of mystery fiction." I pulled the release from my jacket. "Rhonda Fall signed the order for exhumation."

Sam took it and nodded. "We'll get it done in the morning. I've been going over the autopsy report again. What a mess! Dr. McIdiot didn't know his butt from a hole in the ground. And I mean that literally. I'm going to do a complete autopsy on remains almost ten years old. Not sure what I'll find. But I will excise that rib and find out what those metal flakes are."

"Good. I'm heading home to try and get some sleep."

Trenda appeared at the door her eyes as big as saucers. "We've got a call out. Police found a body."

For some reason I picture Mrs. Kosack, lifeless glaring at me saying "I told you so!"

"Jack, care to go with me?" Sam said.

"Why not. I probably can't sleep anyway. I need to make sure it's not Mrs. Kosack."

<hr>

ST. Mark's cathedral had been built in the 1930's. It had once been an architectural marvel in Talako and the center of religious fervor. Three years ago, the church closed and became a refuse for drug addicts. Two police cars sat out in front of the crumbling edifice of this once majestic building. A fine, cold rain fell and lightning cast strobe like spikes of light across the bell tower.

Sanchez met us just outside the yellow crime tape. "I hope your heart is in good shape. Body is at the top of the bell tower."

"Tell me the facts." Sam pulled her hoody up over her multi-colored hair.

"Homeless addict found the body about an hour ago. In one of his more lucid moments ran out into the street screaming at the top of his lungs. Patrol car just happened to be coming by and almost plowed him down. Officer Goode didn't want to believe the man until she saw blood on his hands." Langley joined us.

"Jack! Why are you here?"

"He's my consultant." Sam said holding up her bandaged wrist. "He's helping out until my wrist heals."

Langley nodded as if we had not seen each other just hours before. "Homeless guy is covered in blood. I doubt he had anything to do with the dead body. Goode climbed the stairs and secured the sight. She said it's pretty gruesome."

"You haven't been up there?" I asked.

"We don't want to climb it but once. Crime investigators on the way?"

"Yes. Well, let's get to it. Quasimodo is waiting." Sanchez said, chewing on her ever present toothpick.

It took about fifteen minutes to climb the stairs. Broken brick and stained glass covered the steps. Langley and Sanchez's flashlights mirrored the lightning outside. In places, the side rail had broken away. One misstep and it was a long fall to the bottom. We reached the top of the stairs and moved into the large chamber. Ropes hung from a harness that once held a huge bell. Officer Goode leaned against the wall.

"Glad you're here. I'm heading down. Body's over there. Be prepared. It's nasty." She pushed past us and fairly ran down the stairs.

Sanchez led us around the periphery of the bell tower. Once beautiful stained-glass windows had been broken out. Cold rain blew into the chamber making the floor slippery. We avoided the gaping hole in the center where the bell ropes hung.

Lightning hit somewhere nearby filling the room with blinding light and the thunder afterwards rattled the walls. More broken glass clattered across the floor. In that brief moment of bright illumination, I saw the woman sitting against the wall. Nausea gripped me.

Langley illuminated the body. The woman's eyes were wide open in pain and the skin on her face was missing. I clearly saw the masseter muscles at the corner of her ragged mouth. No lips! No eyelids! Cheek bones gleamed in the white light.

"Well, that's something you don't see every day." Sanchez said pointing with her toothpick. "Looks like the crime scene guys have their work cut out for them. Dr. Francisco? Think this person is alive?"

"I think it's safe to say he's quite dead. But, I'll let the crime scene investigators do the liver temp." Sam glared at Sanchez. "You did have to say it, didn't you?"

"What?" Sanchez asked innocently.

"Have their work cut out for them?" Sam swore and it echoed down the stairway.

I BREATHED through an open mouth as I hurried down the stairs. I would wait at Sam's car for her to finish. There was no way I could do her job! Sanchez and Langley joined me. Sanchez carried an umbrella and Jerry stood just under the outer edge.

"You're going to catch your death of cold." Sanchez said.

I stepped underneath the large umbrella's protection. "I

don't know what to say or think. I've never seen anything like it."

Sanchez was so close to me I smelled the cinnamon from her toothpicks. Jerry leaned toward me. "Death in Motion."

"What?"

"It's an exhibit at the Convention Center." Sanchez said. "Ever seen bodies injected with some kind of polymer and then posed without their skin in various states of activity?"

"What? Yeah, I've seen something like that on the Internet."

"This guy is different. He deconstructs donated bodies and imbeds them in Lucite, or some clear polymer and poses them. From one direction, you see all the parts separated. But step to the right angle and the parts line up looking like a complete body." Jerry said.

"Why are you talking about that?" My mind had already gone to the conclusion. "You think it has something to do with this murder?"

Sam joined us, her hoody beaded with moisture. "Three murders and one attempted murder in less than a week. Jack, I think we're looking at the work of a serial killer."

I tensed and my thoughts instantly went to Mrs. Kosack for some reason. "What makes you think that?"

"Your old professor had his kidneys removed." Sanchez said.

"Then our desk clerk had her eyes removed." Jerry said. "And there was the posed body at the Tiger's Tail with the body parts lined up just right, like the exhibit."

"And now, this woman has her face removed." Sam finished.

"Exhibit comes to town with dissected deconstructed bodies." Sanchez spat her toothpick onto the pavement. "Nutcase killer gets inspired. I've seen it before. All these psychos need is a little macabre inspiration."

"Jack, let's all go home and let the crime investigators do

their job." Sam said motioned for me to get into her car. "Our part of this job is done."

I glanced at Sanchez and Jerry huddled under the umbrella as if the meager protection protected them from the evil up in the tower. "Yours is just beginning." I said to them.

Chapter 28

The next day, we settled into the jury box to hear more evidence from the homicide division. The first witness of the day turned out to be someone who once worked with the medical examiner's office. Toby Taravek stood six foot five with a gaunt skeletal figure. Thick glasses magnified his ice blue eyes in a deeply tanned face surrounded by shoulder length blonde hair. Except for his glasses, he would have passed as a California surfer. He settled into the witness stand and still looked like he was standing. His story, teased out by questions from Mansfield was he had left the medical examiner's office a little less than a year ago right after Sam came on as the new M.E. I sensed there were loads of unspoken details I would have to get from Sam later.

"Mr. Taravek, did you examine the victim's clothing and other residue from the crime scene on February 14th of last year?" Mansfield said.

"I did. The salient feature of my exhaustive examination was the presence of a deformed Hyperspeed 371 crossbow bolt imbedded in the victim's chest. Meticulous analysis revealed the plastic component matched bolts purchased in a lot sold to the local Super-Mart three months before the murder." His voice was so low pitched, he could have voiced a science fiction villain.

"And how did you arrive at these conclusions?" Mansfield asked.

"May I?" Taravek pointed to the remote control.

"Certainly. These are your photographs."

The first image showed a red arrow placed on a white background. "This is a Hyperspeed 371 crossbow bolt obtained from Super-Mart only days after the murder." Next image showed a magnified image of the shaft. Etched along the shaft was a number/letter combination. "This is a batch signifier. Notice the 'ND' and the following two digits? ND means November and December of the year ending in those 2 digits. This batch manufactured during those months has two more numbers, as you can see." He activated the laser pointer on the remote and outlined the two numbers. "This would be arrow 123,227 out of 125,000."

The next image showed a badly warped and burned red shaft. A string of digits could barely be seen. "Notice the number? I used computer analysis and enhanced the number. Notice it is ND113777. This bolt came from the same batch as the first bolt I showed you. That batch was one of five sold to Super-Mart in the last quarter of that prior year."

"I see. So, your conclusion?"

"The murder weapon was purchased at the Super-Mart sometime after September of the prior year. And, when we checked on the list of employees who worked at the Super-Mart during that time, one of them was Rex Eagleson."

"Objection, your honor." Kosinski stood up. "This testimony is going beyond the scope of Mr. Taravek's expertise."

"It's Dr. Taravek." Taravek said.

Ford tapped her gavel. "Dr. Taravek, you will stay quiet until I have spoken. Understand?"

"Yes, your honor. All she has to do is question me about

that in cross and I just thought I'd get it out of the way." Taravek said.

More tapping more insistently. "Any more unsolicited comments and I will hold you in contempt of court."

Mansfield's face reddened and he walked quickly up to the witness stand. "That is enough, Dr. Taravek. No further questions."

Kosinski remained standing. "I have no further questions, your honor."

Maybe only we heard it because Ford did not react. But as Taravek left the witness stand, he scanned the jury and muttered. "I made my point, though. Didn't I?"

I shook my head in dismay. No wonder he didn't work at the M.E. with Sam anymore. She would never have put up with this man's arrogance.

Ford sent us out for a break to let things cool off, no doubt. I snagged a bottle of water and joined Gill in the outer room while the rest of the jury sat around the table.

"Doc, this thing is getting weird. Was Mrs. Kosack being paranoid?" Gill said sipping a cup of coffee.

"We aren't supposed to talk about it."

"Doc, we aren't supposed to talk about what we learn in the courtroom. Don't think you should tell your buddy, Jerry, to go talk to Mrs. Kosack?" His gaze was relentless. "You know it's the right thing to do."

"I saw Jerry last night, Gill. At another murder scene. I can't just walk into the courtroom and talk to him sitting on the first row, can I?" I said tersely.

"Hey, Doc. Calm down, brother. If you don't want to talk about it, I get it." Gill started to walk away, and I grabbed his arm and stopped him.

"Gill, I'm sorry. I'm a little on edge here and that Taravek didn't help matters. This whole thing has me way out of my comfort zone."

Gill shrugged. "It's okay, Doc. I get it. But you are the one who took a job with the coroner's office. I think what they deal in the most are deaths, right? Maybe you should have thought of that before you signed on the dotted line."

"Yeah, you're right. As usual, Gill."

"Hey, Doc. I'm always right. Except when my wife tells me I ain't." He smiled and before I could comment, Joe took us back into the maelstrom.

Dr. Wang took the stand. Today, he wore a white coat with his name over the pocket. Mansfield had him recount his education after coming to the United States from the Philippines twenty years ago.

"Dr. Wang, you conducted the autopsy on Paloma Preston." Menedez said.

"Yes."

"Would you share with the court your findings, please." Zuniga handed the remote control to Dr. Wang.

Before he showed any photographs, Dr. Wang related pertinent information about Mrs. Preston measurements and then, quite abruptly the first image come on the screen. I almost fell out of my chair. It showed a badly burned body in a typical fetal position lying on charred carpet. Clothing had burned and pulled away from cracks in blackened skin on the woman's torso. Bile crept up my throat. I wanted to look away as memories of Janice's badly burned body surfaced. I smelled the burned flesh, the charred wood and plastic. The memories were seared into my brain. And as badly as I wanted to close my eyes and moan in pain, I couldn't take my eyes off the images. Wang went on and on about the condition of the body at Mrs. Preston's home. He showed close up images of the deformed partially melted crossbow arrow.

"And, now I will discuss the findings once I received Mrs. Preston's body in the lab. I performed the autopsy at the medical examiner's office on Grim Drive. Prior to the autopsy, preliminary imaging was performed with a CAT scan."

The next few images will forever be seared into my brain.

I knew them. I recognized them. I looked at CAT scans every day. Wang pointed out the anatomy and I knew the details were as foreign to my fellow jurors as ancient Greek!

"As you can see, the impact point for the arrow was against the inner periosteum of the left eleventh rib in the posterior axillary line as evidenced by this trace metal fragmented from the tip of the arrow after striking the rib." The red laser beam encircled the rib. I gasped. I stood up and pointed to the image.

"Can I see that closer?"

Ford tapped her gavel. "Will the juror please sit down and restrain from comments!"

I looked around at my fellow jurors. Their eyes widened in shock at my behavior. Didn't they see? And in one cold wave of realization, it hit me. The metal fragments! The rib! And I knew!

I stared at Rex Eagleson and slowly, oh so slowly, his eyes widened as he met my gaze with those two-toned eyes of his. And HE knew I knew. I slumped into my chair, shaking.

"I'm sorry, your honor. I'm a doctor and I wanted to make sure of what I was seeing."

"You will allow Dr. Wang to TELL you what you are seeing!" Judge Ford said a little too loudly. If looks could kill, she would be at the defense table instead of Rex Eagleson. But as her gaze locked on mine, she blinked and then slowly turned to look at Eagleson. Then back at me. She knew I knew! And in that moment, I saw it all unfold. Was it a coincidence I was on the jury? Despite the random choices of jury prospects, she knew I was one of the potential jurors. And she had practically begged me to stay on the jury. Had she wanted me to hear what I just heard because she had been at the trial against the surgeon?

I jerked my gaze away from her and Eagleson. Wang cleared his throat and went on presenting grisly photographs of the melted arrow protruding from the charred chest tissue.

Then the open chest showing the heart and lungs pierced by the arrow including soot in the lungs indicating the victim was still alive when the fire was set. I heard Bobble head wretch behind me. Gill actually looked paler when I glanced at him. Wang finally finished his rather emotionless recitation. Kosinski, uncharacteristically quiet, refused to ask any more questions.

My thoughts whirled. Could Eagleson have been the one who shot Mrs. Dixon? I glanced at Rhonda but her gaze was directed at her lap. Jerry and Sanchez still sat on the front row. Should I tell them? What should I do? I had to talk to Sam!

Chapter 29

Gratefully, Ford broke for lunch. When we arrived in the jury room, Joe had provided more pizza and drinks. No one was particularly hungry but most of the jury members grabbed a plate of pizza and went across the hall to the small court room to eat.

I stayed in the jury room and chewed on the pizza. My mind whirled with the revelation from Wang's autopsy. My stomach groaned with acid.

"I never want to eat pizza again!" I said.

"It ain't that bad, Doc." Gill nibbled on a piece. "Look at it this way. It's better than hospital food! Of course, you probably get to eat in the la tee da doctor's cafe."

"It's the same food as in the regular cafeteria. The table-cloths and silverware do NOT make it taste any better!" I said gruffly.

"Doc, this will be over soon."

"I hope so. Only I know things I can't talk about, Gill. Things that have complicated my woeful life!" I tossed the half-eaten pizza onto my paper plate. "I just want a break from the action, you know? Just a chance to stop and catch my breath."

"Well, look at it this way. You're not having to read any radiology studies this week."

"Yeah, but I will be working for someone who gave up their week off to cover for me!" I sat back and crossed my arms over my chest. "Two steps forward and three steps back."

"Doc, you're in the waiting room." Gill brushed crumbs from his hands. "Ever sat in a doctor's office waiting room?"

"Or course I have. Being a doctor doesn't grease the wheels like you think it would."

"I'm sitting there waiting and waiting to see the doctor. Maybe I'm sick and not feeling well. The longer I wait, the longer I suffer. Or maybe I'm waiting for news about that test. Could it be cancer? Answers are all I want and there I sit with no answers. Just a lot of questions. And the longer I sit, the more I ponder on the questions and the more I considered all kinds of answers."

"Your point?" I said tersely.

"My point is you can worry yourself sicker. Or you can spend the time being positive. Think about what you will do if the answer goes your way. And then, plan on what you'll do if the answer goes the other way. Don't waste time worrying. Don't be problem oriented. Be solution oriented. When I'm looking down inside the open gantry of a CAT scanner, I know the problem is somewhere deep in that mass of anodes and diodes and wires and receptors. And there are dozens of possibilities. If I sit back and worry about how long it will take me to dig through all that to find my answers, you would never get your CAT scan to interpret. I have to be patient and MOVE forward and take it one small step at a time."

Gill's words should have brought me comfort. But he had no idea what I had just learned. Big problems, indeed. With no solution!

Gill leaned toward me and put a hand on my shoulder. "Doc, you been through things most people never experience once in a lifetime, not to mention over and over. You lost two women you loved. You died and saw heaven. You thought you had leukemia. You got drunk and lost most of your money at the casinos. You were accused of murdering your own wife! Give yourself a break! Give yourself some breathing room. It will take time to process all of that and it will take time to recover." His brown eyes bored into mine. "And you're not alone, Doc. You got friends, like me, who will be there to help you. You got Lt. Langley. And, even, Sanchez. Not to mention Dr. Francisco." He swatted me gently on the shoulder.

"So, come on, get with the program. Put your mind to work on this trial and make up your mind where we're headed. When we get back to deliberations, you're going to be the smartest man in the room because you work at the medical examiner's office. And you're a doctor. Take all that wasted energy worrying and put it to good use. And guess what? You'll find you're about to walk through the door and out of the waiting room."

"Gill, you have no idea what I have concluded about this trial so far. And what I know I can't say to anyone in the jury. Not even you. I'm stuck in the waiting room until this trial is over!" And then, I didn't yet know what I should do.

Gill leaned back. "It seems to me the only way you could have gotten that far was by sitting patiently in the waiting room. Imagine Jesus in his waiting room."

"Where was that?" I glared at him.

"The garden of Gethsemane. He knew He was about to die. After all, he was God in man form. Imagine never having tasted death? Imagine facing something so unknown, more unknown to Him than to us! He who could never die was about to face the ultimate human fate. No wonder he asked for his cup to pass from him. What was that condition called where you sweat blood?"

"Hematidrosis."

"Yeah, you understand the medical stuff behind it. All I

know is that Jesus was under so much stress so bad it made him sweat blood." He leaned forward again. "Now, I know you've been under a lot of stress in the past year. But have you ever sweated blood?"

I raised an eyebrow and shook my head sheepishly. "No. But I feel like I'm about to after that autopsy report."

"Well, He did. And He was betrayed and beaten and flogged and crucified and he died. He's been through more than you or I will ever experience in a lifetime, Doc. He understands. And here is the truth that should bring you some comfort." Gill put his big, meaty hand on my arm. "He's still in the waiting room with you!"

Well, I wish Jesus would take the wheel and tell me what to do!

Chapter 30

After returning to the courtroom, Zuniga stood at the podium. "Your honor, we now have a stable video connection to our last witness."

A window appeared on the monitor. A gray-haired man sat behind a desk, his eyes surrounded by dark rings. He wore a rumpled red flannel shirt. "Is anyone there?" He said.

"Mr. Rodriguez, this is Mrs. Zuniga with the prosecution. Thank you for your patience in this matter."

"Dang tornadoes! I thought I left them behind when I moved to Colorado." He coughed wetly and pulled a handkerchief from his pocket and wiped his mouth. "Been without power way too long. Life to froze to death!"

The court clerk swore Mr. Rodriguez in, and Zuniga began the questioning. "Mr. Rodriguez, would you tell the court what your relationship to the deceased is?"

"She's my daughter!" He bellowed and shook his head. "I guess she WAS my daughter now that she's dead!"

"Can you tell us about your relationship to Mrs. Preston?"

"My wife and I ran the orphanage in Matamoros. Florence said God had called her. And where Florence went, I followed. Never was too crazy about moving from Pensacola to Mexico. But, once we got there and started the orphanage, the poor children just melted my heart." He wiped at his eyes. "We didn't have children of our own. But we had dozens over the years at the orphanage. But we only adopted one."

He drew a deep breath, and his voice shuddered with emotion. "Florence found the baby on our doorstep one morning. She was wrapped in a coarse handmade blanket and one card was tucked into the blanket with her name and a plea for us to take care of her. As well as the other thing."

He looked away. "We called her Dovey because she cooed like a dove. Sweetest kid we'd every had and Florence was dead set on adopting her as our own. So, we did. But she would have to wait until she was an adult to get her U.S. citizenship. Dovey was so kind and resourceful and grew up to be a wonderful girl."

"Mr. Rodriguez, would you tell us about the disk?"

"The disk! Yes, that thing! It ruined our lives, is what it did. The mother had wrapped it in the blanket. The first time I touched it, I knew it was evil. That carving of a dismembered person and the number thirteen, both smacked of evil. I put it in our safe the moment we found it. We never told Dovey about it until she was thirteen. Florence reasoned since she was coming of age, she should know about it. So, we showed her the disk."

Rodriguez shook his head and covered his eyes. He sobbed for a moment and then wiped the tears from his face. "I told Florence it was evil. Dovey wanted nothing to do with it. Florence said she could sell it one day to pay her way through college. But it wasn't long after that Dovey was kidnapped by traffickers!"

Rodriguez pounded the table. "In Brownsville, Texas of all places. Not in Mexico where you would have expected. Nine months we prayed and searched and hoped. It took an independent tracker to find her. She came home and was never the same afterwards. Florence tried to get her to open up about what happened to her, but Dovey kept it all to herself. By the time she reached eighteen, she seemed to have overcome most of the memories. And that is when that boy showed up!"

"What boy, Mr. Rodriquez?"

"Roy Kingbird. A college student from Tyler came down with a youth group. Every summer we would have a different mission group from the states. They would come and help with construction and clean up and do backyard Bible studies in the nearby villages. This kid was in college and seemed so nice. But what he did to us was beyond forgiveness."

"Objection, your honor." Kosinski stood up. "The defense would like to know what all this has to do with the accused?"

Rodriguez leaned forward as if trying to look out of the monitor. "The accused is Roy, dang it! He changed his name! We found out about that later. Changed it to Rex Eagleson. Just ask him."

Murmuring filled the courtroom and Ford tapped her gavel. "Quiet, please. Mr. Rodriquez, we will address that issue momentarily. Please continue."

I glanced at Eagleson and he avoided my gaze. Was that true? Had he changed his name? And Ford said we would address it, not Zuniga. She knew something we didn't know!

Rodriguez reached out of view of the camera and retrieved a pink and purple bound notebook. "While I was up in the attic trying to get the power back on, I found Dovey's box of memories from the orphanage. Should have given it to her when we moved to Colorado five years ago but that was when Florence got pancreatic cancer and died in six months' time. I opened the box and found her diary from back then. I read it and it tells everything you need to know about Roy and Dovey."

"Objection!" Kosinski had not sat down. "We were not appraised of this line of evidence, your honor."

"Your honor, we only now have heard about this diary." Zuniga said.

"You want to know the truth about what happened, don't you?" Rodriguez said.

Ford nodded to the clerk. "Mute our audio feed, please. Counselors approach the bench." What followed was a heated discussion I'm sure we weren't supposed to hear. But from the body language and tone of voice, the defense did not win this argument. The attorneys returned to their table. Ford turned to face us.

"I will allow Mr. Rodriguez to read some of the diary entries and I will have a U. S. Marshall come to his home and claim the diary in person so it can be entered into evidence. Joe, will you see to that? ASAP?"

"Now, you will hear from Mr. Rodriguez. But, if I determine the entries are not a reliable source of information, I will have them stricken from the record. Also, the defense will have an opportunity to cross examine. Let us proceed." Ford tapped her gavel. I released my breath unaware I had held it.

Zuniga seemed a bit rattled also. "Well, uh, Mr. Rodriguez, obviously we do not want to hear the entire diary."

"Don't worry. I have picked out the most important entries. The first are when she was eighteen and she met Roy." He opened the diary and began to read.

June 9

A new group of students arrived today to work on the addition to the orphanage. They are with a missionary group from a church in Tyler, Texas. They seem nice and kind. One of them, a college boy, is particu-

larly handsome. I guess what attracted me to him to begin with were his eyes. They were of two different colors! I've read about that condition somewhere. He sat by me at dinner, and we had a little talk.

June 10

Roy finished with his part of the construction and asked me if we could go for a walk. It was early in the evening and the terrain around our orphanage is mostly low brush and stunted trees. But an uncharacteristically cool wave had gone through, and I knew of a path through the trees that led to a small pond. It is my special place. So peaceful and quiet. I go there to hear the voice of God. After what I have been through, God is my only comfort. I will never trust any man. But Roy may be different. He seems so kind.

We walked to the pond and sat on a rock by the water. I pointed out one of my favorite birds, a dove that lives in our area. I told him I had been named after a dove. Their cooing is so soothing. He pointed out a gray and yellow bird I had seen many times. He said it was a tropical kingbird. Roy is a birdwatcher, it turns out. He even knew the bird's scientific name and I wrote it down — Tyrannus Melacholicus.

We walked back to dinner and he tried to hold my hand but I wouldn't let him. He apologized for being so forward and I wish I could tell him of my history. At that moment I felt, what is the word? Almost like the bird's name, melancholic. Sad and wistful.

June 11

I met Roy for lunch. He was all dirty and sweaty from working on the building and he took his shirt off to cool off. I tried not to look at him, but he was beautiful especially with those haunting eyes. I found myself trying to explain why I couldn't let myself care for him. I told him I had been kidnapped at age thirteen for nine months and had been the victim of human trafficking. I have had to overcome my trauma, and God has given me the assurance I am a worthy person, not just something to be used. But at times, it is hard to get past those feelings. Roy told me about his childhood. His father was very abusive and beat him most of his life. Now, he is in college and no longer lives with his parents. It seems we both have trauma in common. Perhaps I can trust him.

June 12

Early in the morning, I went for my walk, and I was shocked to find Roy at the pond. He was reading his Bible. Turns out he was trying to understand Revelation! Good luck with that! I have read through the Bible at least twice and when I get to Revelation, I get PTSD with all the violence and death foretold. I told him this and he was very kind. He said that Revelation was about a new kingdom where the rule of God's law would punish those who did not accept God's way. Where was the rule of God when I was kidnapped, I asked him.

I fear violence from humans. My ancestors were Aztec, and their heritage of human sacrifices haunts me. My parents have locked away the gold disk they found with me when I was abandoned on their doorstep. When I was thirteen, I asked to see the disk and the image on it frightened me beyond words.

For some reason I shared this with Roy. I told him about the disk and how touching the disk had filled me with most horrendous sense of evil. One day, I will need the money to finish my naturalization and then to pay my way through college. I will move away from Matamoros and teach children with special needs. Roy suggested we sell the disk. He said he knew someone on the black market who would pay top dollar for the disk.

He smiled, touched my face, and tried to kiss me. I almost let him, but my old trauma surfaced, and I pushed him away. He fell into the pond and when he got out of the pond, I saw something evil in his eyes. I was scared and I ran down the path back toward the orphanage.

I skipped dinner because I knew Roy would be waiting for me. Maybe I overreacted. But the more I think about his actions and his comments about the black market, the more uncomfortable I have become. How does he know about the black market? Just the thought of such a thing reminded me of the human trafficking ring through Mexico and southern Texas. Could he be part of such a thing? But he is so kind. His eyes are filled with understanding and compassion.

One day, I will leave this place and go out on my own. I will owe everything to my Lord and to my parents. They can have the disk. I will make my own way. I dream of changing my name to something more American. Dovey comes from the name left on a card when my parents found me, Paloma. That was my name, and it is Spanish for dove. My parents nicknamed me Dovey. One day, I will go to college and hope and pray God brings that special man He has planned for my husband. I do not know who that man will be. But I do know right now that it will not be Roy Kingbird.

June 13

The worst thing happened today! My father caught Roy in the supply room. Roy had somehow figured out how to open the safe and was stealing the golden disk! He attacked my father and knocked him out. But the adult in charge of the mission group, showed up and stopped Roy. The police came and took him to a Mexican prison and that is horrible. So horrible. Hopefully their chaperone, Mrs. Dixon, can get him transferred to an American jail before they kill him. Americans don't do very well in a prison in Matamoros. Not even Roy deserves that kind of treatment.

June 14

The mission group is leaving early. Roy was beaten to within an inch of his life in the prison and fortunately transferred to a hospital in Brownsville. I hope he survives. He may have tried to take advantage of my friendship to steal the golden disk, but he didn't deserve to be treated this way. I heard his parents are coming down from Tyler to the hospital. I hope his father isn't too hard on Roy!

"This entry is from three years later." Rodriguez said quietly.

June 1

I officially received my citizenship today! I have already enrolled at Northwestern University in Louisiana after meeting my future husband, Benjamin Preston. Today is a very special day. On my citizenship papers, I am officially Paloma Rodriquez. The day was almost ruined by the appearance of Roy Kingbird! At first, I was a little frightened he was there. But he was very kind and told me he wanted to be there for my special day. He never mentioned the golden disk! He told me he had to drop out of college after the incident in Matamoros and his father had died in a tragic accident. He wished me the best of luck with my future. And, like me, he changed his name! Tyrannus Melacholicus was the name of the tropical kingbird, and he said it inspired him to change his name to Rex Eagleson. When I asked him why, he said he needed to put his past behind him and start over.

—

I GLANCED over at Rhonda Fall. Had Rodriguez said Mrs. Dixon was the chaperone? How many Mrs. Dixon's could there be? Rhonda seemed not to have noticed the name, and her eyes were wet with tears.

"Your honor!" Kosinski stood up along with Xavier. "We have no way of being sure any of these entries are true. I don't want to disparage Mr. Rodriguez, but he could have made all this up. My client is not this Roy Kingbird person, but Rex Eagleson. I demand these diary entries be stricken from the record and the jury instructed to disregard what they have heard."

"Your honor." Mansfield stood up. "We acquiesce to the defense's demands. Until we can determine the validity of these entries, we agree the jury should be so instructed."

My mouth fell open. How could I possibly forget what I had just heard? But maybe that was the point Mansfield was making. Give in to the objection knowing we could never forget it.

"Just a dang minute!" Rodriguez held up the diary. "My poor girl was killed by that Rex Eagleson and you just want to sweep her under the rug? I don't think so. What kind of justice is that?"

Ford nodded to the clerk, and she killed the audio feed. Rodriguez continued to rant silently. "Does the defense wish to cross examine?"

Kosinski leaned over to Xavier and they conferred with Eagleson. His gaze met mine and then moved on toward Rhonda Fall. Kosinski stood tall. "We have no questions."

"Mr. Rodriguez, thank you for your time and a U. S. Marshall should arrive any moment to take the diary into custody."

Rodriguez continued to speak silently, and the video image disappeared. My heart sank at what I had just learned. Had Rex Eagleson known Mrs. Dixon, Rhonda's mother?

Mansfield cleared his throat as he took to the podium. "Your honor, the state rests. And we would now like to present the evidence in its physical form to the jury."

The clerk of court stood up and it was only then I noticed she had a rolling cart next to her chair. She rolled the cart up to the jury box. Jerry came forward as well as Dr. Wang and Trenda. Jerry picked up a notebook and came forward. He leafed through the notebook showing us all the real photographs taken at the crime scene. He made sure and leaned between the members of the front row to show the back row. Trenda did the same with her documentation of the DNA and fingerprints. Wang had a larger notebook and presented us with the autopsy photos. I had one brief chance to see the image captured from the CAT scan and yes, the metal fragments were almost identical to the ones in Mrs. Dixon's CAT scan. Finally, Wang passed around a box containing the melted, deformed arrow. The odor of burned plastic and burned flesh still clung to the arrow even months after the murder.

Bile flooded my throat and I managed to swallow it back. My face warmed with anger and I glared at Eagleton. He smugly glared back and then winked. I looked away.

Judge Ford dismissed us for a break. But there was no way I could eat anything!

Chapter 31

The foyer of the jury room was too small. I paced back and forth, my thoughts racing. Joe had laid out soft drinks and a basket of sweet items. I couldn't possibly eat.

"What's up, Doc?" Gill sat on the couch eating a candy bar

"I just realized something, Gill." I paused. And could I tell him? We weren't supposed to talk about the trial proceedings. But, it was Gill. He was my sounding board. I plopped down beside him.

"Gill, I'm going to tell you something in strictest confidence." I turned and looked into his brown eyes. He paused in his chewing.

"Okay, Doc."

"There is another, uh, cold case. I reviewed the CAT scan from that victim taken at the time she arrived at the ER. She died afterwards. I saw the same pieces of metal up against a rib in her CAT scan as I just saw in that courtroom."

"Who killed this patient?"

"It's a cold case. They never found the assailant."

"What? You think Rex did it?"

"I don't know. Coincidence that I see the same changes on that CAT scan as on this one?"

"Doc, I don't know how many murders take place each year, but I would guess between knife stabbings and gun shots, they would all have some kind of metal in their bodies." He turned to face me. "Maybe you're trying so hard to figure out this cold case, you've got tunnel vision. Happens to me all the time. CAT scan goes on the fritz. I open up the gantry and look at that complicated piece of machinery and I'm convinced it's a detector gone bad, you know. So, I test every detector and come to the conclusion we have to replace every one since I can't find the culprit. I go see my boss and he just laughs at me. He knows how expensive it would be to replace all the detectors. So, he goes back and instantly sees a loose wire! Just a loose wire, Doc. You get what I'm saying? Some-times we can't see the trees for the forest. Maybe you're reading too much into this."

My heart sank at his words. Was he right? Was I overreacting? "Maybe so, Gill."

"Look, Doc, this trial is going to come to an end pretty soon. I'd predict we'll be in deliberations by the morning, and we can all go home tomorrow afternoon. Don't complicate things. Don't say something that would lead to a mistrial."

He was right, of course. I got up from the couch and managed to get a sip of water down before Joe came and took us back to the courtroom.

JUDGE FORD TAPPED HER GAVEL. "Is the defense ready to present its case?"

"Your honor, may I approach the bench with state counsel, please?" Kosinski said after we were seated.

Judge Ford nodded and Kosinski and Mansfield stood in front of the judge's desk. Their whispers were loud enough I could make out what they were talking about. Mansfield was agitated and Kosinski quite fervent in their back and forth. Finally, Judge Ford tapped her gavel.

"The court rules in favor of the defense. You may call your witness." She turned to us. "The defense has requested a last-minute addition to her witness list. Normally, this is not allowed. But I will allow it. The defense may proceed."

Ms. Kosinski came to the podium. "Your honor, as you can see, we had three character witnesses scheduled for testimony. But, in view of the discovery of the most recent witness, we waive the appearance of the first three witnesses in lieu of this witness. I will call Mrs. Belinda Atkins to the stand."

Mrs. Atkins approached the witness stand. I recognized her as the woman who had sobbed earlier in the week. She was probably in her early seventies with snow white hair and a thin, wrinkled face. She wore a plain white dress and a string of pearls. Her hair framed her aged face. The clerk swore her in, and she settled into the chair.

"Mrs. Atkins, what is your occupation?"

"Well, I'm retired now, Missy. I live in that fancy retirement complex on the riverfront. Got me a nice condominium where they let me keep my cats. Three meals a day and I don't have to cook or serve a one of them." She said in a heavy Cajun accent. "Me, I was going to move down south with my son, but they don't cotton to me much anymore. I don't approve of his third wife."

Kosinski nodded impatiently. "Before you retired, where did you work?"

"I was a waitress at the Duck and Decoy Diner for twenty years, I was."

I tensed and glanced at my fellow jurors. We all perked up at this information. I glanced at Jerry and he almost stood up. They claimed they could not locate this person and she had been in the courtroom the entire trial!

Kosinski smiled and approached the witness stand. "While working at the diner, did you have recurring customers?"

"Missy, I had my favorites. I also had my cast offs. Some of them did nothing but sit at the counter and complain. Do I look like a bartender, I ask them?"

Someone behind me laughed. Kosinski waited for quiet. "Your favorites came in often?"

"Some of them every day. Some once a week."

"Do you recognize the man sitting at my end of the table?"

"Sure do. Mr. Eagleson."

"How often did Mr. Eagleson come in?"

"Oh, every couple of days. Had a favorite place at the diner. First time I saw him, his eyes creeped me out. But then, I got used to them. He would sit at the end of the counter next to the restroom in the darkest part of the diner. Said his eyes were sensitive to light." Mrs. Atkins nodded. "Me, I let him and got to where I knew when he was a coming. I made sure his stool was empty. He always showed up around 3:30 or 4 when the apple pie was fresh out of the oven." She leaned forward and winked at Kosinski. "Want to know a secret?"

"Yes." Kosinski said nervously. What secret were we going to hear?

"That apple pie recipe came from my grandmother. Uses real lard in the crust, it does. Me, I hate that pie. Got tire of eating it every Sunday dinner after the boudin."

"That's nice." Kosinski said. "Do you remember Valentine's Day of last year?"

"How could I forget. Me, I wanted to hang up some hearts and some cupids, but Rudy said we couldn't. He's such a fickle old fart."

"Rudy?"

"My boss. Runs the diner and does the cooking. Didn't want no Valentine hearts hanging from the ceiling." Mrs. Atkins nodded as if that made total sense.

"Do you recall who was in the diner that day?"

"Sure do. I knew Ms. Judy was coming in. She's alone. What we used to call an old maid. Never married. Lives with a dozen cats, she does." She leaned forward and put a hand next to her lips. "Stinks like them, too! I knew she would be looking for company that didn't squat over a litter box."

More laughter from behind me. This time, Judge Ford tapped her gavel. "Please refrain from reacting, please." She said to us.

"And then, that new couple came in. Always sat in the 'enchanted grotto' on the other side of the restroom hallway. I call it that because of that Frasier episode, you know? No one could see it when they made out. I think they're both married and are having an affair. But me, what business is it of mine if they pay for their meal and leave me a good tip? I think it's to keep my quiet, don't you know."

Before Kosinski could say anything, Mrs. Atkins pointed to Eagleson. "And, of course Mr. Eagleson was there sitting in his usual place waiting for apple pie."

"Mr. Eagleson was at the diner about what time?" Kosinski asked.

"It must have been from about 3:30 to about 6 I'd say." She pointed to the front row. "If you'd have the bailiff bring me my purse, I have the receipt from that day."

Mumbling came from the people sitting in the courtroom and I glanced at Gill. Judge Ford tapped her gavel. "Quiet please. Joe, would you get Mrs. Atkins's purse for her?"

Joe retrieved an enormous black purse and brought it to the witness stand. "Now, it's in here, somewhere. Me? I kept it because of what he wrote on the back of the receipt." She began to unload objects from her purse, placing them on the railing: an ancient flip phone, a bottle of aspirin, a banana, a hairbrush filled with gray hair. Finally, she pulled out a tattered envelope.

"Here they are. I keep all my most precious receipts, me

do." She took receipts from the envelope and held out one. "Here you go, Missy. If you look at that receipt, Mr. Eagleson ordered his apple pie at 3:48 P.M. on Valentine's Day and I ran his credit card through at 5:35 P.M."

Kosinski handed the receipt to Xavier. "Your honor, we would like to enter this receipt into evidence. Mr. Xavier will prepare it."

"I will allow it."

"If you look on the back, you'll see his sweet note. 'To my favorite cherub.' He's so sweet. There's no way he could have killed anyone."

"Objection, your honor. Speculation." Mansfield said.

"Sustained. Mrs. Atkins, response only to the questions."

"Mrs. Atkins, thank you for your time today. I have no further questions." Kosinski moved back to her table.

I could hear the gears turning in the minds of my fellow jurors. If he was at the diner, there was no way he could have killed Paloma Preston. Mansfield whispered to Zuniga, and she nodded. Zuniga approached the witness stand.

"Mrs. Atkins, thank you for your time. Can I ask when you retired?"

"Well, I came into some money last March. It was enough to supplement what little retirement my boss had allowed me to save up. He took all my tips and kept half of them! The leach!"

Zuniga looked back at Mansfield who was studying something on his laptop. He motioned for Zuniga to come back to the table. "Your honor if you would give me a moment to consult with my colleague?"

"Make is snappy, Ms. Zuniga."

Zuniga leaned over the laptop and whispered to Mansfield. She pointed to the printer and a piece of paper emerged. She took it and read it while walking back to the witness stand. "Mrs. Atkins, my colleague and I were just studying the Louisiana Lottery site from March of last year and we found this." She handed the paper to Mrs. Atkins. "Would you tell the court what you're holding?"

"Me, I'm beaming proud of this photo. Lord, I look old in this photo. They didn't give me a chance to put on my makeup."

"Can you tell the court why this photograph was taken?"

"I won the lottery, Missy. One hundred thousand dollars! And the lottery office insisted on taking my picture and posting it on the Internet."

Zuniga stepped closer and pointed to the document. "So, you recognize this posting and can verify its authenticity?"

"Yes, Missy."

"Can you read the third sentence in the last paragraph?"

"I never bought a ticket before, and this winning ticket was left as a tip from one of my customers." She nodded. "That's what I told them all right."

Zuniga took the document and handed it to the clerk to put into evidence. "Mrs. Atkins, who gave you that ticket?"

"Why, Mr. Eagleson did. Me, I think if he'd a known it was a winner, he would have kept it. Fact is, he gave it to me the day the drawing took place. All he had to do was check the numbers and he would have known he was a winner. I still think he knew, and he was just so kind, he wanted me to have that money so I could retire. I had told him so many times how hard it was working at the diner with my arthritis and all. He was an angel, Missy. An angel!"

Zuniga glanced at us and smiled. "I see. Very convenient, wouldn't you say?"

"Objection." Kosinski growled.

"I withdraw the comment. Now, Mrs. Atkins, you said Mr. Eagleson always sat at one end of your counter?"

"Every time."

"And why was that?"

"I done said, sweetheart. His eyes. He had to stay away from the light."

"And you know about the condition of his eyes?"

"Yep. Two different colors. I bet one of Ms. Judy's cats have eyes of different color. Cats can do that, you know?"

"On Valentine's Day what was Mr. Eagleson wearing?"

"What he always wore. Black New Orleans Saints jacket. Black tee shirt and his black cap. Every time, he wore the same thing. I think it was supposed to bring good luck. But it hadn't worked for the Saints this season, has it?"

More chuckling behind me. Ford tapper her gavel and never had to say a word. Zuniga paused, deep in thought. "Mr. Eagleson wore his cap that day?"

"Yes."

"Did you see his eyes?"

"What?"

"Did you see his eyes, Mrs. Atkins."

Mrs. Atkins paused and glanced over at Eagleson. "I never got a good look at his eyes cause he always wore his sunglasses. I only seen them that one time when he first came in."

"So, on Valentine's Day, you saw a man in a black jacket, black tee shirt, black cap wearing sunglasses sitting at the end of your counter in the darkest section of the diner?"

"Yes."

"And you are sure it was Mr. Eagleson?"

"Well, it had to be. He came every Tuesday and Thursday."

"Did he speak to you?"

"Missy, he didn't have to speak. I knew what he wanted. Black coffee and a piece of MY hot apple pie Ala mode."

"Mrs. Atkins, this is very important. Did the man sitting at the counter on Valentine's Day speak to you?"

Mrs. Atkins's face twisted in confusion, and she blinked. "Well, come to think of it, I don't know that he did. But it was him. I know it was him."

Zuniga returned to the table. "Your honor, one more moment."

"This is the last delay, Ms. Zuniga."

She studied the laptop with Mansfield and the printer whirred again. She took the paper and handed it to Mrs. Atkins. "Mrs. Atkins, this is a handwritten account of Mr. Eagleson's whereabouts on the day he was questioned by Lt. Langley. He was asked to write down his activities on that day on a legal pad. It is a part of the official record."

"Okay, if you say so."

Mendez motioned to Mansfield and he tapped on his laptop. The document appeared on the monitor. "Here is a scanned in version for the court to see. Are these the same documents?"

"I would say so."

Zuniga approached the clerk. "May I see the receipt, please?"

The clerk handed a clear plastic sheath containing the receipt. Zuniga brought it to Mrs. Atkins. "You testified this was the receipt you received from the man at the counter on Valentine's Day."

"Yes. Mr. Eagleson."

Zuniga handed the receipt to Mansfield and he took a photo of it with his phone and uploaded it to the laptop. "Your honor, we have just made a digital copy of the receipt as witnessed by everyone in this courtroom and we would like to place it on the monitor for the jury to see. Do we have your permission?"

Judge Ford glanced over at Kosinski. "It was your evidence, counselor. Any objections?"

Kosinski sat with her arms crossed over her chest. "None."

The receipt appeared on one side of the screen next to the handwritten page. "Now, Mrs. Atkins, I know you are not a handwriting expert. But would you say these two documents were written by the same person?"

"Objection, your honor. This is ridiculous."

"Your honor, Mrs. Atkins has testified that she knows Rex

Eagleson so well he left her a note on a receipt. I would assert that she is well acquainted with his handwriting. While not an expert, I would like to know her opinion of the receipt handwriting compared to the account obtained by Lt. Langley. And we readily acknowledge that Mrs. Atkins is NOT an expert witness."

"It ain't the same!" Mrs. Atkins blurted out. "I know his handwriting anywhere. Me, I never thought of it. But any person with good sense can tell that."

"Objection, your honor, again." Kosinski stood up. "We protest this cheap trick! Mrs. Atkins is not an expert handwriting analyzer."

"We withdraw the question, your honor." Zuniga nodded to Mansfield, and he took the images down.

I heard whispers around me. I glanced once at Gill and he shook his head nothing one word, "Accomplice?"

Kosinski stood up after Mrs. Atkins left the stand. "Your honor, the defense rests."

Murmurs broke out in the courtroom and Ford pounded her gavel. "Silence in the courtroom." She drew a deep breath and studied her laptop. "It is now 3 P.M. and I will not proceed today with closing arguments. We will reconvene tomorrow at 10 A.M. for closing arguments and then the jury will proceed with deliberations."

Chapter 32

Missy looked up from her desk as I burst through the door to the M.E.'s office. She touched the Bluetooth speaker at her ear.

"Just a minute, Roxie. Dr. Merchant?"

"I need to see Dr. Francisco now."

"She's in her office. Go on back."

A body lay spread out on a table when I stepped into the main lab area. The skin was desiccated and tight against bone. The chest had been laid open. I stopped at the awful smell of death and decay.

"Jack?" Sam said from her office. "Are you done?"

"Closing statements tomorrow." I put my hand to my nose. "Mrs. Dixon?"

"Yes. Come in and close the door. I need to show you something."

I shut her office door behind me. Her side bench, usually stacked high with folders and papers had been cleared. She pointed to a microscope with a view screen. "Take a look."

Against the backdrop of stained tissue small dark flecks stood out. "From her rib area?"

"Yes. You were right. These are some kind of metal and Trenda should have the spectroscopic analysis any minute."

As if on cue, the door opened, and Trenda froze. "Dr. Merchant?"

"The defense has rested. Closing statements in the morning. Is that the spectroscopic analysis?" I pointed to a document in her hand.

"Yes." She handed it to Sam. "The defense must not have had much to say."

"Stop!" Sam put up a hand. "Do not discuss the trial, Jack. Trenda was a witness, and we don't want a mistrial." She studied the document. "Traces of aluminum, stainless steel and some kind of carbon product."

"Not typical for a bullet?" I said.

"No. Not sure what could have caused this."

"I have an idea." I said.

Sam looked up at me and frowned. "Wait a minute. How would you have an idea about these results when you just saw them?"

"I can't say." My heart raced. "Trenda, if you drive over to the Super-Mart and pick up a Hyperspeed 371 cross bolt arrow and compare the tip contents with this specimen you might find a match not only from the tip but from the shaft."

Trenda's brow furrowed. "What?"

Sam studied me for a moment and placed the document on her desk. "Trenda, go. Now."

Trenda nodded and left. Sam motioned to a chair. "Sit. What can you tell me that won't endanger your status on the jury?"

"Okay, before we get to that, reconstruct the crime for me. You've revised what police report and the autopsy results. What happened to Mrs. Dixon?"

Sam leaned back and nodded. "I'll need coffee."

"No prune juice?"

She glared at me. "My bowels are already in an uproar."

A coffee maker on a back table provided us with a fresh brew. Sam sat down and told me what she had learned.

"Mrs. Dixon taught kindergarten at Sunshine Christian Academy, a private school. One week prior to the murder, a visitor to the school created chaos. A man in a black hoodie with a heavy black beard and sunglasses entered the school without permission and made it to Mrs. Dixon's room. The children were gone for the day but a janitor heard them arguing about Aztec artifacts and Mexico."

I froze. "Aztec artifacts? Go on."

"The janitor intervened and the man cursed him out and stormed out of the room. One week later she was dead. The police didn't take it seriously. This is what happened. An off-duty deputy sheriff with Talako parish police was fishing on Talako Lake. It was about sunset, and he was heading in to the dock for the day. He was using a trolling motor which is pretty quiet, and he attributes this to his ability to arrive just as the murder occurred."

"Go on."

"Deputy Firth heard a gunshot just as he pulled around the bend. He kicked his motor into higher gear and when he arrived at the dock, saw Mrs. Dixon's body in the parking lot. A cloud of dust down the road was the only testimony that someone had been there. His wife was supposed to come pick him up and he called her as he left the boat at the dock. She was about ten minutes out."

"He found Mrs. Dixon lying in a pool of her own blood with a gunshot wound to the abdomen. He called 911 and tried his best to stop the bleeding. His wife appeared in their truck just then and they loaded her up and started down the lake road to the highway. An ambulance met them halfway to Fairmont Central and took Mrs. Dixon the rest of the way. The rest you know."

"What did the investigation show?"

"No eyewitnesses to whatever vehicle the assailant used.

No bullet casing at the sight. No DNA. No fingerprints. Nothing to go on. There were truck and car tire tracks all over the place and any fresh tracks were obliterated by the deputy's wife arriving. Basically, the case grew cold. A reward posted by the daughters went unanswered. No one was ever caught. No leads on the man who came to her school. It became a cold case. The official conclusion by the police department was the assailant was the man who stormed the school."

I stood up and paced the room. "What if I might know who did this?"

"What?"

"Let's just say you were right about the jury. The past few days on a jury have allowed my mind to work differently. I mean, up until now, as radiologist, I've been an investigator looking at evidence for disease in my imaging studies. Seeing how the law works and how evidence is collected and analyzed has rounded out my ability to think and consider this case."

Sam sipped more coffee. "Stop right there. I know where you're going with this, and you can't possibly say another word."

"I know you know what I'm hinting at, don't you?"

"I'm not saying anything else. What is your theory?"

I paced some more. "The CAT scan from the hospital revealed two diverging tracts. And you said the autopsy report showed a strange stippling pattern at the entrance of the bullet. So, what if our assailant shot Mrs. Dixon with a crossbow arrow. Then he heard the approaching motor from the deputy and realized he was not as alone as he thought. The arrow would lead anyone back to him. So, he pulled the arrow from the victim, placed the pistol in the wound and fired to cover up the fact she had been shot with an arrow. If the wound had been identified as an arrow that would have narrowed the search for the murderer. He then, as you would say, policed his brass, took the arrow out of her, and left in a hurry leaving her to die."

"And the arrow impacted the rib leaving a tiny amount of metallic residue at the impact sight?"

"Yes. It makes sense. Now, if you could re-open the case with that knowledge, you could begin looking for an assailant that might have used a crossbow."

"Why did you say crossbow and not a bow and arrow?" Sam asked.

"She was shot up close, right? A bow and arrow would have been too wieldy. A smaller crossbow is more like a pistol."

"Why would our assailant use a crossbow?"

I paused and sighed. "He had a personal vendetta against her. He wanted to punish her up close. This was no random killing, Sam. He wanted vengeance!" I stepped up to her desk. "I'll give you a hint and then I'll leave you it, so I don't bias you anymore. Look up the passage about the white horseman and see what weapon he used."

"What?"

"In Revelation." My heart was pounding with excitement. I finished off my coffee. "Now, I'm starving, and I need a good night's sleep before tomorrow's deliberations. I have a feeling they won't be short. And, according to a very reliable source, I will be the smartest man in the room!"

I STUDIED my phone after crawling into my bed. Should I call? I dialed the number for Fairmont Central and asked for CCU.

"This is Dr. Merchant. Is Pam working?" I asked the clerk.

"Pam is about to leave. Her shift is over in an hour. She's with a patient. Let me get her." The clerk said.

I waited impatiently and my heart quickened. "This is Pam."

A chill ran down my spine and I croaked when I tried to talk. "Pam? This is Dr. Merchant."

"Hey. What's up?"

"I, uh, was calling to check on Mrs. Kosack."

"She transferred out to a step down unit this afternoon. I checked on her about an hour ago. She's fine. Still worried about the trial. How are you?" Her voice sent more chills down my spine.

"I, uh, well, I'm fine. Tired. The attorneys wrapped their case this afternoon and closing arguments are in the morning. Then we deliberate. This trial should be over by tomorrow afternoon." I cleared my throat. "Maybe you could share that with Mrs. Kosack for me and that might ease her anxiety."

"You sound pretty anxious, Jack." She said.

"Yeah, it's been a rough week. How is our dialysis patient?"

"Almost back to normal. One of your partners, the surfer, upgraded his catheter to an indwelling so he will be going home tomorrow." Pam said. "Thanks again for doing what you didn't have to do."

"No problem." I said. "Hey, maybe sometime we could get some coffee?"

Silence. I cursed and slapped my forehead. "That would be nice, Jack. After this trial is over. Give me a call."

"Sure. I will. Talk to you later." I ended the call and let out my breath. "Jack, you are so rusty!" And, for the first time, in a long time I smiled.

Chapter 33

"Doc, you look you've been rode hard and put up wet." Gill said as we settled into our seats in the jury room,

"I didn't sleep much last night."

"Worried about Mrs. Kosack?"

"Worried about a lot of things." I drank my coffee hoping the caffeine would kick my brain into high gear. "She's fine. I called and checked on her last night."

"Anything you want to share?" Gill said with a grin on his face. "Was Pam still there?"

"Not now, Gill. Maybe after this trial is over."

I felt his gaze focused on me, but I refused to look at him. I couldn't give anything away about Mrs. Dixon or Pam .

Joe led us back into the courtroom and we settled in for what we hoped would be the final step in this trial that had lasted all week. Judge Ford gave us some instructions on the scope of closing arguments, but I never heard a word. All I could do was focus on Rex Eagleson. Once or twice, he would look directly at me, and I refused to look away. We didn't exactly have a staring contest but if it had been, I won.

Mansfield came to the podium and motioned to the monitor behind him. A photograph of Paloma Preston surrounded by adults and children filled the screen. She smiled at the camera.

"Paloma Preston belonged to a loving, Christian family. Her greatest love in life was teaching these kindergarten children. You see her class and the children's parents. Imagine having the job of shaping the lives of young boys and girls and loving every minute of it. That was Paloma Preston. But her life was cut short by Rex Eagleson. A man devoted to extreme religious views, his differences with the teachings of Paloma Preston to her class motivated him to attack her and eventually kill her as he sought a priceless golden disk. As the evidence has shown, Rex Eagleson had a verbal argument with Mrs. Preston at the Christian Life Bookstore where she met with these children every day. You have seen video footage and heard testimony to this event."

"But Rex Eagleson could not let it go. He had one last argument with Paloma Preston, abducted her, and then drove to her home. He hoped to find a golden disk he had tried to steal years before. In his angry moment, he decided to take Mrs. Preston's life and retrieved a crossbow from his van and shot her in the chest. When he realized he had been discovered, he set her body on fire while she was still alive to cover his tracks."

"You have seen abundant evidence to the truthfulness of our position. A partial fingerprint found at the crime scene. DNA evidence retrieved at the crime scene belonging to Rex Eagleson. Fire damaged clothing recovered from the hospital he was taken to after being hit by a driver. And where did Rex Eagleson get his weapon of death? You have seen evidence the arrows came from the same batch sold at the very area in Super-Mart where Rex worked. Ladies and gentlemen of the jury. Take a long look at that smiling face surrounded by happy parents and children. Paloma Preston will never have the chance to teach another child. She will never have the chance to spend time with her family. She will never see her friends and colleagues at Christian Life Bookstore ever again. She will never have a family of her own. Rex Eagleson, in a fit of religious fervor while trying to locate and steal Mrs. Preston's golden disk, took her life and he should not walk free. He should spend the rest of his life at hard labor without the possibility of parole and we ask that you find him guilty of second-degree murder. Thank you again for your careful attention and your valuable time and I ask that you find justice for Paloma Preston."

Mansfield returned to his seat. My eyes roved over the courtroom to see how they reacted to the closing statements. Mrs. Atkins from the diner sat on the front row, her cheeks streaked with tears. Jerry Langley and Gloria Sanchez sat on the right side of the room. Other family and friends of Paloma Preston sat behind them. The only person possibly mourning the fate of Rex Eagleson was Mrs. Atkins!

Kosinski arose and moved gracefully to the podium. "I also want to thank the men and women of this jury for your attention and your patience. I would like to ask you if there has ever been a time in your life when you were mistaken for someone else? Maybe someone showed you a friendly face until they realized you were not their friend. Or, hopefully not, you were attacked angrily by someone who thought you were a person who had mistaken you for a villain in their life."

Kosinski turned and pointed to Rex Eagleson. "Mr. Eagleson is the recipient of this kind of treatment. Did he have an honest difference of opinion on the interpretation of a Bible verse? Yes, he did. Should he have handled it differently? Yes. But let's use some common sense. Who kills someone for a simple disagreement over Biblical interpretation? If that were so, we would have violence in every church on every Sunday. Instead, the Christian attitude is to agree to disagree in love and patience. Not violence. Mr. Eagleson is a Christian and he knows full well what Jesus taught and that is to never repay evil for evil or hatred for hatred. Love you enemies, He taught."

"The state has asserted Rex Eagleson abducted Mrs. Preston and then went to her home and attacked her and shot her with a crossbow after failing to find some kind of nebulous, questionable Aztec artifact. And yet, we have only circumstantial evidence to that effect. A faceless man in a black cap, black coat, and sunglasses was seen leaving from Mrs. Preston's house to drive away in a white van that was never recovered. I did a little Google search. It turns out that over 10,000 New Orleans Saints caps were sold in North Louisiana in the last year. The jacket is even more popular and 15,000 has sold. I bet if you pay attention the next time you go to the store, you probably see a dozen men wearing dark caps and dark coats. And let's face it. Louisiana is the 'Sportsman's Paradise' and hunting, particularly by bow and arrow, is common."

Kosinski pointed to Mrs. Atkins sitting in the front row. "And we have testimony that Rex Eagleson arrived at the Duck and Decoys Diner for his usual apple pie on the afternoon Paloma Preston was killed. No, Mr. Eagleson may have had a disagreement on the interpretation of verses in the book of Revelation. But this was insufficient motivation for murder. Frankly, the circumstantial evidence is very weak and if you use common sense and a careful analysis of that meager evidence you will find that there is insufficient cause to find Rex Eagleson guilty of second-degree murder beyond a reasonable doubt."

Kosinski walked calmly back to her end of the table. I noticed some of the jury members around me nodded quietly. Kosinski had been very convincing. If only I could shout to the mountain tops what I knew about this man! But I couldn't.

Judge Ford turned to face it. "This trial is now at its conclusion. To reach a verdict, whether it is guilty or not guilty, all of you must agree. Your verdict must be unanimous on each count of the indictment. Your deliberations will be secret. You will never have to explain your verdict to anyone. It is your duty to consult with one another and to deliberate in an effort to reach agreement if you can do so. Each of you must decide the case for yourself, but only after an impartial consideration of the evidence with your fellow jurors. During your deliberations, do not hesitate to reexamine your own opinions and change your mind if convinced that you were wrong. But do not give up your honest beliefs as to the weight or effect of the evidence solely because of the opinion of your fellow jurors, or for the mere purpose of returning a verdict. Remember at all times, you are judges—judges of the facts. Your duty is to decide whether the government has proved the defendant guilty beyond a reasonable doubt. When you go to the jury room, the first thing that you should do is select one of your number as your foreperson, who will help to guide your deliberations and will speak for you here in the courtroom."

"A verdict form has been prepared for your convenience. This form states the indictment as read to you at the beginning of this trial. The foreperson will write the unanimous answer of the jury in the space provided for each count of the indictment, either guilty or not guilty. At the conclusion of your deliberations, the foreperson should date and sign the verdict. If you need to communicate with me during your deliberations, the foreperson should write the message and give it to the court bailiff. I will either reply in writing or bring you back into the court to answer your message. Bear in mind that you are never to reveal to any person, not even to the court, how the jury stands, numerically or otherwise, on any count of the indictment, until after you have reached a unanimous verdict. It is now 11 A.M. and lunch will be supplied for you. You will be confined to the jury room until you reach a verdict or declare you cannot do so. Bailiff, please escort the jury to the jury room."

Chapter 34

My mind was in a whirlwind. What should I do? I knew beyond a reasonable doubt Rex Eagleson had killed Paloma Preston. But he had also killed Rhonda Fall's mother, Eartha Dixon! But I couldn't share any of that with the jury! We had to find a verdict based on the evidence presented to us. But what I could do was make sure I steered everyone in the direction of a guilty verdict. Once Eagleson was behind bars, Jerry could re-open the old murder case and bring him to justice. Again.

The jury room reeked of pizza and I almost retched. No way I could eat pizza again. I plopped into my seat and Joe rolled in a white board. "You requested this?"

Henry Crenshaw, the retired computer program met him and nodded. "Yes, thank you."

"What's that for?" Consuela Giddens asked pointing with a tattoo covered arm.

"I need this to outline the evidence." Henry said in clipped tones. He wore baggy jeans and a wrinkled shirt and his salt and pepper hair was combed in front but in disarray in the back.

"Who put you in charge?" Consuela said, wagging her head.

"We have to choose a foreman and I'm the obvious choice." Henry said.

"No! I want to be fore-PERSON!" Autumn said. "Hey, everybody, look at that wall." She pointed behind me. I turned. "Now, look back at me."

I looked back at her and I know my expression was as perplexed as anyone else. "See, I have leader written all over me. You all did what I said!"

"How old are you?" Henry asked.

"Nineteen. Sophomore in college and my major is law enforcement. That is why I'm so excited to be on this jury." Autumn said.

"I nominated Autumn for fore-PERSON." Consuela said, emphasizing the last word while cutting her eyes at Henry.

"I second that." The snarky blonde said. "I'm Zenia Rick-etts and I want to get on with this. We've been here five days and it's time to go!"

"All in favor?" Consuela said.

Everyone but Henry and Aaron Fields, the engineer raised their hands. I raised mine. With Henry in charge, we would be here for days!

Autumn produced the paper handed to the jury by the judge. "I have the paper. So, let's start by asking are any of you in doubt of Rex Eagleson's guilt?"

"I am. Dante Marshall. Bank executive." Dante said.

Rhonda raised her hand. "Me, too."

"I want to see the transcript of the interview of Rex Eagleson with that homicide detective." Dante said.

"Fine." Autumn went to the door and knocked. Joe stuck his head in, and Autumn talked to him for a long while. The door shut and she returned to the table."

"Joe said he'd ask the judge if we can have it. So, there's

enough questions, Henry." She plopped down. "The floor is yours. For now."

"If you would be patient, Autumn." Henry said condescendingly, "I have a question that is very important to our deliberations. And, if you don't mind, I want to write it on this white board so everyone can see. Do you object?"

"No objections!" Autumn said, mimicking Judge Ford.

Henry wrote three words across the top of the white board. "Motive, method, and opportunity are the key elements of a murder."

Consuela groaned beside me and reached for pizza. "Looks like we'll be here a while."

Henry didn't respond and underlined the word, motive. "Here's my problem. The prosecution claims Eagleson's main motivation for the murder was a disagreement over interpretation of a Bible verse." He turned to us and pointed the marker at the board. "Logically, differences in interpretation of a Bible verse would never rise to the level of homicide. Something is missing here. The prosecution failed to convince me of a reasonable motive behind the murder."

Gill raised his hand and Henry pointed to him. "Yes, uh, what was your name?"

"Gill will do." Gill glanced at me, and he had the 'look'. Whenever Gill and I would have discussions about anything ranging from religion to politics, he had the uncanny ability to ask me the most pointed and revealing question I had ever heard.

"Mr. Crenshaw, I take you're an atheist."

Henry froze. "How did you know that?"

"Just an assumption. You're logical, a computer expert, no doubt relying on science to answer all questions."

Henry took the bait, and I groaned within. It was going to be a long day. "Well, of course, science answer all questions, Gill! There is no room for the supernatural in the logical explanations of reality."

"And you claim to understand the book of Revelation?" Latonya, aka, Bobble head said. "You have no grounds for voicing any opinions when it comes to Bible interpretation."

"That's because it is nothing but fairy tales!" Henry said. "Written over thousands of years, by dozens of authors and changed by the church hundreds of times."

"Not so." Dante said. "The Bible is substantiated by almost 6000 ancient manuscripts some dating back to the first century with 99.7% correlation! And those discrepancies that are present are minor things like tense and punctuation. None of those differences change the basic tenets of theism."

"Ah, I take it you are a Christian apologist?" Henry sneered.

"And you miss the truth, Henry. You said you're a computer programmer? How then did the programming of the DNA occur? Chance? Huh? DNA IS programming and behind programs are programmers and that means an intelligence despite the foolishness that you, a programmer, are showing right now!" Dante was standing at this point.

"Hang on a moment!" Latonya stood up. "We don't need science and DNA in our churches. The Bible said it and I believe it."

Rocky Drayden stood up slowly. "And now you see why as ex-military we had to maim and kill religious zealots over there. Works of religion are the root cause of all wars!"

Voices raised in anger and heat. I looked at Gill. "You started this."

"And I'm going to stop it." He whistled loudly and everyone stopped talking. "Sit down! All of you! Let me ask you one question. How many of you were angry enough you wanted to lash out at someone with whom you disagreed? Huh?"

Silence reigned. Gill nodded. "That's what I thought. I think we just proved to Mr. Henry here that differences over religion can lead to violence, including homicide. I'm not a preacher, but I am a minister of the Gospel. I work with homeless people who live down on the riverfront. They got that way from fighting wars they didn't understand. Some of those wars were with other nations. Some were with themselves. Someone once asked me," and here he looked right at Dante, "and our Christian apologist will understand this: How can a good God allow bad things to happen to good people? Well, the answer is: there are no good people. We are all rotten to the core and capable of the most heinous violence under the right conditions. That doesn't excuse what Mr. Eagleson is accused of. But it proves that with even what would seem the slightest motivation, we can quickly devolve into our most destructive behavior and kill! It's called sin. I think Judge Ford mentioned heat of blood? When we are angry, our blood is hot and so is our violent nature." Gill nodded and sat back. "Does that answer your question of motive, Mr. Henry?"

Henry stood with his mouth open and nodded. "I guess you proved your point, Gill."

"And there is the issue of that golden disk." Latonya said. "A thirteenth evil spirit?"

"Regardless of what the disk portrayed, evil spirit or otherwise, I can tell you from an engineer's perspective, the construction of such a disk even in the early 1800's would make it very valuable. Pure speculation that such a disk exists would have motivated anyone to investigate." Fields said.

"How about just pure greed." Zenia said. "Best motivation."

"But the prosecution never produced the disk." Henry wrote disk under motivation and then religion under that. "Where's the disk?"

"Mrs. Preston never had to actually have the disk." Dante pointed out. "All Eagleson had to do was suspect she had it because of their history together in Mexico."

"No one ever established Roy Kingbird really changed his

name." Henry pointed out. "Either the prosecution didn't know about that little fact, or it doesn't exist. Either way, they are a bit incompetent when it comes to that point."

I had to get things back on track. "Well, I have a problem with the method, Henry. Why kill with an arrow? Most murders of passion and anger are personal. I'm a consultant with the medical examiner's office and I've only been there three months, so I wasn't around when this murder took place. But I've seen the nature of killing from a purely emotional point. With men, it's always strangulation or blunt force trauma." I paused because what I was about to say walked very close to a line I couldn't cross. "But an arrow? I'm sorry but this murder doesn't seem to be spontaneous but pre-meditated. I'm surprised the prosecution didn't press for first degree murder and the death penalty."

Everyone began to murmur, and Autumn wiped pizza residue from her mouth. "Hey! Let's be sensible about this. One at a time."

"Can we change the charge to first degree murder?" Zenia said sourly. "Because I believe the SOB did it!"

"I don't know, can we?" Latonya nodded.

"Just a moment!" Henry underlined the word 'method'. "Let's not chase rabbits. Why would he kill with a crossbow?"

"It was convenient." Rocky said. "On the front lines, if we lose our equipment, we are trained to kill with just about anything we can find, including our hands. Eagleson had the crossbow and arrows in the van. What did the judge say about the heat of blood? He was angry and went back out to the van. He had time to cool down and when he saw the crossbow, he made the decision to kill." He looked at me. "I'm sorry, Dr. Merchant, but I don't think he's guilty of first-degree murder."

But you don't know what he did ten years ago, I wanted to scream. "But you do think he is guilty?"

"I do have some more questions." A quiet, blonde haired

woman in a fashionable dress sat up from the corner. She had been most inconspicuous the last few days. "I'm Sybil Shepherd and my husband runs Paradise Cay. I haven't said much but I do have something that bothers me. What about Mrs. Atley and the diner? How could Mr. Eagle be in two places at once."

"Mrs. Atkins." Henry corrected her. "His presence there seems very convenient. Contrived, like most of the Bible."

"So, you think some of it is true?" Dante wasn't letting it go. "Historical accounts outside the Bible corroborate a historical Jesus who taught, performed miracles, was crucified, and was seen alive by his disciples after his death. And their conversion from good Jewish men to followers of their Messiah is also mentioned in these historical accounts."

"Can we not have a Sunday School lesson?" Zenia said caustically. "I, for one, want to get this over with. The two of you can have your debate at the nearest coffee shop after we've reached a verdict."

"She was obviously a plant." I said. "Eagleson made sure she was in the audience and showed emotion and sympathy toward Eagleson. A lonely woman enamored by a man with two tone eyes who pays her attention twice a week and complements her apple pie recipe."

"There was the issue of her retirement." Consuela said. "Remember, she said she lived in a nice condominium now. Who do you think paid for that? How can a retired waitress from a diner afford a nice condominium? I think Eagleson paid her off."

"How could Eagleson get her a winning lottery ticket?" Consuela asked.

"Oh, that's easy." Sybil waved a hand in the air. "My husband knows how to get his hands on winning tickets. Not the big money ones. But the smaller ones."

"Regardless of the issue with Mrs. Atkins, the defense had several witnesses ready who also saw Eagleson at the diner that day." Henry underlined opportunity. "If he was there, he couldn't have been the man who killed that woman."

"Paloma Preston." Latonya. said. "Say her name, Henry."

"Mrs. Preston." Henry said quietly.

I glanced at Gill, and he nodded. "What if Eagleson had an accomplice?" Gill said. "Someone who wore the cap, coat, and sunglasses?"

"Yes!" Rhonda said. "I thought of that myself."

"No! We have to stick with the evidence." Autumn spoke up. "Judge Ford's instructions were clear. We can't speculate."

"Thank you." Henry nodded. "Very logical and reasonable."

"The prosecution raised considerable doubt in my mind about the identity of the man in the diner." I said slowly. "Accomplice or not, there is a possibility he was NOT Rex Eagleson."

"Okay, let's take a straw poll right now." Autumn announced. She took a notebook out of her purse and tore out twelve pieces of paper. "Write down your verdict as of right now. We'll do secret ballot so no one will feel coerced."

We passed the papers around, and I wrote 'guilty' on mine without hesitation. Autumn collected the papers and looked at each. "Well, we do not have a unanimous decision yet."

Joe appeared in the foyer. "I have the transcript. I am instructed to give it to one person to review."

"Mr. Marshall asked for it." Autumn pointed at Dante.

Joe handed the documents to Dante. "Here you go."

"It will take me some time to review it."

"Let's take a thirty-minute break." Consuela said. "Take some time to think about the evidence. Let's face it, we haven't had an opportunity to be alone with these final thoughts, right?"

Joe pointed to the door. "I can allow you to go across the hall to the small courtroom and spread out. But you'll have to stay in the room at all times."

"Most of the people here are old school." Autumn said. "Can you bring you some paper and pens since we don't have our phones? Everyone can write down the sequence of events and tease any areas you still have questions."

Well, the college student turned out to be the most reasonable one of us all!

Chapter 35

Gill and I sat next to each other at the judge's desk in the small courtroom. He leaned toward me. "Doc, maybe I shouldn't have mentioned the possibility of an accomplice."

"A lot of us were already thinking in that direction. You just voiced what we were thinking." I glanced at him. "I know something, Gill. And what I know didn't come from the evidence presented at the trial or from Mrs. Kosack."

"Okay. Then you can't share it, can you?"

"Not even with you."

"But whatever it is has convinced you beyond that reasonable doubt Eagleson is guilty?"

"Yes."

Gill leaned away. "You trust me, Doc?"

"Sure."

"I mean I'm just a bio-rad engineer with half a college degree. You are a medical school graduate and trained in radiology and all that. But something has happened with us."

I smiled. "We've become friends. Unlikely, but there it is."

"You know what bridged the differences for me?" He raised an eyebrow.

"What would that be?"

"You're not Henry or Dante. You're open to the possibility that there is more to this universe than chance. I like that. I can work with that."

I nodded and smiled. "I had a near death experience, like you did. That changes a person. When you taste what's on the other side and realize there is something beyond death, it makes you more open, Gill."

"I heard Sanchez came to church with you."

I laughed and if felt good. "Yeah, and the roof didn't collapse." I grinned at him. "You know what, Gill. She danced in church!"

"So?"

"Well at Jerry's church let's just say there isn't usually any dancing."

"Doc, I spend most of my time on Sundays with the men and women at the riverfront. But if you want to see a worship service that'll knock your socks off. Come to church with my wife. Dancing's pretty tame for us."

"I might do that if you go with me."

"It's a deal, Doc." He shook my hand.

We sat in silence for a while. I reviewed all the evidence from the trial trying my best to ignore what I knew about Rex Eagleson from his prior murder. Rhonda Fall sat apart from everyone else and every now and then she would glance at me and then back at her lap. She scribbled on her paper. I desperately wanted to tell her that the man who had killed her mother sat in the courtroom waiting for our verdict!

A painfully long hour passed before Dante was ready to go back to the jury room. The pizza had been removed and bottles of water sat in the center of the table. I glanced at my watch. It was almost two in the afternoon. Would we finish today?

Autumn drank from a bottle. "Don't like plastic water bottles. All you older people have brains filled with microplastic but I can't be choosy. So, if you still have doubts about Eagleson's guilt, speak up."

Henry went to the white board. Beneath motive he wrote "religious fervor". Under method he wrote, "convenient crossbow". Under opportunity he wrote a question mark. He turned to us. "Where is the van?"

Rhonda asked. "Why was he walking on a country road and if he left his van somewhere nearby, why didn't they find it? And how convenient there was a fire in that ditch to contaminate his clothes?" She looked at me and I nodded. She was getting it. The accomplice. Which meant someone else capable and culpable of murder was still out there. I thought of Mrs. Kosack and her spiked drink. Someone took her out of the picture to try and sabotage the jury. But I couldn't say anything about that. My head was about to explode! I made a decision.

"I would like to say something." Everyone looked at me. "Shooting someone with an arrow in the chest isn't immediately deadly. A bullet traveling through tissue would pulverize the tissue with shock waves and disrupt the heart, blood vessels, lung tissue and bone. But an arrow from a crossbow shot at the right angle would miss the heart and prolong the victim's death." I looked around at these members of the jury. What I was about to say would condemn a man to prison for life. And that was too good for him!

"There was a small detail mentioned by the pathologist that probably many of you missed. He said there was soot in Mrs. Preston's lungs. Do you realize what that means?"

Rhonda gasped and put a hand to her mouth. "She was alive when he set her on fire?"

"Yes. He wasn't trying to cover up the evidence! He was going to burn her alive. Dante, you said you were a Christian apologist? What can you tell us about the source of their religious disagreement?"

Dante reached into a backpack and pulled out a Bible. "I

don't have my cell phone but I do have a real Bible. Let me read that passage for you. It begins actually with the throne room scene. The lamb of God, Jesus Christ, appears as a sacrificed lamb before the throne of God and this is what it says:

"And whenever the living creatures give glory and honor and thanks to him who is seated on the throne, who lives forever and ever, the twenty-four elders fall down before him who is seated on the throne and worship him who lives forever and ever. They cast their crowns before the throne, saying, "Worthy are you, our Lord and God, to receive glory and honor and power, for you created all things, and by your will they existed and were created."

"Now this is very important to understand based on the next passage." Dante said.

"And I heard every creature in heaven and on earth and under the earth and in the sea, and all that is in them, saying, 'To him who sits on the throne and to the Lamb be blessing and honor and glory and might forever and ever!' And the four living creatures said, 'Amen!' and the elders fell down and worshiped."

"So here John sees this vision of the great throne room in heaven and only Jesus is worthy to sit on the throne. All seems so good! Happy ending! But the narrative doesn't stop there, and I think these next verses are the ones Eagleson and Paloma Preston had disagreement on."

"Now I watched when the Lamb opened one of the seven seals, and I heard one of the four living creatures say with a voice like thunder, 'Come!' And I looked, and behold, a white horse! And its rider had a bow, and a crown was given to him, and he came out conquering, and to conquer. When he opened the second seal, I heard the second living creature say, 'Come!' And

out came another horse, bright red. Its rider was permitted to take peace from the earth, so that people should slay one another, and he was given a great sword. When he opened the third seal, I heard the third living creature say, 'Come!' And I looked, and behold, a black horse! And its rider had a pair of scales in his hand. And I heard what seemed to be a voice in the midst of the four living creatures, saying, 'A quart of wheat for a denarius, and three quarts of barley for a denarius, and do not harm the oil and wine!'"

"When he opened the fourth seal, I heard the voice of the fourth living creature say, 'Come!' And I looked, and behold, a pale horse! And its rider's name was Death, and Hades followed him. And they were given authority over a fourth of the earth, to kill with sword and with famine and with pestilence and by wild beasts of the earth."

"No doubt many of you have heard of the four horsemen of the apocalypse. In his interview Eagleson talked very specifically about the white horseman."

"Yeah, what was that all about?" Autumn asked.

"More nonsense." Henry crossed his arms and stood before his white board.

"Maybe to you." Dante said. "But not to Rex Eagleson. Here was a man different from ordinary men. He had eyes of different color. Maybe he thought this made him unique. He certainly seemed to indicate that in his interview. He thought of himself as special. I believe he saw himself as the man on the white horse. Now scholars have come up with dozens of different ways to interpret that passage. The key to knowing how Rex Eagleson understands it comes in a comment he made about the millennium."

"Preach on, brother." Latonya said.

"I wasn't paying much attention to him during all of that." Zenia said.

"Which is why I think it was Providence I was on this jury. The millennial kingdom signifies a thousand-year reign by Jesus Christ over humanity. Some think it will come after the rapture, an event when God takes all his followers from earth to heaven in the blink of an eye."

"Left Behind. I saw that movie." Rocky said. "There were many times I wished for the rapture in the battlefield. It was hell over there."

"I feel for you, Rocky. Now you know a little bit about what the followers were feeling at this point in Revelation. The other interpretation of the millennial kingdom is it's already here in the time of the church on earth. And that is key to understanding Rex Eagleson. If you adopt a post rapture millennial view then the four horsemen are seen as supernatural beings wreaking havoc on the remnants of humanity preparing them to follow the charismatic leader, the Anti-Christ."

"But if you are an amillenialist then the horsemen are already here. The home schooling association Paloma worked for prescribed to the former view, not the latter. It's on their website and I knew this long before this trial, so I didn't look it up. I spoke to their high school students on more than one occasion on defending the Christian faith."

"Brain washing. Propaganda." Henry said.

"Shut up!" Rhonda said ferociously and everyone jerked at her sudden forceful demeanor. "You had your chance. Let Dante finish."

"The key to understanding Rex is in his mention of one name." Dante picked up the sheaf of documents. "In his interview he said he was a reconstructionalist postmillennialist."

"What?" Henry said.

"Christian reconstructionists advocate a theonomic government and libertarian economic principles." Dante said.

"Christian nationalism?" Aaron said, "I've seen what that has done to our country."

"Not exactly." Dante tapped the papers. "The founder of this system was mentioned by Rex. Rushdoony. This belief systems advocated the reinstatement of the Mosaic law's penal sanctions such as stoning."

Sybil shook her head. "My heavens!"

"Under such a system the list of civil crimes which carry a death penalty would be things like idolatry, false prophesying, and public blasphemy. When Paloma Preston disagreed publicly with Rex, she committed that crime in his eyes. Under the system that Rex believed in, the Bible advocates such justice, and the biblical punishments prescribed for crimes are the maximum allowable to maintain justice." Dante stood up and held up the documents. "And there is the account of a man named Haman, who was killed by impaling."

"Impaling?" I said. "Like with an arrow?"

"A parallel, perhaps." Dante sat back down and shook his head as he spoke. "I believe Rex saw himself as the white horseman. He said as much in that interview. He is a form of an anti-Christ and his job was to enforce that view on those who do not believe him. How does he do it? What was the weapon used by the white horseman?"

"Bow and arrow." I said quietly.

"And what was given to him?" Dante asked.

"A crown." Aaron said.

"He came out conquering and to conquer." Latonya said.

"And bear in mind, Rex is Latin for 'king'. My friends, no matter what you believe about this Bible, Rex had his twisted interpretation, and I believe he would do anything to make sure his crown was never challenged. And he did that by conquering his enemy with the bow and arrow. It all fits his personality. And all of this is based on his own testimony. I think that is evidence enough to find him guilty."

"But what about the golden disk?" Rhonda asked.

"Icing on the cake." I said. "Maybe finding that disk was the final push he needed to go after Mrs. Preston."

"Another straw vote still lacked one vote from being unanimous and the dissenting vote had a note written at the bottom. "Can we have another thirty minutes of quiet?"

Joe took us to the courtroom again. I sat in the corner next to Gill. My mind was a whirlwind of thoughts. White horseman of the apocalypse? A golden disk with an evil thirteenth evil spirit? Who was Rex Eagleson? Why had he done the things he had done?

"Gill, what is this Mosaic Law Dante mentioned?" I asked Gill.

"Like he said, eye for an eye. Try to read Deuteronomy and Leviticus and you will find about so many laws for everyday life of the Israelites. Break the law and you could die. Stoning, for instance. You remember the first martyr?" Gill said.

"Uh, Steven?"

"Yep. And Saul of Tarsus held cloaks while the good Israelites stoned a man of God. Or, how about the woman caught in the act of adultery brought to Jesus?"

"I remember that one. Let he who is without sin cast the first stone." I nodded. "This is what Eagleson wants to go back to?"

"Yep. Eye for an eye. Tooth for a tooth. But God also said vengeance is mine. It's not our place to carry out God's justice." Gill tapped his chest. "Doc, Jesus took all that away when he preached the sermon on the mount. It's more important what is in our minds and hearts BEFORE we act than the act itself."

"Gill, I did a lot of things I'm not proud of."

"You told me that already, Doc."

"I know. Janice and I had a tough time in our marriage and when my old girlfriend showed up and wasn't dead after all, I almost left Janice for her." I swallowed hard. "I've never told anyone this."

Gill merely grunted. I glanced at him. "But I didn't go through with it. Keri wouldn't let me. She had a fiancé at the time. Instead, I went to work on our marriage. Janice and I got through the rough spots." I sat back in my chair and looked out over a room filled with quiet, pensive jury members.

"And then, Keri came to me out of the blue. Asked me to meet her at a coffee shop the day Janice died." I blinked back tears. "Her fiancé had died, and she wanted me to come back to her. I couldn't, Gill. I didn't want to ruin what Janice and I had worked so hard for." I looked at Gill. "I lied to Janice. I told her I was going to the store for some snacks. Instead, I met an old girlfriend. I wasn't there when Janice needed me. No, I was there for Keri. And Janice died." I gasped for a moment, suppressing the wave of emotion. "I should have never left the motel room. My last words to Janice were a lie. I deserve to be stoned."

I wiped tears angrily from my eyes and Gill put a hand on my shoulder. "Doc, I'm not a priest. I don't take confession. But I am your friend. Isn't it strange God brought us together. We don't have anything in common except for a love for the Lord." He leaned forward and glanced at me. "At least, I think you do."

I smiled. "I'm getting there."

"Life can be full of regrets. You should hear what my friends on the riverfront are carrying around. I think some of those memories they have would have crushed me if I had been in their place. I can't understand what you've been through. But let me tell you one thing." I turned to look him full in the eyes. "When you see Jesus face to face, you realize he has already dropped your rock. He's not going to stone you. So, Doc, drop your own rock because your target is yourself."

"Wise words, my friend." We both looked up at Dante standing before us. "Sorry. Couldn't help overhearing. Gill, you are truly a minister of God."

"I'm not a preacher, Mr. Marshall."

"No, but you have the words of God to speak to all of us. I thank you for that." Dante sat beside him. "Now, who do you think is the hold out?"

I looked around the small courtroom. "Sybil?"

"My thoughts exactly. I'm thinking she has a hard time thinking for herself. I know her husband. He uses our investment strategy, and he is a control freak. She needs him here to tell her what to think."

"She's waiting for an intervention." I said. "Like the woman caught in the act."

"I'll go talk to her." Gill stood up. "Give her a word of encouragement."

Gill moved across the room and sat beside Sybil. Dante looked at me. "What do you think, Dr. Merchant? Is Eagleson truly guilty?"

"No doubt in my mind."

"You know something the rest of us don't?"

I nodded. "Yes. If I share it, there could be a mistrial."

Dante nodded. "I'll tell you my main concern."

"What's that?"

"Eagleson claims to be the first horseman. What if there are three others?"

A sudden chill ran down my spine as Dante patted my knee and walked away. Three more killers like Eagleson? After what I had seen the past week, I didn't doubt him for a second.

By the time we returned to the jury room it was 4:30 P.M. Gill must have been successful with Sybil. This time, the vote was unanimous. We found Rex Eagleson guilty of second-degree murder.

Chapter 36

"Has the jury reached a verdict?" Judge Ford asked.

"We have." Autumn Coleman said.

I was once the thirteenth juror. Now, as an active member of the jury, I had joined my colleagues in sending a man to prison. I had no doubts about Rex Eagleson's guilt. As Autumn handed the verdict to Joe, I stared unblinkingly at Eagleson. He glared at me and frowned, then looked away. Joe took the verdict to Judge Ford. She unfolded the paper and studied it through her reading glasses. She handed the verdict to the clerk of court.

Everyone seemed to be holding their breath. I looked over at Langley and Sanchez sitting nervously on the front row. Family and friends of Paloma Preston filled the rows behind them. And alone on the front row of the far side, Mrs. Atkins perched on the edge of her seat.

"We, the members of the jury find Rex Eagleson guilty of second-degree murder." The clerk read out loud. Time stood still and then all hell broke loose.

Mrs. Atkins screamed and ran from her front row seat directly toward Rex Eagleson. "No! Not my Rex. He didn't do it, I tell you."

Joe tried to stop her, but she shoved him aside. Jerry Langley ran after her and that was a mistake. No one paid any attention to Eagleson. He rose quickly and shoved Mrs. Atkins toward Langley. When Langley caught her, Eagleson snared his side arm and jerked Kosinski to her feet. He hugged her to himself with the pistol planted against her right temple.

"All right, listen up. No one move or she dies. Joe, lock the doors. Now!"

Joe hurried to the double doors and locked them from the inside. "You." Eagleson nodded toward Langley. "Give your handcuffs to Dr. Merchant."

Langley glanced at me, his eyes wide in shock. "Why?"

Eagleson shoved the pistol deeper into Kosinski's head. She moaned and tears ran from her eyes. "Ten seconds. Ten, nine, . . ."

Langley motioned to me. I actually hopped over the jury box railing. Langley handed me the handcuffs and for a moment our eyes met. I nodded. "I've got this." I whispered.

Eagleson motioned to me. "Put one handcuff on her left wrist and the other on your right wrist."

I swallowed hard and crossed to Kosinski. She looked at me with open fear. "Please. Help me?" She whispered. Where was her bravado? Her arrogance?

I merely stared at her as I closed the handcuff on her wrist. I closed the other on my right wrist loosely. My heart hammered in my chest. Eagleson peeked around Kosinski's head, and his different colored eyes focused on me. "Tighter."

I gritted my teeth and tightened the handcuff on my wrist. Eagleson backed toward the door beside Judge Ford's desk.

"Joe, open the door. Now!"

Joe slipped past us and for a second, he glanced at me. Instead of calm assurance and control I had seen throughout this week, his eyes filled with fear.

"I hear one person come through that door and they die. You got it?" Eagleson said.

"We do." Ford said. She looked down on us and for a second her eyes filled with profound sorrow as her gaze drifted to mine. "I'm sorry." She said silently.

We got through the door and Joe shut it. Eagleson pointed to a slide lock. "Lock it from this side." I slid the bolt closed. He turned us away from him and shoved us toward that rear entrance we had used before. He grabbed the handcuff chain and pulled our arms painfully behind us.

Kosinski screeched in pain, and she looked at me with desperation. "Open the door, Merchant." Eagleson growled.

I opened the door and he pushed us ahead of himself, quickly down the stairs to emerge on Texas Street right in the middle of a parade. People standing along the street had no idea a killer and his hostages had just emerged from the courthouse. Eagleson pulled me close pressing his mouth against my ear. "Say one word and you're dead."

"You got what you wanted. Let her go." I hissed.

"Yes. Let me go!" Kosinski said, her face streaked with tears.

"Oh, no! I'm not done with you the two of you yet. I need to know what you know." He shoved us down the sidewalk and we passed person after person screaming at the top of their lungs, "Throw me something, mister!" Parade floats in gaudy purple, gold, and green filled Main Street. Giant heads with beaded masks and fancy headdresses emerged from each float. Flashing lights circled the float perimeters. Pulsing, loud music came from each float with a distinct Creole beat. The crowd moved and milled and jumped to catch necklaces of multicolored beads. Those multicolor gold, green, and purple beads rained down around us and Eagleson ignored them.

We reached an intersection and crossed without ceasing behind the crowd and ended up down the sidewalk toward the riverfront. The parade had turned along the parkway. The crowd was impenetrable at this point. Eagleson pulled us back into a recessed doorway. I looked up at the nearest float to see

Sam standing at the forefront, a golden crown on her head. She was flinging beads with her good hand. A giant caduceus, two snakes wrapped around a pole, towered from the back of the float and wings flared out from the top of the pole. Multicolored lights coursed along the snakes' bodies. The symbol of medicine marked the float as Sam's royal vehicle. Did Sam see me? All I had to do was call out.

"Isn't that the medical examiner?" Kosinski said.

"Yes." I glanced at Kosinski. At least six rows of people separated us from the parade route. No one seemed to notice two handcuffed people and a man with a pistol. Where were the police?

"I can kill your ME with one shot." Eagleson said. I felt the cold muzzle of his pistol on the nape of my neck. Beads continued to cascade around us. A set of beads landed on Kosinski's head and settled around her neck. I put a hand over her mouth before she could scream. She glared at me and bit my hand.

"Get your hand off me, Merchant."

"Really? You scream and he kills us both."

"He's right." Eagleson pushed his face between ours. People moved and writhed in ecstasy down the sidewalk as the parade progressed. I realized there was no way police could make it through this crowd and find Eagleson. The loud music pulsed and the people danced and moved to the rhythm. No one could hear us!

Sam's float came even with us and tucked into the shallow doorway, she could not see us. "What do you want, Eagleson?"

"You go with me willingly, silently, and without provocation down the alley in the next block. Say a word and I will not only kill you, but I will make sure your precious medical examiner dies in front of hundreds of parade goers." Eagleson whispered in my ear.

"We'll go with you." I said and my heart thundered in my chest.

Eagleson pushed us gently out into the stream of moving people. We made it across an intersecting closed off street and walked within six feet of a policeman chatting with a patron of the parade. Eagleson ushered us down the alleyway past rancid garbage filled dumpsters to a tattered wooden door.

"Open the door and go inside."

I pulled the door open, and we stepped into darkness. Moist musty air filled my nostrils, and he shoved us across a debris laden floor toward a white van. Yes, *the* white van.

He turned us to face him. His eyes glowed with malice. "Now, what do I do with the two of you?" He tilted his head. "Ms. Kosinski, not even a valiant effort, I'm afraid. There was so much more you could have done. But what can I say? Pro bono work? Worthless."

"I hope you rot in hell." She hissed.

"Oh, I will. And I will not be alone." He put the pistol up to her forehead. I don't know what got into me. It was Kosinski, right? My enemy? Right? Love your enemy, Jesus said. How could I possibly love Kosinski? She had made MY life a living hell!

"Wait!" I put up my free hand. "No need to kill her, Eagleson. Let her go. You wanted me for some reason. You got me. Let her go."

Eagleson glanced at me and smiled. "What a hero! To the end! You don't care about her! I know what she tried to do with you. She told her partner all about it thinking I wouldn't hear. Or care."

Kosinski should have been trembling. She should have been begging for her life. Instead, she glared at him. "Go ahead, you worthless piece of crap! I'm so tired of your whining and preening and two different colored eyes. I jumped through hoop after hoop to try and save your worthless life."

Eagleson smiled and licked his lips. "You're right, Merchant. Killing her would be a relief to this world. I will not exact my justice on her. I'll leave her here to make more people's lives a living hell." He whacked her in the side of the head with the pistol, and she went down, dragging me with her.

Eagleson raked the pistol, dripping blood across my forehead and down my arm. He paused with the pistol touching the chain. He fired and the explosion deafened my right ear. Stunned, I fell back onto the floor and my right hand was free. Kosinski lay unconscious beside me. Eagleson grabbed me by the shirt and pulled me to my feet.

"Open the back door and climb in." He pointed to the back of the van. I opened one of the doors and climbed into the interior.

"Over there on the wall, grab a set of wrists restraints and put them around your wrists."

I took a loop of plastic restraints and put both hands through. The remaining handcuff still encircled my right wrist. Eagleson cinched the restraints tightly. I kept my wrists slightly bent to prevent the restraints from tightening all the way and I prayed that in the dark interior he would not notice.

"Now, get in the passenger seat."

I climbed awkwardly out of the back of the van, and he opened the door. I glanced once more at Kosinski. Her chest rose and fell so she was alive. I climbed up into the van and sat in the seat. He closed the door and before I could move, had circled the front of the van and sat behind the steering wheel. He kept the pistol in his right hand and started the van.

Eagleson drove through hanging plastic sheets into the alley. We passed across several streets always keeping to the alleys until he reached Grim Drive. Instead of turning north toward the M.E.'s office, he turned back toward downtown and soon, pulled off the drive onto a rutted dirt road running through a lot for sale hidden by overgrown weeds. We passed an old, abandoned house covered in vines and he pulled up to the edge of the Choctaw River.

The river rolled from recent rains up north just a few feet below the edge of a bluff overlooking the red waters. Eagleson killed the engine and turned partially to face me. Lights from the casinos across the river reflected off the rolling river. Shards of light played across his face and his eerie eyes.

"Now, what do you have on me?"

"What do you mean?" I said hoarsely.

"I know you know."

"Know what?"

He lashed out with the pistol against my left temple. I saw stars and bit my tongue. Blood trickled from my mouth. I shook my head to chase away the pain.

"Let's try that again. What do you know?"

I glared at him praying for my blurred vision to clear. Did I need a CAT scan of the brain? Blows against the temple can cause skull fractures leading to an epidural hematoma. "I think I know."

"She knows, too?"

"Who?"

Eagleson raised the pistol again and I put my hands up. "Okay! No, she doesn't know just yet. She's reviewing the evidence."

"But you think I killed Mrs. Dixon, don't you?"

I looked out over the waters of Choctaw River. "I suspected it after I reviewed her CAT scan from ten years ago. I was the radiologist who did her angiogram. Her daughter is on the jury, and she asked me for help in finding the real killer."

"Why didn't you stick with your medical practice? Huh?" Eagleson growled. "No! You had to go poking your nose into a cold case from ten years ago. Don't worry about Rhonda. I'll take care of her later. I'm assuming you've told her."

"No!" I shouted. "She has no idea it's you. I couldn't talk about anything outside the evidence from the trial. I swear."

Eagleson sat back and rubbed his chin with his left hand. "He's not going to be happy about this."

"Who?"

"My student."

"Your accomplice?"

Eagleson glared at me. "Everyone else on the jury was just stupid. But they had to put someone with smarts on the jury. Someone who worked with the coroner's office. I tried to tell Kosinski to get you off the jury. But she wanted you there for some reason."

"How much did you pay her to defend you?"

"I didn't. She was assigned to me. She had to take a pro bono case. Then you show up on the jury. She said the two of you had a history."

"She was the one who accused me of being a liar." I sighed. I was having a casual conversation with a killer! "What are you going to do with me?" Buy some time, I thought. I slowly wiggled my right wrist. With the handcuff still on, the restraint had loosened. Just a little. Maybe enough?

"I'll let the other one decide. He'll be here soon."

I jerked in surprise. The other one? "Who?"

Eagleson looked out the windshield at the river. "We met on an online forum for people with *heterochromia iridum*. That's the formal name. It can be caused by a number of factors which you, as a physician, should be aware of. Are you?"

I slowly slid my hand further out of the restraints. "I'm a radiologist, not an ophthalmologist."

"My condition is a genetic mutation. My, uh, student's condition is due to chimerism. Do you know what that is?"

Keep him talking. Work on your wrists. "I remember something about that from medical school. Basically, two fraternal twins fuse during the embryonic phase and the final person has two different DNAs. And possibly lots of other genetic abnormalities."

"Ah, but most human chimeras go through life without realizing it. Unless they get tested for their DNA!" Eagleson chuckled. "Imagine trying to track down a criminal from the wrong DNA sampled when they have two DNAs! Brilliant way to escape detection."

"So, your student is two people in one?"

"Yes. One blue eye and one brown eyed person." He glanced in the side mirror. My heart raced with fear and panic. Stay calm, I told myself. I had been in a similar situation with the man who had killed Janice. Keep him distracted. "Where is the disk?"

Eagleson snorted and glanced at me. "What?"

"The disk. You stole it from Paloma, I know."

Eagleson laughed. "It's right behind you in the toolbox."

"Why did you kill Mrs. Dixon?"

Eagleson stared at me with his two-toned eyes. "Want to know what happened to me in that Mexican prison? An American, hated and reviled by members of the drug cartel. I was violated in so many ways! I was in there for only two days, but it seemed like an eternity. And who was to blame for that? Mrs. Dixon! She didn't have to call the police! She could have taken me home to my father and his punishment would have been bad enough. But, no, she had to be self-righteous and report me to the Mexican police!"

Eagleson breathed hard and looked out over the river. "It took me a couple of months to get my strength back and then my father decided it was his turn to punish me. He took me to our remote hunting cabin and pulled out his whip. Yes, a real whip! But I was prepared. After the first couple of strokes, I tore my way out of his restraints and choked him with the whip. Just enough to make him unconscious. I had planned this moment for years. I put him in the driver's seat of our jeep and drove down to the river, just like now. There was a rickety old bridge that led to our property, and I steered from the passenger's side and ran through the side of the bridge. We hit the water and my father woke up. He was too groggy to get out of the seat belt." Eagleson leaned toward me. "I stayed in my seat while water filled the car, and I watched him drown. I watched the life leave his eyes! And that is when I knew what really fulfilled me. A power unlike anything I had ever experienced!" His eyes filled with insanity. "I had a vision. The dismembered woman on the disk! I saw it! I had to find that disk and claim that power."

His breath came fast, and he laughed. "So many! So many! Each time perfecting my craft. I attracted a couple of followers on the Internet and one, in particular, proved to be very promising. He helped me with this ruse. He was the other man at the diner." He looked at me. "And he has two different colored eyes, too!"

Eagleson laughed again and shook his head. "One day, he will approach my level of expertise."

"You got arrested." I said. "That doesn't speak highly of your level of expertise."

Eagleson growled and hit the steering wheel. "*He* screwed up! I wasn't supposed to be walking on that road. He was supposed to pick me up in the van."

"Maybe he has exceeded you." I said, desperate for more time. I had almost pulled one of my hands from the loose restraints.

"Are you saying he will betray me?" Eagleson laughed. "No! I would implicate him in a heartbeat. I have secrets collected on him! Kill me and they will be revealed." He nodded as he glanced at the side mirror. "No, we'll just move on west of here and start over. New name. New story. New victims."

"Does your student like cutting out people's organs?"

Eagleson stopped and glared at me. "What?"

"There has been a string of murders lately. Victims having their organs removed."

Eagleson thought for a moment and shook his head. "No, he is beyond that kind of amateurish activity. Too obvious. I taught him better."

"Why did you screw up with Mrs. Dixon?"

Eagleson froze. "That was ten years ago. I've gotten better since then. How was I to know, of all people, a policeman would pull up in a boat? I almost had the location of Paloma. I knew she would have kept in touch with Mrs. Dixon. A few more minutes and I would have known."

He chuckled. "It took nine years but wasn't it unlucky for Paloma I wandered into the bookstore? There she was all righteous and pretty and teaching children her religious drivel! I couldn't help but argue with her. And she didn't recognize me! Me! Roy Kingbird! Rex, like the kingbird, is king. I am the bearer of the crown on the white horse. I give out justice to those who deserve it! Like Mrs. Dixon!"

"Like Paloma? She didn't do anything wrong!"

"She refused to give me the disk. It was mine. It was the source of my power and conviction! It spoke of the evil of the thirteenth demon, and I had to find that power!"

"Did you?"

Eagleson looked away. "It is not over. We are still looking and one day, now that I have the disk, I will find it and it will give me unprecedented power to fulfill my destiny." He reached behind him and pulled the toolbox into his lap. He opened it and for a moment a red light issued forth, painting his face in bloody shadows. He reached in and retrieved something wrapped in a cloth. He pulled the cloth away and held up the golden disk.

I felt the evil flood over me like the waters in the river. He pointed to the obscene image. "The next victim will look like this."

"I thought you said dismembering was amateurish." My hand was almost free.

"Oh, this is not on the scale of your copycat killer. This is ascension. This will be my crowning glory. And the police will not find it in this van." He leaned toward me, his eyes burning with crimson fire. "The van is going into the river." He motioned to the bluff with his gun and put the van in neutral gear. We lurched a bit but he kept his foot on the brake.

The sun had set, and darkness engulfed us with only the shimmering reflections of the casino riverboats across the river casting occasional shards of light through the windshield. Suddenly, a brighter light bounced off the side mirror into Eagleson's face. He tucked the disk into the inside pocket of his jacket.

"He's here." He climbed out on his side. It was time! I pulled my right hand free of the restraint. Eagleson stood in the open door and the light from the vehicle behind us lit up his face. "I have him." He shouted.

With a sickening "thunk" an arrow sank into his chest. He looked down at the arrow with shock and surprise and slumped sideways onto the driver's seat. The movement provided enough push to start the van rolling toward the river. I tried to open my door, and it wouldn't unlock! We rolled closer to the edge of the bluff, and I launched myself out of the seat toward the open driver's door. Eagleson's body blocked my way. His brown and blue eyes stared back at me, and I grabbed the arrow protruding from his chest to pull myself across his body.

With a sickening lurch, the van rolled over the edge of the bluff, and we fell. The van hit hard, and the momentum threw me up against the steering wheel and windshield and then we hit the water.

Icy cold water gushed through the open door and Eagleson's body kept it from closing. The van rolled in the current and plunged beneath the surface. The shock of the cold water drove air out of my lungs, and I sucked in muddy water. Choking and coughing, I rolled across the windshield and onto the roof, now the floor of the van.

I pulled against the steering wheel toward the door and shoved and shoved to push it open. Something gripped my wrist, and I looked down through the murky water at Eagleson's eyes. He was still alive! Amidst the panic and fear, one overwhelming desire surfaced. Vengeance is mine!

I shoved the shaft of the arrow deeper into his chest and his eyes widened in pain. His mouth opened in a scream but only sucked water. I finally extricated myself from the front seat, out the open door and swam toward the surface. The cold water sucked the warmth and life out of me and my arms and legs grew numb and useless.

I flailed against the current toward the surface. My head broke through and I sucked in cold, welcome air. A light blinded me, and I waited for the inevitable plunge of an arrow into my chest. Instead, I saw the face of a woman chewing on a toothpick.

"Give me your hand, Merchant." Sanchez said from the front of a police boat. I reached toward her only then realizing I had pulled the arrow from Eagleson's chest.

Chapter 37

"That's two times I saved your life, Jack." Sanchez hovered over my stretcher in the emergency room at Fairmont East.

"How do you figure that?"

"I saved you from Korskin."

"By blowing up the MRI! And you could have killed us both." I coughed again, my chest burning after near drowning. "However, thank you for pulling my butt out of the river."

"Dr. Francisco saw you and Kosinski head down an alleyway with someone. She noticed the handcuffs and knew you weren't into that kind of kinky stuff. She called the police and Langley went looking for you." Sanchez said. "I overheard a policeman reporting seeing a white van roll into the river. I hightailed it to the riverfront where we had two patrol boats. Langley said lots of parade goers ended up in the river! Too much to drink! I saw the van rolling on the water and then it went under."

"Thanks for coming for me. I don't think I could have lasted any longer in the cold water." I shivered again beneath the heated blanket. Dr. Mary Belasco came in. "Looks like you'll live, Jack. Chest X-Ray is clear."

"I'll be the judge of that." Roger Montana strolled in behind Belasco.

"You came out just to check on me?" I said.

"No, he was putting in a dialysis catheter." Belasco said. "Moon Dog was tied up at Central. If you feel like going home, I'll get you signed out. If you start coughing and feel like your lungs are filling up, come back in and I'll give you an I.V. antibiotic." She patted my hand and left the room.

"Jack, I think you're spending more time with Sanchez than with your partners." Montana said.

"Yeah, I've seen way too much of him this week." Sanchez said.

"Jack, you set a new standard on how to end your jury duty." Montana said.

"We found him guilty." I coughed some more.

"Of course, we don't know where Eagleson is." Sanchez said.

I glanced at her. I had seen the life leave his eyes. I recalled his words about his words of seeing the light leave his victim's eyes. Was I no better than Eagleson? I realized I still held a stone in my hand. I shivered again. "He's dead. His body will wash up. What did you do with the arrow?"

"Police took it to the crime lab."

"Arrow?" Montana asked.

"It's complicated." I tried to sit up and my head swam with dizziness. "Did you make it to Bayou City Medical this week?" Eager to change the subject.

"Yeah. Good thing you didn't go after all. I spent all week putting out fires. But, come Monday you'll be there with Masters. If you're up to it, I'll meet you over there tomorrow morning and show you around and get your credentials caught up for the PACS. Say, around ten?"

"Sure. I'm looking forward to doing something normal. Like going home and sleeping." I said.

"Okay, I'll take your statement later so I'll get out of your muddy hair." Sanchez said.

"Wait! What happened to Kosinski?" I asked.

"She's at St. Alexander." Sanchez put a toothpick in her mouth. "I think she's in surgery."

"She had a temporal bone fracture and an epidural hematoma." Montana said. "I heard it from the ER nurses in the hall."

"Could that come from a pistol whipping?" Sanchez asked Montana.

"Yep."

"And just what is an, epipen whatever?"

Montana raised an eyebrow in irritation. He never liked answering a lot of questions. "Hitting someone on the temple can break that bone and there is an artery that can be transected. It starts bleeding on the surface of the brain. Because it's an artery under pressure, the blood collects quickly and expands and compresses the brain. It can kill you in no time."

"Noted!" Sanchez ran a hand along her own temple. "I'm pretty sure that's what happened when I got shot. They bored a hole in my skull and let the blood squirt out." She looked at me. "Right?"

"Yes, that's right. You and Kosinski have something in common." I said.

Sanchez snorted. "I want nothing to do with her." She glanced at Montana. "Although I wish her God speed. Or, whatever you say here in the South."

"Bless her heart." Montana said sarcastically.

I laughed. "Yes, just bless it."

Sanchez looked back and forth between us. "Ya'll are weird."

Montana actually laughed. "I'll see you in the morning, Jack."

"I'll be there, Roger."

"Good. Take care." He strolled out.

"He's married, right?" Sanchez asked.

"Hopelessly. Did anyone see who shot that arrow?"

"We only have your word on it, Jack. Police are checking on it now."

"What about the van?"

"Patrols are searching the river."

The door opened and Dr. Sam Francisco waltzed in wearing her full royal regalia with her golden crown perched atop her purple and green hair. A shiny gold gown with green sash and purple belt completed the ensemble.

"You okay, Jack?" She came to my bedside and took my hand. I winced only then aware of its tenderness from the restraints.

"Yeah. My nerves are shot." I looked up into her eyes. "Eagleson was going to shoot you if I didn't cooperate. We were just a few feet away from the parade float."

"I thought I saw you and Kosinski going into an alleyway in handcuffs. I knew you weren't THAT cozy with her and then I heard about Eagleson's escape on the police scanner."

"Police scanner? On the parade float?"

Sam just shrugged. "What? I take it everywhere." She pulled up a chair and sat beside me. "Tell me what happened." I did.

"Whoever shot Eagleson was probably the person he called 'one of his students'." Stinky river water trickled down my forehead and I wiped it away. "That means he had an accomplice. And he admitted to killing Mrs. Dixon. Turns out she was a chaperone on a mission trip to Matamoros, Mexico the summer he met Paloma Preston. He had planned to torture Dixon to find Paloma and her golden disk. Paloma had married, and he couldn't find her when she came to the states."

"That fellow at the diner that looked like him must have been an accomplice." Sanchez said.

"Not to mention the blood sample from Mrs. Kosack confirmed her fears." Sam said.

"She was drugged?"

"Yep. One of those CIA drugs that kills almost with no trace. Which means the same man from the diner must have been after her."

"Think he shot Eagleson?"

"Cover your tracks." Sanchez said. "I'll see you around, Jack. Lots of paperwork." She left the room and as the door closed behind her I glanced up at Sam standing over me. Maybe it was the dissipated adrenaline. Maybe it was the lack of playful banter. My jaw trembled and my eyes welled up with tears. I grabbed Sam's right hand and she swore from the pain.

"Sam, I can't go on doing this." My voice was thick with emotion. "I just can't."

Sam leaned toward me. "Jack, look at me."

I blinked away unshed tears. "I was so scared."

"When I saw you and Kosinski with that man I was terrified. I didn't want to lose you, Jack." Her eyes brimmed with tears. "You're more than just my consultant. You're my friend."

I smiled and wiped moisture from my eyes. "I'm still scared, Sam."

"Jack, you can do this. You're a natural puzzle solver. And," she nodded at me, "you may not want to admit it, but you enjoyed it."

"What?"

"Ah, come on! Danger always makes you feel more alive. Face it, you've been suffering for the last year. You want to feel alive. You thrive under this kind of stress."

I shook my head. "I don't see it that way." But I couldn't help but smile.

"Oh, you will. Tell you what. I'll get Wang to cover on Mardi Gras and you can go to New Orleans with me."

"I have to work, Sam."

"It's one day, Jack. I'll get Lamb to fly you down Monday evening on the hospital airplane and then fly you back, oh, about 3 AM Wednesday morning. You'll miss only one day. Surely someone can cover for you for one day."

"3 A.M.?"

"Might have a little break in the action by then." She grinned.

My heart rate slowed and the fear subsided. "Dr. Charles owes me for taking his call."

"There you go. You can spend the nights at my brother's apartment on Bourbon Street."

I raised an eyebrow. "You have have a brother?"

"Yes. Two brothers."

"And he owns an apartment on Bourbon Street?"

"It's been in the family for decades."

"How will you get Dr. Lamb to agree to fly me down?"

"I know where one of his skeletons is hidden." She winked and stood up and she patted my hand. "I've got lots of paperwork and I'll save yours for next week."

"Great!"

"No such thing as a free lunch, Jack. Now, I've got to get out of this regalia. This gown is about to choke me!"

I lay back on the stretcher after she left but the door opened again. A face appeared surrounded by blonde hair. Rhonda Fall stepped into the room. "They told me you were about to go home but I had to talk to you before you left."

"Hey, Rhonda. You okay?"

"I'm fine. What about you?"

"A little beat up."

"I just saw Dr. Francisco in the hall. She said to ask you about my mother."

I pointed to a chair. "Have a seat, Rhonda. I'll tell you all about the man who killed your mother. It was Rex Eagleson." She sat down and tears rolled down her cheeks.

"I had forgotten about my mother going on those mission trips. I was only nine or ten. But I remember now that one time, she came back all upset and said she couldn't go with the kids anymore. I was too young and too self-centered to ask her why. I was just glad my mother was free to take us on a summer vacation!" She took a tissue from the table beside me and dabbed her eyes. "Thank you, Dr. Merchant. Tell me everything."

Chapter 38

Bayou City Medical Center's parking lot was almost empty on Saturday morning. I moaned and groaned as I climbed out of my car in the doctor's parking lot at Bayou City Medical the next morning. Montana waited for me at the emergency room entrance, and I followed him into the structure. I thought Fairmont Central looked worn and old. BCMC looked positively ancient. We arrived in the radiology department and Montana introduced me to the personnel. He showed me the equipment, some of which was relatively new. Dr. Lamb had promised to replace most of it.

The reading room, where the radiologists sat before their monitors to "read" studies was big enough for three reading stations. Masters sat at one of them.

"Gabe, this is Jack Merchant." Montana introduced us.

Masters was shorter than me and a bit portly with dark skin and short hair. He wore clear rimmed glasses. "Jack, good to meet you."

"Same." I said.

"I look forward to working with you next week." He said.

"How do you feel about this takeover business?"

Masters shrugged. "Way overdue. The city council runs

this place and most of the employees are relatives or friends. Lamb will clean house and upgrade the equipment so it can only get better."

"What happened to you two partners?"

"One joined the group in Shreveport. The other St. Alexander's group. I prefer to stay here."

The door to the room opened and a tall, hulking man lumbered in. He wore a wrinkled white coat over drab, gray scrubs. His salt and pepper hair stuck out from under a surgeon's cap. "Masters, where the heck is my report?"

"I'm finishing it up right now, Dr. Alton."

Alton paused and glared at Montana. "Still hanging around, I see."

"I'm not going anywhere." Montana said tersely.

"Who's this moron?" He pointed to me. I tensed.

"Moron?" I said.

"You're a radiologist, right? Nothing but a glorified photographer and don't you forget it."

"How could I?" I said. "I'm Dr. Jack Merchant."

Alton stared at me with a cold, calculated look. "Shadow merchant, eh?"

"I've heard that one before. From one moron to another."

A lop-sided grin twisted his lips. "Well, we'll see how long you last around here."

Masters motioned to his monitor. "I'll show you what you're operating on."

Montana steered me toward the door, and we went out into the hallway. "Now you see what a mess Lamb had gotten us into."

"And you want me to spend the next few weeks here?" I said.

"You've been dealing with the criminally insane, Jack. This will be right up your alley." I think he was trying to be funny!

I WAS HALFWAY across the bridge back to Talako when the text came over my phone. I glanced at it and waited until I reached a red light. The message came from Judge Ford. She wanted to know if I could meet her for coffee.

She sat at a table in the corner when I walked into one of our local coffee shops. Ford motioned to a chair.

"I got you a vanilla latte. Sam said you preferred it over the green swill she drinks."

I sat before the coffee cup. "Better than prune juice. You talked to Sam?"

"Yes. I'm glad we finally have a more than decent medical examiner!" In blue jeans and a tee shirt, Ford would never be mistaken for a judge. "I wanted to talk to you about this past week."

"You knew I would be on the jury." I sipped my coffee. "Did you put me on the jury?"

"No! I have no control over that, believe it or not. Can't even begin to think about going there." She looked away. "But when I saw your name on the list, I realized it was more than coincidence. I call these kinds of things divine circumstances."

Ford tapped her coffee cup with a painted fingernail. "You see, I had an idea of who killed Mrs. Dixon. Problem was, when I was practicing law, Rex Eagleson had retained my firm to defend him against a civil suit from a neighbor who claimed he killed his dog." Her gaze focused on me. "With a crossbow."

"Really?"

"And, once he retained us, there would be a problem of confidentiality. I knew I couldn't reveal my suspicions, even if I could prove them."

"But no one knew Dixon had been shot with a crossbow!"

"I know that. He just made some very telling remarks about a fight with a school teacher over teaching the Bible in class. I thought he meant he was against her teaching it. Now,

I realize it was because he differed with her interpretation of the Bible."

"Religious violence knows no boundaries." I said.

"It didn't take me long to get away from that firm. But I had to sign a non-disclosure agreement. When Paloma Preston's case came up I had this sixth sense I should preside and I volunteered to take the case. I had this poorly defined intuition that Eagleson had something to do with Dixon's death. And, when your name popped up on the list, I realized that maybe, just maybe having a connection with the medical examiner's office might give you a suspicion also. Particularly since Mrs. Dixon's daughter would be on the jury. I knew it wouldn't take her long to ask you about her mother's death. She had been asking the D.A.'s office to reopen the case for years."

"So, you hoped her asking me would prompt me to look into it."

"And, maybe, if we were lucky find out for sure that Eagleson was connected." She drank more coffee. "I'm sorry it almost cost you your life."

"I'm getting used to that by now. So, what's next? Will Mrs. Dixon's case be closed formally?"

"Later this week, Lt. Langley will get your formal statement. The police are going back over Eagleson's apartment again now that we suspect he was connected to Mrs. Dixon's death. We'll find a connection and give Rhonda Fall and her sisters the closure they need." She stiffened. "Oh, they found the van. Lots of evidence to sift through."

"Eagleson's body?"

"Not yet."

I looked out the window and shook my head. "He had that disk he stole from Paloma in his pocket. He showed it to me." I looked back at her. "Evil."

"I see evil every day, Dr. Merchant." She sipped her coffee. "But I see good when the law prevails and justice is served."

"I think in this case, justice was served indeed." Carried out by me, I almost said. My hand tingled where I had pushed the arrow into Eagleson's body. I felt the stone in my hand again! "What about his accomplice. His 'student'?"

Ford sat back. "Yeah, Langley ran that one by me. I hope it's not true. We can't have Eagleson's evil twin running around the city shooting people with arrows."

I smiled. "Evil twin, eh? Eagleson said his student was a chimera so he started out as twins!" I stood up. "I'm going to check on Kosinski. Thanks, Judge."

"You can call me Tamika. But only at a coffee shop!"

ST. Alexander, unlike Fairmont Central or Bayou City Medical Center had been updated and renovated many times. The newest tower of glass and white exterior towered twenty stories into the air and arose from the older, squatty original buildings of the hospital. A huge foyer filled with plants and lots of light greeted me as I walked through the doors. A young woman in blue scrubs met me and smiled a thousand watt smile.

"Good afternoon. Welcome to St. Alexander. How may I direct you?"

I looked around at touch point kiosks. "I'm Dr. Merchant. Can you direct me to the SICU. I'm looking for a patient, Madeline Kosinski."

She looked at my name on my white coat and studied a tablet in her hands. "Of course, Doctor. Third floor in the annex. Take the second bank of elevators and follow the signs."

The 'annex' turned out to be the older section of the hospital. When I arrived, a cluster of people waited outside the door to the surgical intensive care unit. I glanced at my watch. Five minutes until visiting hour.

The doors opened and a man dressed in pale green scrubs greeted everyone, asking who they were visiting. I waited until the group had entered.

"Hi, I'm Dr. Merchant. Is Madeline Kosinski in the unit?"

"Dale," according to his name tag, froze. His eyes widened and he blinked quickly. "Dr. Merchant? I saw you on the news last night. You're the man kidnapped by that killer."

"Yes I am."

"Then you were with Ms. Kosinski?"

"I was. I need to see how she's doing."

Dale cleared his throat. "Well, normally only family is allowed. But Ms. Kosinski doesn't have any family."

"He may go in." Someone said behind me.

I turned and Mr. Xavier walked up. He nodded to me and his dark eyes were hidden by his tinted glasses. "It seems I'm the only one who has permission to go in, Dr. Merchant. You can go with me."

"Of course." Dale motioned us in.

"How is she?" I asked Xavier as we entered SICU.

"Alive. No thanks to you." He said quietly.

I paused. "What?"

Xavier turned and faced me. His tinted glasses had cleared now he was out of the sunlight. "Let me make one thing clear, Dr. Merchant. Once Madeline is out of the hospital, we will be filing a civil lawsuit against you for damages from her kidnapping."

My face heated with anger. "What? I saved her life, Xavier. Eagleson was going to shoot her point blank and I talked him out of it. I volunteered to go with him if he would leave her behind!"

"That's not how she remembers it."

"He hit her in the head with his pistol. She has had brain surgery. She probably doesn't remember things clearly if she remembers them at all!" I shouted. Dale appeared behind Xavier.

"Please keep your voice down." He said.

"This morning, she seemed very clear on what she remembers." Xavier continued in that calm, deep voice of his. It irritated the crap out of me!

I huffed and hurried down the line of rooms until I saw her name. She sat halfway up in her bed with her head wrapped in bandages. She opened her eyes when I came into the room followed by Xavier.

"You!" She hissed. "What did you do to me?"

I gripped my hands into fists. I clenched my teeth. To think I had prayed for her recovery. "I saved your life, Kosinski!"

"By letting him hit me in the head!"

"Yes! He was going to shoot you point blank!"

"That's not how I remember it." She said hoarsely and put a hand to her head. "Oh, my head!"

"Perhaps you should leave." Xavier said from the opposite side of the bed.

"Not yet." I looked at her. "Eagleson had us both hand-cuffed when we arrived at that warehouse. He planned on shooting you and then taking me to his accomplice. I talked him out of shooting you and then he hit you with his pistol."

"Why would he want to kill me?" Kosinski glared at me.

"Because you did a crappy job of defending him. That's what he said. The man was a psycho, a lunatic! The only reason you are alive is because of me!"

"I doubt that." She closed her eyes. "Now, leave before I call security."

I exhaled and fought for control. "I'm telling the truth. You hate me so much, you refuse to listen."

Kosinski opened her eyes. "I have a reason for hating you, Merchant. You ruined my life ten years ago. That little stunt in the courtroom cost me a partnership position with my firm. They let me go. Xavier here took my place. I had to form my own legal firm. I no longer have the pull and influence to keep me from pro bono work with scum like Eagleson. Now I have the chance for payback. And it will come in spades!"

I turned to leave and fought for control. I felt the "stone" in my hand. If only I had one! But then I would be no better than Eagleson. I turned back to her. "One thing I'll say and that is all. I'm not your enemy, Kosinski. You are your own worst enemy. Put me on the stand when you take Monique's case to trial. I'll gladly throw you a bone. Not for your sake. For Monique's sake. She needs long term care. I'll cooperate in any way I can. Now if that doesn't prove to you I'm not your enemy, I don't know what will."

"Get out!" She said forcefully. "I'll see you in court."

Downstairs, I paused just outside the door. The air was crisp and cool and the sky a clear blue. A warm breeze promised the coming of spring. A rock garden spread out away from me planted with magnolia trees. I reached down and picked up a white, smooth stone the size of a plum. I held it in my hand and thought about the woman caught in the act of adultery. That woman was Kosinski! I felt the hatred and the need for vengeance fill me. I gripped the rock, ready to toss it at her perfect face!

I closed my eyes and felt the breeze caress my cheeks. I felt the warm sun on my face. I couldn't give into this hate. I would be no better than Kosinski. No better than Korskin. No better than Eagleson. Are you there, God? Can I feel you? Can you give me some peace in this moment?

I DROVE to the parkway and traced the tree line to where the van must have gone over the bluff. I found the dirt road and drove past the rickety house for sale. Yellow crime tape stretched across the road. I stopped and got out of my car and walked toward the bluff. My heart raced at the memories of the restraints on my hands, the sick fear washing over me as I waited for certain death. Tire tracks had been marked with orange cones. I stood where Eagleson had stopped the van and followed the tire tracks to the edge of the bluff.

Below me, Choctaw River churned red and swollen like a pustule about to burst. I swallowed back nausea and calmed my breathing.

"Jack?" I turned and Jerry Langley and Sanchez walked toward me. "What are you doing here?"

I stepped away from the crumbling bluff. "I don't know."

"We were following up on leads." Sanchez said, spitting her toothpick into the grass.

"And we saw a car pull off onto the road and we had to check it out." Jerry said. They halted in front of me. I swallowed again and looked away.

"Jerry, I almost died. Right here." I said hoarsely. "I almost died." I turned and looked across the river at the towering casino hotels in the distance. "And, I almost died *there*." I pointed to the casino hotel. "A slow, lingering death."

I felt his hand on my shoulder. "But you didn't, Jack."

Sanchez stood at my other side. "I almost died, too, Jack. It changes your perspective."

We stood there quietly, while the overwhelming desire to find that lonely, smoke filled corner of the casino in front of the noisy slot machine filled my mind with desire. I tasted the wet drink on my lips. I yearned for the mindless abandon.

"Kosinski is going to sue me." I said.

"What?" Sanchez said.

"Shouldn't surprise me. No good deed goes unpunished."

"What do you mean?" Jerry asked.

I glanced at him. "I tried to be a hero and she can't see it. I told Eagleson I would go with him if he would spare her life. Why did I do that?"

"Because you're an idiot." Sanchez said. "An idiot with a conscience. It's why I like you." I looked at her and her eyes flared with humor.

"I've been called that once today already." I said. "I'm about to go to work in enemy territory."

"What does that mean?" Jerry asked.

"Our hospital system bought Bayou City Medical Center and the medical staff there are not excited to see me sitting in one of the chairs that belonged to one of their prior radiologists. I'm not wanted."

"I know that feeling." Sanchez said. "Only I wasn't wanted by my own people. People!"

"Sanchez, why are you really here?" Jerry leaned past me to look at her. "No bull. Just the truth."

Sanchez pulled a toothpick from her pocket and tucked it into the corner of her mouth. "I don't like people, Jer. Never have. Never will. That's the problem with this world. People." She smiled at me. "But I like the people here in Louisiana. Sometimes we just need a fresh start." She patted my chest. "Jack, you are in the midst of a fresh start. Facing death kind of does that to you. We can wallow in fear and despair. Or, we can find a reason to move on and make it better this time."

"This time?" I looked into her intense gaze.

"Until you almost die again!"

Epilogue

Gill sat in the passenger seat of my car and looked out the window at the tombstones spreading out in the darkness. Night had fallen and the latest murder images were still fresh in my mind. The promise of spring had unwillingly yielded to another winter rain.

"You're doing the right thing, Doc."

I gripped the steering wheel unwilling to take the next step. "I finished him off, Gill." I looked at him and felt the old guilt surface. "I thought Eagleson was dead from the arrow and then his eyes opened while we were under water." I swallowed. "I shoved the arrow deeper. I watched him die."

Gill's silence and stillness said volumes. "Vengeance is mine says the Lord."

I looked away out over the cemetery. "Gill, I am a doctor. I don't take lives. I save them."

Gill squeezed my arm, and I jerked at his touch. "Doc, we all have skeletons in our closets. Paul killed dozens of Christians. David had Uriah killed so he could marry Bathsheba. And God still called him a man after His own heart. Some decisions we make are full of selfish sin. And we have to live with the memory even though we are forgiven. Now, go do what you have to do."

The oldest cemetery in Talako held bodies from as far back as the mid 1800's when Talako was founded. When Janice had died, I had her body transferred to the cemetery and buried in a plot hastily purchased. We had not made any "exit" plans. We had been too young to think about burial plots and head stones and such.

At Sanchez's request, Janice's body had been exhumed and re-examined by the more capable Dr. Sam Francisco. Her findings had been the key to unlocking the cause of Janice's death. Shortly after Christmas, Janice had been laid to rest once again in her grave.

I made my way through the tombstones, slick with the cold misting rain toward the back corner of the Talako Memorial Cemetery. At the time I had chosen Janice's burial plot, her life insurance had given me plenty of money to buy a plot beneath a spreading oak tree. The grounds keeper told me the tree was almost one hundred and fifty years old.

The cold drizzle soaked my hair to the scalp and fogged my glasses. Light from the distant interstate highway gave a low-level glow to the mist and the fog hovering over that end of the cemetery.

"The plots along the back are less desirable but there are more trees," The funeral director had told me.

"Why are they less desirable if there are trees?"

"The noise from the interstate." He said. "So loud some people think it would wake the dead."

He only smiled after that. Mortician humor!

I arrived at Janice's grave. It had been almost two months since we had reburied her and the red clay dirt still showed through meager grass growing over the mound. January and February were not the best months to grow grass in Louisiana!

"Hey, there." I whispered, kneeling at the end of the grave in the cold, wet dirt. "I just had to come and talk to you."

My voice croaked with emotion and more moisture from my eyes misted my glasses even more. I took them off and rubbed my eyes.

"You wouldn't believe what I'm involved in. Working with the medical examiner's office! Trying to keep my job with my radiology practice! Jury duty! But I'm trying church with Jerry and Faye. We really should have given that a try when you were still alive."

I groaned and shook my head. "What if you're not there? What if you didn't make it to heaven?" I looked up. "We talked very little about the afterlife. We talked even less about God. But you told me you were baptized when you were eleven, so I have to hope that was enough."

I sat back in the wet dirt and cried. My sobs echoed among the tombstones.

"Janice, I messed it all up. Bad. I lost the money. I got hooked on gambling, drinking, anything to fill the void and avert my attention from a world without you. And then, Keri showed up again and brought it all back to me. The loss of love and happiness! The profound emptiness now that both of you are out of my life."

I gasped and wiped snot from my nose. The cold rain fell even harder, and I shivered. "I have to find a way forward to move away from this darkness I've wrapped myself in. That means I may have to move on from, well, us. It's hard and it hurts. But I have to choose between dying with you or living with your memory. Gill is helping with that. And, to some extent Jerry." I suddenly chuckled. "And believe it or not, Sanchez. You would have liked her spunk."

I stood up and pointed to the head stone. "Can you believe she actually thought I had killed you? I mean, come on. We've had fights but really?" I wiped rain from my face and shook hard from the cold. "Anyway, I loved you and I miss you. But, I'm moving on with my life. And I think," I paused.

"No, I *know* you would want me to do that. Goodbye, sweetheart."

I reached into my pocket and took out the stone. I look at it and dropped it by the grave. With warm tears mixing with the cold rain on my face I bent over the headstone and kissed the cold granite. I turned my back on the past and walked away into the darkness.

Afterword

If you enjoyed Dr. Jack Merchant's adventures so far, check out these other books.

In "Death By Darwin" a murderer is featured who is related to the events in "The 13th Juror".

In "The 7th Demon: The Pandora Stone", "The 5th Demon: Demoneyes", and "The 4th Demon: The Trial of the 3rd Demon", Dr. Merchant is a major character. By the time these books occur, Dr. Merchant has spent a few years in Talako and moved to Shreveport, Louisiana when his radiology group merged with a group in that city. To say he might have done so because a certain nurse also moved to Shreveport is possible!

Preview of "Slice Fatigue"

Here is the first chapter from the third book in the Jack Merchant Medical Mystery series: "Slice Fatigue".

Chapter 1

Twenty five years ago.

"Hey, Doc."

Roger Montana turned from his light boxes at the young man standing in the door of his office. He was irritated at being interrupted. He had only been in this radiology practice for a year and so far, his struggle to control his anger had not gotten much better.

"Who are you, again?" He growled.

"Virgil Brown. I'm new. One of the engineers."

Montana massaged his beard and mustache. He ran his hands through his mullet and crossed his arms. "What is it?"

"Sorry to interrupt you. But I found something I didn't know what to do with it." He placed a large bucket in the center of the room. He wore rubber gloves stained a pitch black. "They called me to the surgery dark room because the drain was stopped up."

Montana grimaced at the odor from the bucket. "What is this?"

"That's what I was wondering. I found it in the drain to the developer." Montana looked at the black on Virgil's gloves. The X-omat as it was called developed the Xray films. Films were loaded in the top of the X-omat in the dark of the dark room. The films ran through the developing process and dropped out the bottom. Because of the silver nitrate in the films, the fluid from the X-omat were pitch black and went into a special drain. Montana flipped on the overhead lights which normally were off because of the need to read films in the dark. He looked into the bucket. A smooth, round structure was surrounded by black fluid.

"What the?" He took a pen from the desk behind him and poked at the black structure. It was rubbery and resilient. "That looks for all the world like a liver."

Virgil nodded. "That's what I was thinking. It looks organic. What should I do with it? I can't just throw it in the trash."

Montana's curiosity was now full blown. "Could have been a piece of an organ from surgery, maybe? Why don't you take it to pathology and let them look at it?"

Virgil shrugged. "Okay, Doc."

Montana watched him walk out the door of his office and down the hall toward the lab.

⊏⊐

A week passed and Montana returned to Fairmont Central from a week working in a small town at a smaller hospital that needed a roving radiologist. He saw Donna, the chief tech and when he sat behind the desk, he paused before going into his office.

"Donna, did Virgil ever find out what he found in the surgical dark room drain? He took it to the lab."

Donna froze, and her face paled. "I don't know what you're talking about."

Montana frowned. "What aren't you telling me?"

Donna looked over her shoulder. "We were told not to talk about it. It was a liver. No one knows how it got in that drain."

Montana sniffed. He sat in his office chair and shook his head. "I always thought there was a serial killer in Talako."

Acknowledgments

There will be those in the medical field who will object to sections of this story that pull back the curtain on the medical legal aspects of medical practice. Most people are unaware of the Medical Review Panel Process although information about this process is readily available to anyone searching the internet. I have personally been on many such panels and the case discussed in my story is NOT one of those. Again, I would not disclose privileged information.

On my very first panel, I hated the process. I resisted the demand for me to do all the work sifting through the medical records so the attorneys did not have to. The payment was a mere pittance and is still such. However, over the years I have learned that our unique process in the state of Louisiana gives the patients and the doctors valuable information before the case ends up in court. Although I do not like being on a panel, I recognize it gives the plaintiff's attorneys the opportunity to better understand the processes that led to their client's case. And it gives the doctors a chance to clarify the medical records.

I have benefitted from such panels and I support the process, however painful it may be to the doctors involved. I believe, like being on a jury, it is a necessary evil, an unwanted job that must be done to guarantee justice is carried out fairly.

About the Author

Bruce Hennigan grew up in Northwest Louisiana and became a physician practicing in the field of radiology. He was a church drama director for 15 years and wrote over 150 plays. He is a certified apologist, or one who defends the truthfulness of the Christian faith with Reasons to Believe and with the North American Mission Board in the role of a Certified Apologetic Instructor. He speaks on this topic on a regular basis. Bruce is also the author of ten books in the supernatural thriller series, "The Chronicles of Jonathan Steel" as well as "Death by Darwin", "The Homecoming Tree", "Our Darkness, His Light", and, with Mark Sutton, "Hope Again: A Lifetime Plan for Conquering Depression" and "Shadow Merchant: A Jack Merchant Medical Mystery".

Together with Mark Sutton, he participates in a seminar based on the book entitled, "Conquering Depression". For more information on the book and tool, "LifeFilters" go to www.conqueringdepression.com.

Bruce is married to the most incredible woman in the world, Sherry. They have two adult children and they live in Shreveport, Louisiana. Bruce and Sherry along with their daughter, Casey, are strong advocates of support for epilepsy patients and their caregivers.

For more information on books: hopeagainbooks.com

Also by Bruce Hennigan

Death By Darwin

Volume 1: The Chronicles of Jonathan Steel: The 13th Demon, Dark Covenant; The 12th Demon: Wolf Dragon; and The 11th Demon: Chimera

The 10th Demon: Children of the Bloodstone

The 9th Demon: Time of the Cross

The 8th Demon: A Wicked Numinosity

The 7th Demon: The Pandora Stone

The 5th Demon: Demoneyes (7th and 5th books include story of the 6th demon)

The 4th Demon: Trial of the 3rd Demon (includes the story of the 3rd demon)

The 2nd Demon: Tales of the Grimvox

The Homecoming Tree

Our Darkness, His Light

Just a Bite of Something Sweet: At Christmas

Shadow Merchant: Book 1 of the Jack Merchant Medical Mysteries

Hope Again: A Lifetime Plan for Conquering Depression with Mark Sutton